HIS FIRST GIRLFRIEND

BOOKS BY NORA VALTERS

Her Biggest Fan

Now You Know

Here For You

The Party

The New Girl

HIS FIRST GIRLFRIEND

NORA VALTERS

bookouture

Published by Bookouture in 2026

An imprint of Storyfire Ltd.
Carmelite House
50 Victoria Embankment
London EC4Y 0DZ

www.bookouture.com

The authorised representative in the EEA is Hachette Ireland
8 Castlecourt Centre
Dublin 15 D15 XTP3
Ireland
(email: info@hbgi.ie)

ISBN: 978-1-80550-239-5
eBook ISBN: 978-1-80550-240-1

For my mum, Ann

PROLOGUE

I know what you did. I know who you really are. And I promise to make you suffer.

And I always keep my promises.

And after the suffering? Well, then it's the end. For you, that is. Not me.

You know, people tell me I'm obsessive. But I just like to think that I get things done. I can't understand these people who start things and then don't finish. I couldn't have lots of half-done tasks hanging around in my head, weighing me down. I think I'd suffocate.

People also tell me I'm a planner. I do like to make meticulous plans. Why? Because I don't like it when things don't go my way. If I have a well-thought-out plan and execute it precisely then things go right. And I'm happy.

People have told me a lot of things over the years. Mostly that I'm not right in the head. Well, screw you all. I'll do whatever it takes to get what I want. How many people can truly say that? To me, you're all the fucked-up ones. Meandering through life without any clear direction.

Well, my first priority is *you*.

The obsession has kicked into gear.

The plan has been planned.

I'm ready to make you – and everyone you love – believe the lies.

CHAPTER ONE

PRESENT DAY – OCTOBER 2024

'They'll be here any minute,' I say to my husband.

I bounce around the kitchen getting ready for the arrival of my son and his first girlfriend.

Lily, her name is. That's all we've heard for the past six weeks since Seth started at university. Lily this, Lily that. *I'm going over to Lily's. I'm meeting Lily after lectures. Lily and I are going to a gig...* They met at the freshers' fair during freshers' week. She's a first-year too.

And then yesterday, Seth asked me if his 'girlfriend' could come round. Girlfriend! It was the first time he'd called her that. Obviously, I squealed YES! I'm excited to meet her. And curious. And apprehensive.

Seth isn't naturally a people person. Don't get me wrong, he's a wonderful boy, and I couldn't have asked for a better son. But he's an introvert, and, like me, has some quirky passions that stray from the mainstream. He has one close friend from primary school, and that's about it. I was worried about him starting university, worried about him making friends. But I shouldn't have been. He found his tribe pretty quickly. And, not only that, but he met a girl. He's had a couple of female friends over the past year or two but nothing serious and no one he's referred to as his *girlfriend*.

I pull my well-loved, home-baked honey cake from the oven and put it on the side to cool. The delightful smell fills the kitchen. I drizzle my homemade honey and rosemary mixture over a tray of peanuts and cashews and pop it in the oven to roast.

I'm desperately proud of Seth for getting into university. He's blossomed into a sensitive, funny, passionate eighteen-year-old. I still pinch myself that we live in this house and have this life. It could've all turned out very, very differently.

But the less I think about all that, the better.

'Fancy a top-up?' I ask my husband and hold up a bottle of my homemade mead.

Todd sits on a high stool on the other side of the kitchen island bobbing his head to a pop song on the radio and watching me. This is our little thing. He sits while I'm cooking in the kitchen, and vice versa. It's our chatting time. We have lots of chatting time – when we work out together in our home gym, when we're in the car or at night in bed before sleep. We have endless things to say to one another. And have done since we first met. Conversation never runs dry with us.

We tell each other everything. Well, *mostly* everything, in my case.

It's Todd's thing to constantly have the local radio on. He presents a football show on this radio station twice per week, so is a loyal listener. I prefer silence, but he's not very good with quiet when he's awake.

Todd picks up his empty glass. 'Yes, please.'

He slides off his stool and comes around the kitchen island to stand behind me and put his hands on my waist. He nuzzles into my neck and gives me a little kiss.

I pause what I'm doing to fully feel his embrace, to welcome in his love, to pay all my attention to this man, my one and only, my true love. I'm blessed to have met him.

His aftershave fills my head and takes me back to when we first met. It's the same stuff he's worn for years; it's his scent.

He pulls away and puts his glass on the counter. I fill our glasses with my alcoholic honey brew. He goes back to sit in his spot, flashes me his big grin and takes a swig.

He only drinks alcohol on a Friday night. And occasionally on a Saturday if he's socialising. But it's rare. Todd has his quirks too. He's a fitness fanatic and obsessed with doing Ironman challenges and other endurance feats. He does them for charity and raises significant sums.

Todd is a year older than me at forty-five, and to the outside world, we're like chalk and cheese. But on the inside, in our close relationship and tight family unit, Todd happily pursues his passions. Hobbies he likes to keep to himself and only share with those close to him.

He's a very attractive man with deep-brown eyes, dark hair that's going grey at the temples and salt-and-pepper designer stubble. He has a square jawline and a pleasingly symmetrical face. My husband is a retired professional footballer. I never thought I'd say that, but here we are. Other players used to call him Pretty Boy, still do. He's shorter than me by one inch at five foot nine. He has a smile that makes women – and men – go weak at the knees. He also looks impeccable in a suit.

I, on the other hand, am tall and long-limbed, with the loathed and unoriginal nickname of Beanpole when I was younger. I also have brown eyes. My long, wavy, brown hair is going grey. I'm fully embracing it. I have never dyed my hair and am not going to start now. I usually have it up in a low ponytail. I never wear make-up. Haven't touched the stuff in eighteen years. I have a smile to match Todd's – big and warm and friendly. I'm no beauty. I'm not your typical footballer's wife stereotype.

And that's exactly what Todd loves about me. At the height of his fame, women threw themselves at him. All the same kind of women – beautiful, yes, but as Todd describes it, with bland personalities. Then he met me. We immediately clicked and slotted perfectly into place.

Todd is a legend in Southampton, the city where we live in the south of England. He played for Southampton Football Club for sixteen years. He's famous. People chant his name. He has a very public persona and does a lot of media and publicity. I, however, hate the public eye and actively avoid any kind of attention. Initially, I told Todd I didn't want to date him because I never, ever wanted to have my photo in a newspaper or do a personal 'family life' article in a glossy magazine. I'm intensely private. This was refreshing for Todd – he'd dated too many women who were just with him for the fame. He likes to keep his family life private.

Women still throw themselves at him at any opportunity. They do it while I'm standing right next to him. But I'm not jealous or worried. I look closely at his face. It disgusts him. 'I'm only truly me when I'm with you,' he likes to tell me. I know he'd never cheat.

He loves the sanctuary of our small family unit, of this house, of us in this house, as much as I do.

He bought the land and designed and built this property when he was in his early twenties and earning a substantial footballer's wage. It's worth a few million pounds now, but he'd never sell it. We'll live here until we die. It's in an exclusive area of Southampton called Chilworth and set in a discreet, tucked-away spot at the end of a lane. It backs onto woodland and has almost an acre of grounds. The two-storey house is modest in that it only has three bedrooms and three reception rooms, but each room is huge. Our bedroom is vast with a large dressing area and en suite bathroom. There's also a one-bedroom two-storey annexe, a separate little building that houses the gym and

Todd's 'office' upstairs, and a huge garage. The open-plan kitchen and dining area is in the middle of the downstairs with a large lounge off to one side and the family room – now Seth's telly room – off to the other. Todd didn't want loads of rooms that no one ever went in; he wanted fewer rooms that were bigger and got used.

'The nuts need another few minutes, and then you can get started on dinner,' I say and sip my mead. The fragrant, sweet liquid goes down smoothly and warms my insides. I hold my glass up to admire the golden colour. This was an especially good batch.

'Seth and Lily aren't eating with us, are they?' Todd asks.

'No, they're going to order pizza. Seth thought a quick hello would be enough for our first meeting. He didn't want to put her through dinner with us too.'

Todd laughs. 'Fair enough.'

'Your son is very thoughtful,' I say.

Todd beams proudly.

I wipe down the counter and check on the nuts. 'These are done.' I pull them out and leave them next to the cake to cool. The smell is divine.

I point at Todd. 'You're up.'

He gets to his feet and heads into the kitchen. As we switch places, we kiss each other and smile. I perch on the stool, warmed nicely by his rather lovely bum.

Todd rubs his hands together. 'Your favourite coming up. Lasagne with your homegrown tomatoes and homemade garlic bread.'

He gathers what he needs. He made the bread yesterday. He's obsessed with his bread maker.

'What shall we watch later?' I ask.

Friday night is movie night. It's a family tradition. Well, it was a family tradition but then Seth got older and wanted to do his own thing, so now it's mine and Todd's tradition. Sometimes

Seth sits with us, but more often than not he's out on a Friday night.

The sound of the front door opening makes us both freeze and look at each other. I clap my hands excitedly.

'Hey, we're back,' Seth shouts from the hallway.

I eagerly listen to the rustle of coats and shoes being removed and two lots of footsteps padding down the hallway.

Seth appears in the doorway. He stands to one side and gestures for Lily to come in. I immediately jump up and give Seth a big hug. I'm a hugger. I go to hug Lily, but Seth gives me a look as if to say, *too much, Mum.*

So I back away and smile.

Todd comes to stand next to me. He flashes Lily one of his winning smiles too.

Lily smiles back shyly. She pulls at the cuffs of her oversized hoodie to cover her hands. She's stunning. There's no other word for it. She has naturally blonde hair that has been cut in a fashionable shaggy style with a long fringe. Her bright-blue eyes sparkle like the sea on a sunny day. She's petite, perhaps five foot three, and Seth towers over her. She has radiant skin without a trace of make-up, a slim figure and a heart-shaped face. She's like a little doll. Her nose is wonky and fat at the tip, and just out of proportion to the rest of her face.

Seth is an attractive lad in an unusual way, with a wide forehead, square jawline and small eyes. He's tall and lanky like his mum but with a bit of muscle on him from working out with his dad. He has brown eyes, dark hair and olive skin, like me. His hair is floppy and wavy, and he has a Shawn Mendes vibe about him. He also has a killer smile.

They look great together.

'Mum, Dad, this is Lily,' Seth says. He puts his arm around her shoulders and brings her forward a little. It's a tender, protective gesture that melts my heart. Immediately, I can see they are an adorable couple and very in tune with one another.

'Lily, this is Jen and Todd,' Seth says.

'Hi,' she says with an awkward wave, as if she changed her mind about it halfway through.

'Hi, Lily. It's an absolute pleasure to meet you,' Todd says.

I beckon her further into the kitchen and pick up the bottle of mead and a glass. 'Welcome! Come in, come in,' I say. 'Would you like a glass of mead?'

'Mead?' she asks and glances up at Seth.

'It's an alcoholic drink made with honey,' I say.

'Mum keeps three beehives at the bottom of the garden and harvests the honey and makes all sorts with it,' Seth explains.

Lily takes a tentative step forward. 'Sounds amazing. Yes, please. I'd love to try some.'

'Excellent. Seth?'

Seth shakes his head. 'No thanks, Mum. I'm driving Lily home later so not drinking tonight.'

I pour Lily a glass and hand it to her.

'Thank you, Mrs James,' she says. She takes a tiny sip. Smiles. 'It's delicious.'

'Please, call me Jen,' I say. 'I've made your favourite nuts,' I tell Seth.

I pour the tray of roasted nuts into a bowl and place it on the counter. Seth comes forward, leans against the cabinet, grabs a handful and throws them in his mouth.

Todd takes his seat at the kitchen island. 'Honey-roasted nuts,' he tells Lily.

Lily steps further into the kitchen to stand next to Seth. Her eyes rove slowly around the room, taking it all in with wonder. 'You have a lovely home,' she says.

'Thanks,' Todd and I both reply at the same time. And then chuckle in unison.

Lily looks at me. 'Thank you for inviting me here. Seth mentioned you aren't all that keen on strangers in your house.'

I raise my eyebrow at Seth. 'Did he now?'

'Yeah. Do you remember that time you freaked out when Dad turned forty and had a party,' Seth says.

This is a running family joke.

'That was because your father said he'd invited five people, and then fifty people turned up,' I say.

Seth and Todd both snicker. I purse my lips in mock annoyance.

I turn to Lily. 'It's true, I get a bit funny about people I don't know coming to the house because this is our safe place, and I'm very protective of it. But you're not a stranger anymore and are welcome here any time.'

She blushes and looks around the room again. She points at the large pinboard next to the fridge. 'Are those Seth's drawings?'

'Ha, yes. One of the three of us and one of a frog. They've been up there since he did them when he was a toddler.'

'Aww. And look at all those pictures.' She takes in the framed photos of Seth as a baby and of Todd when he was a footballer or at special events. 'There's none of you, Mrs James.'

'Mum has a fear of having her photo taken,' Seth chips in. 'Doesn't have social media, or anything like that.'

'Oh.' Lily nods, accepting this immediately.

I don't *really* have a fear of having my photo taken. I just don't *want* my photo taken. Ever. I can't risk it appearing in the wrong place or being seen by the wrong person. So I gladly stoke this perception.

'He was such a lovely boy,' I say and pinch Seth's cheek. 'Always with his head in a pond.'

'Mum,' Seth says, rolling his eyes.

Lily smiles. 'They don't call him PondGuy for nothing,' she says proudly and nudges Seth in the elbow.

Seth is obsessed with the ecosystem of ponds and has a social media following for his videos on frogs, toads and the like. Just one of his quirky passions. I love that Lily doesn't find that weird. Todd and I have always encouraged Seth's hobbies and interests. We give him our full support to be and do whatever his heart desires. There was no insistence that he follow his father into football or anything ridiculous like that. Zero expectations from us other than to be himself and to love his life.

Seth pretends to jump away from Lily and grins playfully. She grins back.

'Anyway,' he says. 'We're going in the other room. Gonna order pizza.'

'I've made honey cake for dessert, if you want any,' I say.

Seth gives me a thumbs up – it's also one of his favourites – and shows Lily into his telly room. She takes the glass of mead with her. He closes the door.

Todd kisses my cheek. 'She seems nice.'

'She does,' I reply happily. 'He's done well.' I cup Todd's face. 'And I hope we've made a good impression on her.'

Todd grins as I squeeze his cheeks. 'Of course we have. How could anyone not love Todd and Jen? We're ace parents.'

A few hours later, after a delicious husband-cooked dinner, Todd and I are curled up together on the sofa watching a Jason Statham action movie. We haven't heard or seen much of Seth and Lily. The doorbell went not long ago so they've got their pizza.

'Mum!' Seth comes running into the lounge.

Todd pauses the movie.

I sit upright. 'What is it?'

'Where's the cleaning stuff? We dropped pizza on the carpet.'

'I'll grab it,' I say. I do like a clean house. We have a weekly cleaner, but I keep things topped up. I get the cleaning spray and a sponge from under the sink. One thing Todd insists on is light-coloured carpets so I'm used to scrubbing stains off them. Todd and Seth always give it a go, but don't ever do it properly.

'Show me,' I say.

Seth lopes off towards the telly room, and I follow him. Lily is hovering by the end of the sofa looking anxious.

'I'm so sorry, Mrs James,' she says and wrings her hands.

'It's not a problem. We're used to tackling spillages in this household. Where is it?'

She points at the carpet near her feet. Seth waits behind me. The dropped slice is folded on a tissue on the coffee table, so at least they picked it up quickly. I kneel and spray the stain – a greasy, bright-orange, cheesy pepperoni smear – and give it a scrub with the sponge.

'I'll do it, Mum,' Seth says.

'It's no problem, be done in one sec. Could you get a plastic bowl of warm water with a few drops of washing-up liquid and a cloth from under the sink?'

'Sure,' he says and dashes out.

Lily nervously picks up her plate of pizza from the coffee table and takes a bite.

I scour some more.

'Oh no,' she squeals.

I look at where she's looking. A second slice of pizza is on the carpet. We both move to pick it up and bump hands.

'Mrs James, Jen, I'm so sorry! I'm a bit tipsy off your mead. And I'm being clumsy...'

'Honestly, not to worry, Lily.' I pick up the slice and put it on top of the other folded one and spray the second spot with cleaner.

I dab at the second stain, and Lily stands over me. Her shadow falls across my face. I glance up. She's mortified, close to tears.

Seth arrives back and hands me the bowl and cloth.

She reaches for him. 'I dropped another slice,' she says, choking up.

He puts his arm round her. 'It's fine. Don't worry.' He asks me, 'Can we help, Mum?'

'No, almost done.' I give the stains a rub with the warm soapy water and pat at them with the cloth. 'That should be fine for now.'

I stand up.

Lily steps towards me. 'I'm really so sorry,' she says. 'What a terrible impression I'm making. I've ruined your carpet.' Her eyes well up.

'Lily, it's absolutely fine. No harm done. I'm pleased you liked my mead.'

Spontaneously, she hugs me. 'Thank you for being so kind about it,' she says into my shoulder.

She releases me and blushes, realising what she's done.

'She's a hugger too,' Seth says with a laugh.

Lily and I smile at each other, one hugger to another.

As I look into her sweet and innocent face, I know she'll never have to do what I had to do. She'll never have to scrub clean her past like I just scrubbed stains from the carpet.

CHAPTER TWO

The following Friday, Todd is away overnight in London for a speaking gig. Lily has been over to the house three times in the week, and I've said a quick hello. But earlier, Seth asked if she could stay the night. And I asked if they would have dinner with me so I could get to know her a bit better. We both said yes to one another.

Seth volunteered to cook spaghetti bolognese and is chopping onions. Lily asked if she could help, but he told her he had it covered. She then asked me, but I'd already laid the table. So, as Seth takes charge in the kitchen and there are no other tasks that need doing, Lily and I sit on the high stools around the kitchen island with large glasses of red wine in hand and nibble on my latest batch of rosemary and honey-roasted nuts.

'What are you studying at uni, Lily?' I ask.

'I'm doing computer science with modules in artificial intelligence and cybersecurity,' she replies.

'She's a computer genius,' Seth says as he puts the onions in a frying pan, turns on the gas and clicks the igniter.

Lily blushes. 'Well, I don't know about that...'

'Come on, you are,' Seth insists. The onions begin to sizzle, and he stirs them while looking back to us. 'She brings her laptop everywhere with her. We all bring our mobile phones, but she has her laptop.'

'Is that right?' I ask.

'Yes. I just have these coding ideas pop into my head at the most random times and want to immediately try them out.' She gives a little laugh. 'Very nerdy, I know.'

'We're all nerds in this household,' I reply.

'Too right,' Seth says.

Lily smiles. I take a sip of wine.

She fiddles with the cuffs of her baggy jumper and takes a breath. It looks like she's building up courage. Tentatively, she asks, 'How long have you and Todd been together?'

'Around two decades now,' I reply.

'And how did you meet?'

'It was all because of ThunderCats,' Seth says.

'ThunderCats?' Lily asks.

'It's an eighties cartoon,' I explain. 'Todd and I both love eighties cartoons.' Because we were both mostly ignored by our parents or, in Todd's case, parent, growing up and were plonked in front of the telly and told to shut up and watch. But I don't tell Lily this. 'I was working for a women's shelter charity in Southampton at the time – well, I still work there – and they had organised a fundraising event and invited lots of people. They'd extended an invite to Southampton FC, not expecting anyone to come. But Todd has always been passionate about charity work and decided to attend. The shelter bosses asked their staff if anyone would volunteer to help out with welcoming guests and serving food and whatnot, and I said yes.'

Seth adds the mince to the onions, and the pan spits loudly. Lily and I both glance there momentarily, and I sip my wine. She looks back to me eagerly, obviously keen to hear the rest of the story.

I continue, 'I'd just moved to Southampton and have never

had any interest in football. I had no idea who Todd was or anyone there, for that matter. I had a tray of canapés and happened to be handing them around to a group of people. Todd was in that group and telling a story. Everyone else was listening intently. He came out with a ThunderCats reference. I laughed. But nobody else got it. We exchanged a knowing look, and I walked off to hand out food around the room.'

I pause to graze on some nuts. Lily leans forward, hanging onto my every word.

'And then what happened?' she asks.

'Later on that evening, Todd came and found me. I was at the back with all the other staff and volunteer helpers. The first words he said to me were, "Thunder, Thunder, Thunder, ThunderCats, HOOOO!", which was one of the cartoon's famous catchphrases.'

Seth shouts, 'Hoooo!' while opening a cupboard to find a pan for the pasta.

Lily chuckles.

'Anyway, we chatted about eighties cartoons. As I say, I had no idea who he was. But we just got on so ridiculously well. I wasn't wearing any make-up – I never do – and hadn't made any kind of effort. But he asked me out. And that was that. We've been together ever since.'

'That's so cute,' Lily says. 'And what about Seth?'

Seth does a little silly dance at hearing his name.

'Seth came along very quickly. He was two when we got married. Made an adorable page boy.'

'Aww.' Lily concentrates and appears to be counting on her fingers. 'So, if his birthday is in April 2006, then he must've been conceived in July 2005?' She watches Seth with love-struck wonder on her face.

Seth doesn't notice, too busy putting the pasta into the boiling water. He's never questioned his parents about timings, his precise conception date or exactly when we met. And that's a good thing. Because it doesn't quite add up.

'Something like that,' I say vaguely, with a doting smile at my darling boy that matches the intensity of Lily's googly eyes.

Seth isn't Todd's son, not biologically anyway. I met Todd in 2006 and he adopted Seth when Seth was a few months old. Todd is the only father Seth has ever known and will ever know. Todd loves Seth as if he was his own blood. But Seth doesn't know he was fathered by another man. Todd and I didn't intentionally not tell Seth. It's just that the years flew by, and we never quite got round to it. There's never been a reason for Seth to see his birth certificate – I organised his first passport. And then, suddenly, he was a teenager, and the moment had passed. Todd and I both know the fallout would be catastrophic if we told him now. We know we've left it too late.

Seth is oblivious. He looks just like me.

His Greek heritage overrode all other genes. It was inevitable, really. I look like my Greek mother, and my mother looks like my Greek grandparents, and probably on and on down the Greek line. But Seth will never meet that side of the family – or any of my family whatsoever.

Lily drags her gaze from her boyfriend to face me again. There's a brief pause as we both think of what to say. She beats me to it. 'So, you and Todd met in 2005?'

I know she's only continuing the conversation and is perhaps one of these people who like to know exact dates and facts, but I really can't get into this. I smile broadly at her, in a way that neither confirms nor denies, and stand. 'Seth, shall I get some serving dishes out? Looks like it's almost ready.'

'Yeah, please,' he replies, draining the cooked pasta in a colander over the sink.

I get some dishes out of a cupboard and put them on the side for Seth. He puts the pasta into one of the dishes and the sauce in the other. Lily jumps up. Together we bring everything over to the dining table and get seated. Seth dishes up and grates Parmesan over everyone's plates with relish.

'*Bon appétit,*' he declares.

We all tuck in. I'm about to give my compliments to the chef when Lily says, 'It's delicious.' And gives Seth a quick kiss on the cheek.

I decide to steer the chat onto safer topics. 'Where do you think your love of computers came from, Lily? Was there any moment or thing in particular that sparked your interest?'

Lily finishes her mouthful, and her eyes light up. 'Yes, it was from my dad. He used to build and repair computers for people. I became obsessed with taking them apart and putting them back together and getting them to work. I got a real thrill from seeing all the different components. Slotting them into place was like a puzzle.'

'Your parents must be very proud of you doing this course at uni,' I say.

Her face collapses. 'I wouldn't know...'

Seth drops his knife to squeeze her hand. 'Lily's an orphan, like you and Dad.'

Lily bumps her shoulder to his to communicate her thanks for his support. 'My mum died when I was eight, and my dad died about a year ago now. I have an aunt, but no other family.'

I lean across the table and pat her hand gently, briefly. 'I'm so sorry, Lily. That must've been so tough for you. Losing a parent is devastating, but when you were only a child – gosh, so awful.'

She nods. 'Yes. Seth said your parents died in a car crash. So you must understand.'

I arrange my face into a well-practised sadness, blink as if chasing away tears and steel myself with a deep breath – the manner I always deploy whenever there's talk of my deceased parents.

'I do. Todd didn't know his father, and his mum died when he was nineteen.'

'None of your family are still alive?' Lily asks.

I shake my head.

'Not one?' she insists.

'No,' I reply.

'And you don't have any siblings?'

'No, no siblings.' I gulp back the dregs of my drink and pick up the empty bottle of red. 'More wine, Lily?' I ask.

She shakes her head. 'No, thank you. I'm so lucky to still have my aunt.'

'You are,' I agree. Lily looks like she's about to ask me another question so I get in quick. 'Seth, do you want another bottle of beer?'

He picks up his bottle and checks how much is left. 'Yes, please.'

I stand, head over to the kitchen and grab another bottle of wine and a beer out of the fridge. I don't really want to open another bottle, but needed to get Lily off that train of conversation.

I open Seth's beer, screw the top off the wine and sit back at the table, topping up my glass. Before Lily can ask anything else about my family, I say, 'What made you pick Southampton University? Are you from this area?'

Lily tucks her hair behind her ears. And then untucks it. 'Kind of. I was born in Ashford, Surrey, but grew up around this area – Bournemouth, Basingstoke, Winchester. My mum was from Southampton. When Dad died, I lived with my aunt but wanted to study here.'

I nod.

She asks brightly, 'How come you moved to Southampton? You said you'd just moved here when you met Todd.'

'Yes. I moved from Milton Keynes. I was staying at the

women's shelter because I'd been in a toxic relationship, he'd thrown me out and I wanted a fresh start in a new place.'

Her eyes widen. But Seth doesn't bat an eyelid. He knows this. He just doesn't know that he was also staying at the shelter with me. He helps himself to more pasta and sauce.

'Wow. Intense,' Lily replies. 'And before MK?'

'Before?' I ask, surprised.

'It's just you've got a bit of an accent so I thought you'd maybe grown up somewhere else...' She trails off and blushes, realising she's pried a little too deeply in her eagerness to get to know her new beau's mum and strayed too far from polite chit-chat. She has a slight social awkwardness about her, which reminds me of Seth.

Todd and Seth think I moved to Southampton from Milton Keynes. As far as they're concerned, there's no 'before'. I grew up there and had a decidedly boring and decidedly average childhood. So dull, in fact, that we rarely talk about it. And I'd like to keep it that way. I invented a full backstory, of course, for when Todd and I began dating and we shared 'everything', and for when Seth was young and asked a million questions: 'What was your first job?' 'Where did you go to school?' 'Who was your favourite teacher?' I kept it rooted in the truth, so I didn't trip myself up, but omitted and changed a few major details.

I dodge Lily's astute observation with a smile and quick shake of the head and direct the discussion elsewhere. 'While I was staying at the hostel, they offered me the receptionist position at the charity's office. And I still work there now,' I say.

I love my job. I don't need to work, Todd earns plenty enough to cover our living costs, but that place took me in with no questions asked when I rocked up bruised and battered with a baby in my arms and with no luggage or identification. They also willingly gave me a job with no need for references or any kind of previous employment paperwork – they knew I didn't have it on me and it was highly unlikely I'd be going back to the place I'd run from to get it.

'You work part-time now, right?' Lily asks as she finishes up her meal and puts her knife and fork neatly on the plate.

'Yes. Suits me perfectly.'

'Cool,' she replies, dragging out the word. 'Did you work full-time before you had this one?' She nudges Seth in the side, but he's too busy gobbling down his dinner to do more than waggle an eyebrow in her direction.

I didn't work full-time because I *did* have Seth and job-shared with another woman with a baby at the shelter. While I was working, she looked after her baby and Seth, and when she was on, I looked after Seth and her baby. But no one needs to know that.

'I job-share with a wonderful woman,' I reply with no further explanation and focus on finishing up my meal.

Lily politely dabs at her mouth with a napkin, folding it and putting it on her plate. She sits up straighter, a keen and interested look on her face. It's obvious she wants to make a good impression, which endears me towards her even more.

Seth takes a third helping of pasta and sauce. 'Do either of you want any more?' he asks.

Lily and I indicate we're full, so he spoons the last of the food onto his plate.

'That boy has hollow legs,' I say, and laugh. 'You're like your father, both of you can put away food that's enough for three people.'

Seth snorts through a mouthful.

'You mean Todd?' Lily asks.

I frown. *Who else does she think I mean?*

But Seth chuckles, understanding immediately what she meant. 'Yeah, Dad eats loads. I know, you wouldn't believe it because he's still so lean and fit.'

Lily laughs with him.

I decide to completely change the subject. 'Has Seth told you where his passion for ponds came from?'

Seth rolls his eyes.

Lily jiggles in her seat and tickles Seth in the ribs. 'No, he hasn't. Go on, please tell me.'

I move my empty plate to one side and clasp my hands on the dining table. 'When he was younger, he loved to do anything outdoorsy. I took him to a local nature reserve that had a pond expert in to give a demonstration to the kids. The expert pointed out the tadpoles and explained the different life stages of frogs and showed them all sorts to do with the different animals that live in ponds and freshwater. Seth was obsessed. When we got home, he went straight out to our pond in the garden and poked and prodded. I scooped out a jar of tadpoles, and we brought them inside and watched them grow into baby frogs.'

'And that was that,' Seth says with a big grin. 'PondGuy was born.'

'We discovered there was a zoology course at Southampton. And that's what he's always wanted to do.'

'Yep,' he replies. He rises to clear away the plates. Lily and I get to our feet to help.

Seth continues, 'And I knew from early on that I'd focus on freshwater ecosystems and conservation.'

Lily adds, 'It's your calling.'

He beams at her.

The three of us move around each other tidying up and putting things in the dishwasher.

'What are you two up to later?' I ask.

'We're going to make placards,' Lily says.

'Placards?'

Seth nods. 'There's a protest tomorrow in Portsmouth. The council is considering giving an area of protected nature reserve to a building developer to build houses on.' He raises his voice.

'A *protected* piece of land!' He angrily punches his fist into his other palm. 'And that land has lots of freshwater habitat and some rare birds that nest there. It's disgusting.'

'That's terrible,' I reply.

'Oh yeah, I forgot to ask...' Seth slides over to me and puts an arm around my shoulder. 'Please could you give us a lift to the train station in the morning? After the protest, a few of us are going for drinks at Gunwharf Quays, so I don't want to drive.'

'Of course, what time?' I reply. I'm used to being a Mum Taxi.

He squeezes me into him to show his appreciation. 'Nine-ish?'

I nod.

'Thanks, Jen,' Lily says sweetly. 'And what are you up to tonight?'

Her interest in my evening is touching. 'I'm going to have a laptop night. I've got some cucamelon seeds and need to research the best way to store them to sow next year.'

'Cucamelon?' she asks, intrigued.

'They taste like cucumber but look like teeny-tiny melons,' I reply.

'Cool,' she says.

Seth steers her into the telly room. 'Let's make some signs, baby!'

She grins up at him. Just before they reach the doorway to the telly room, she turns back and says, 'Thanks for letting me stay over, Jen.'

She has impeccable manners, and I can't help but really like her.

I'm certain her curiosity is sated now, and she won't be asking any more questions about exactly what happened in 2006.

There are some questions best left unanswered. Permanently.

CHAPTER THREE

18 YEARS AGO

DAILY TIMES
Monday 3 July 2006

BRUTAL MURDER SHOCKS COMMUNITY – POLICE APPEAL FOR WITNESSES

A murder investigation has been launched after a man was found dead at an address in Southampton

Police are appealing for witnesses to come forward after the brutal murder of Jerry Ward, 69, at the weekend. Mr Ward, a father of two and grandfather of three, was discovered in his house on Becker Road by his daughter on Sunday evening after phone calls had gone unanswered all day. It's believed his time of death was on Saturday evening (1 July) around 9 p.m.

Mr Ward had lived his entire life in Southampton and had only recently retired.

Detective Chief Inspector Rohan Bhatia of Hampshire and Isle of Wight Constabulary commented: 'The nature of this crime was particularly brutal, and we want to speak to anyone in the Freemantle area who saw or heard anything suspicious on the evening of Saturday first of July.'

Mr Ward's eldest daughter, who asked not to be named, said: 'We loved our father dearly, and my kids loved their gramps. The entire family is absolutely devastated. What an awful way to go. What was done to him was shocking. Who could do that to an old man?'

According to his daughter, Mr Ward separated from his wife soon after his second daughter was born but remained in close contact with his children and subsequently their children. He worked in various roles for the post office for many years, including as a letter carrier and in the sorting warehouse.

She also told reporters that Mr Ward's 'throat had been cut with a large kitchen knife' and that 'after, when he was dying and already dead, he'd been stabbed multiple times with that same knife in a frenzied attack.' The police have not confirmed this.

DCI Bhatia added: 'Our officers remain at the scene and will continue to carry out enquiries in the area over the next few days. We fully appreciate the concern this incident will cause within the community, and local officers will be carrying out more high-visibility patrols. We're looking for a potentially very dangerous individual. Please do not confront or approach any suspects, please call the police immediately.

'Our thoughts are with Mr Ward's family at this incredibly distressing time.'

CHAPTER FOUR

I shiver myself awake. It's early in the morning. I'm not sure exactly what time, but my usual 6.30 a.m. alarm hasn't gone off yet. There's a weight missing from the bed. It's not Todd, because Todd is staying away in London. It's the duvet. It's missing. It's not even over my feet.

I must've got hot and kicked it off. In the darkness, I pat around for the duvet on the bed. It's nowhere within grabbing distance. I sit up and reach further down. It's not there. It must've fallen off and is on the floor.

I swing one leg off the bed and tap with my foot on the floor. No duvet. Urgh. I'm just going to have to turn the bedside lamp on. I scrunch up my eyes, switch it on, wait a moment for my eyes to adjust and look around the bed, first at the end and then on Todd's side. No duvet.

Huh?

Our bedroom is vast. It takes up most of the first floor and is over the huge triple garage downstairs. On the other side of the room is the crumpled-up duvet.

How did it get all the way over there?

There's no chance I could've kicked it that far. I must've

woken up hot and half-asleep and put it over there for some reason. I shrug and walk the few paces to collect it and bring it back to the bed.

I shake it out onto the bed and get under it to warm up. It's cold to the touch, so I must've taken it off a few hours ago. I check my phone. It's almost six, so my alarm will be going off soon. I'm not too good at staying in bed once I'm awake, so I get up.

Off the bedroom is a dressing area. It's a separate room with massive wardrobes and huge mirrors. I don't use it as a dressing room. I'm not that bothered about what I wear or checking myself out in the mirror for hours on end. Todd has more clothes than I do. Instead, I've converted a little corner into my 'propagation station', as Todd calls it. I'm obsessed with house-plants. And propagating plants into new plants. I love watching the little white roots grow out of the bottom of cuttings. I'm not so fussed with outdoor plants. I adore my vegetable and herb patch, but we have a gardener who looks after the rest of the grounds. He steers well clear of the beehives though. They're tucked away right in the furthest corner that backs onto woodland.

Most of my baby plants I give away to work colleagues and to women passing through the shelters who are being rehoused and would like a plant to brighten up their new space. Occasionally, Todd will take some into the radio station or when he's going into the club to see his PA. I've got all kinds of plants around the house and sometimes I get requests. Seth's best mate's mum asked me for a polka dot begonia cutting once, and I was only too happy to oblige.

I get changed, potter with my plants for a while and head downstairs for breakfast. It's an unseasonably warm October day, so I plan to get outside to tend to the bees and work in my veg patch. I'll have a few undisturbed hours because Todd isn't due back until early afternoon.

As I'm making scrambled eggs, Lily comes into the kitchen.

'Morning,' she singsongs. 'Seth's just getting out of the shower, and I thought I'd put the finishing touches to our placards.'

'Would you like some scrambled eggs?'

'No, thank you. We're going to get something to eat on the train.' She heads into the telly room.

My toast pops, and I turn off the gas hob. I leave the eggs in the pan and dash to the downstairs loo for a quick wee before I eat them.

Just as I'm finishing up, I hear a scream. I run back into the kitchen.

Seth pinches the edge of a tea towel and holds it up and away from him.

It's on fire. The flames lick up the cloth and towards his face. His eyes are wide, and the flames cast his skin in an orange tinge. Smoke billows.

I yell his name.

He spins and chucks the tea towel into the sink and shoves on the cold tap. Water gushes over the material and quenches the flames. 'Mum, you set a tea towel on fire!'

'Whoa,' Lily says.

She stands between the dining table and the kitchen island. It must've been her who screamed.

Smoke drifts through the kitchen. The fire alarm clicks on and blares.

'Are you okay, Seth? Did you get burnt?' I shout over the din.

'Nope. All fine,' Seth replies and splashes the tea towel with water to make sure it's definitely out.

I place a dining chair under the alarm. I stand on it and press the button on the unit. The wailing stops. I climb down, go over to Seth and take in the charred remains of the tea towel in the sink, now completely drenched.

Seth looks at me over his shoulder. 'You could've burnt the whole house down. How many times have you told me not to leave the gas hob unattended? And not to put a tea towel anywhere near it?'

'I didn't leave the hob on or put a tea towel near it,' I insist. My heart pounds.

Seth shrugs. 'Well, you must've done.'

I blink at him. I'm certain I didn't. But there's no other explanation. Perhaps I've got brain fog from getting hot in the night and not sleeping too well.

He punches my arm lightly. 'Are you still okay to give us a lift to the station in a bit?' he asks nonchalantly, as if he hasn't just saved the house from going up in flames.

I nod. I glance at Lily. She's still open-mouthed and rooted to the spot. She looks as shaken as I feel.

'Are you okay, Jen?' she asks as Seth passes her and gestures towards the telly room.

'Um. Yes.' I decide to make light of it. 'Don't need any coffee now because that's certainly woken me up.'

She smiles and follows my son into the other room.

I pick up the sodden, blackened tea towel and put it in the bin. I don't usually make silly mistakes like that. If there'd been a fire here that got reported in the news, talked about online... there's a risk they'd use a photo of me or a nosy bystander might recognise me.

I need to be more careful. One wrong move could bring this entire life crumbling down on top of me.

CHAPTER FIVE

The next day, I pull into the large car park of a chain pub that boasts an all-you-can-eat carvery for a bargain price. It's Sunday afternoon and busy. I finally find a space and turn off the engine, taking a very long, deep breath before getting out of my car.

I've passed this pub countless times over the years but have never been in. Busy places are not my thing. Plus, there's a small hotel next door, which means travellers and businesspeople and out-of-towners popping into the pub for a drink or dinner. The kind of people I actively avoid.

But this afternoon is different. An adorable couple from work are hosting their baby shower here. He's in accounts, she's in procurement. They got together at a work Christmas party a few years ago and got married soon after. They announced they were expecting and everyone at work was deliriously excited – a work baby! But there were complications at the birth and the baby died a few days later. It was devastating. The entire office felt their pain. It took a long time for either of them to come back to work. But they did. And then a few weeks ago they announced they were expecting again. And this time it was twins.

So I really wanted to come to celebrate with them. But I won't stay long. Work organised a lovely gift but I also baked them a honey and orange cake this morning and have a jar of honey for them. I'll give them both a big hug, get one drink and sit out of the way.

As I get closer to the front door of the pub, I hear a male and female arguing outside but just around the corner. Clearly a lover's tiff.

I put my hand on the door and am about to pull it open when I hear a man say, 'Calm down, Miranda.'

Then a woman screeches, 'Don't you dare tell me what to do, Simon!'

And I know immediately who this couple is. My best friend and his girlfriend. Simon and I work together and met there eighteen years ago. He's been with Miranda coming up for a year and a half now. Miranda and I don't like each other. Initially, I was excited to meet her. But she took an immediate dislike to me, and, after I saw how poorly she treated Simon, the feeling became mutual.

She's pressuring him to move in together, to sell their respective flats and buy a house. But he's resisting. I think it's because he knows deep down that she's not right for him. He says it's because he likes his own space and is coming around to the idea of living with someone else. She thinks he's stalling and messing her around.

Although I've only met her a few times, I know my best friend can do better.

'No! Don't do that,' I hear Simon say, desperately, and I let go of the door handle and jog around the side to see Simon cowering against the wall of the pub and Miranda with her hand in the air. It looks like she's threatening to hit him.

Simon's short and stocky with a rugby player's build. He's almost completely bald. But he has a full beard, a blend of blond and grey. He's only a year older than me but looks much older. The heavy drug-taking in his teenage years, which he's openly told me about, has taken a toll on his skin. But his smile lines make up for it – they direct your gaze towards his eyes, which are a bright blue and always seem to sparkle. He has a lovely smile and is quick to laugh. People warm to him immediately. Although I'm sure he's incredibly strong, his passion for CrossFit keeps him fit, he has a gentle, kind energy.

Miranda, on the other hand, is hard. Sharp features, severe blunt bob, average height and build but with an air of someone who knows that if they decide to kick the crap out of you, they'll win, no matter the opponent. She's got two older kids from a previous marriage and, according to Simon, some unresolved trauma related to her father from many years ago that she hasn't fully processed and which negatively affects her behaviour when triggered.

I've witnessed the verbal and emotional abuse, but physical abuse – this is new.

'Hey!' I shout. 'What are you doing, Miranda?'

Her hand drops, and their faces spin to me.

'Oh, hey, Jen,' Simon says, cheerily. His face always lights up when he sees me, as I expect mine does when I see him. We get on so well.

Miranda makes a noise of disgust from the back of her throat and rolls her eyes.

'Are you okay?' I ask him.

'Yeah, of course. Why wouldn't I be?' he says.

I give him a look, that says, *I know you're not*. Then I glance at her.

She spears me with a glare. Leans forward and grinds out, 'Why don't you mind your own business?'

'Chill out,' I reply.

Simon wedges his body between us. 'Miranda, stop. Jen, are you okay?'

Miranda shouts in his ear, 'Why are you worried about *her*? You should be worried about *me*!' She shoves him aside to jab her finger at me. 'Fuck off! Just fuck right off. Fucking bitch!'

My heart leaps, the adrenaline churning. Am I about to get into a pub brawl? At 3 p.m. on a Sunday?

'Miranda!' Simon grabs her wrist so that her finger doesn't connect with me. He looks pointedly at me. 'I'm okay. You head inside, and we'll see you in there.'

While looking at Simon, I hold up my hands in an attempt to pacify the wild beast frothing at the mouth that is Miranda. 'Are you sure?'

'Yes,' he says. 'I'm sure.' He nods at me.

'Call me if you need me.' I give him a long look and head back to the front door.

'Just bore off already,' Miranda shouts at my back.

I head inside, heart racing, and am hit with the noise of the heaving pub. All the tables are full and there's people everywhere: waiting at the bar, standing in the queue for the carvery, milling around tables, running after restless kids. And the smell is a slap in the face. Roasted meat. Vegetables kept warm for too long on hot trays. Gravy, slightly congealed, stewing.

Nausea rushes up my throat as a painful childhood memory whooshes into my mind.

This is the kind of place my family came to. Cheap. Busy. A bit rough around the edges.

A feeling overwhelms me. Of being left. Of being forgotten. Of not being picked up for hours and hours. Of being so unimportant to people I should be important to. It cracks me in two.

Then a laugh pierces through the chatter of patrons and clatter of cutlery. A woman's cackle that sounds way too familiar.

It's followed with a man's voice, saying her name. Telling her to *rein it in*. As always.

I swallow back the bile and take a few steps further inside the room. I look around and see a man at the bar, his back to me. His broad shoulders covered with a Southampton FC shirt; my husband's name splashed across the top.

It can't be...

He turns, a pint in each hand, and heads right past me towards a table at the front.

It isn't him. It isn't them.

I take a deep breath. Steady myself. Push down the memory. *They're gone. They're gone. They. Are. Gone.*

Glancing around, I spot the baby shower in the corner. Balloons and a table loaded with gifts the immediate giveaway. I hurry there, hug the couple, give them the cake and honey, chat for a while, say a brief hello to colleagues.

And leave.

I don't even have a drink.

Simon and Miranda are gone when I head for my car. Before I set off home, I send him a text to check in. He replies almost immediately:

> *All good here. Miranda had a few too many wines. She's sleeping it off, and I'm watching a movie xx*

> I respond: *I'm worried about you xx*

> Simon: *It was nothing. She just gets a bit wild when drunk. She's a great girlfriend otherwise. Just that one little glitch. We all have them! I know I do! Well, not you, you're perfect LOL. See you tomo xx*

Simon is very good at putting himself down and at the same

time bigging me up. We've talked about it before. I'd love for him to be more confident, but it's just his way.

A few minutes later, and I'm home. Coming through the front door immediately calms my shredded nerves.

'Hey, you,' I say as I come into the kitchen.

Todd is sat on a high stool around the kitchen island tapping on his laptop. He looks up at me, his face goes white, and he snaps his laptop shut. He swallows guiltily, as if I've just caught him up to something.

'You're home sooner than I was expecting,' he says.

'Yeah. Miranda was really aggressive and told me to fuck off. I thought she was going to hit me.'

'Miranda, as in Simon's girlfriend?'

Todd has never met Miranda, only heard about her from me. 'That's the one.'

'Why would she tell you to fuck off?'

'She's not a nice person. Simon said she was drunk. But I think she might be physically abusing him.'

'That's awful. Poor chap. Why doesn't he get rid of her?' This is Todd's default response whenever I bring up Miranda.

'I don't know. But it's not ever that simple, is it?'

He shrugs. 'I guess not. But as you've said to me before, he could do so much better. If he ditched the bitch then that would free him up to find the perfect woman for him.'

'Exactly.' I hug myself and rub my arms. 'Anyway, that shook me up and then I had a weird turn and didn't want to be there.'

He jumps up and comes to hug me. 'I'm sorry, my love. What happened?'

I melt into his embrace. The ridiculous passing thought that he was doing something nefarious on his laptop disappears. I just surprised him. This man is my world. He'd never do anything to hurt me.

'That place reminded me of somewhere I went to as a child... with my... parents.'

'Oh, Jen. Grief is a bugger, isn't it? It creeps up on you out of nowhere.' He squeezes me tighter.

'Yes,' I mumble into his neck.

But I'm not grieving.

CHAPTER SIX

Five days later, on Thursday evening, Todd and I are in his 'office' after dinner. It's the floor above the gym in the little outbuilding. It has a desk with a laptop on it in one corner but is almost entirely filled up with Todd's model railway. There are two large tables placed together in the middle with a huge model on top. In the other corner is his workbench with shelves full of modelling tools and bits and pieces. There's also a small sofa, which I sit on with my laptop on my knee.

The model is growing too large for the space, and I've suggested relocating it into a corner of the garage, which Todd is pondering. It'll be a big effort to move it all. But then he'll have lots more room to expand.

Todd has his back to me. He's hunched over his workbench making trees out of wire and gluing all the tiny leaves on. He can spend hours building models and playing with his trains in this room. He has a bright spotlight shining on his work area and looks at what his hands are doing through a magnifying glass attached to the worktop. He has the radio on next to him, tuned to his radio station. Every now and then he hums along to a song or chuckles at the presenter's quips. He recorded his

Saturday morning football show this morning, plus a few teasers. Every time a teaser plays, he says, 'That's me!' as I say, 'That's you!' It makes us both laugh.

I take a sip of mead – it's from a particularly potent batch – and open a browser. I search for winter sun holidays and peruse the websites that come up. Todd and I are going away in January. We usually go away in the February half-term, but Seth has said he doesn't want to come this year because of his uni work and because he's eighteen now. He told me that he and Lily might save up to go away in the summer, which is very sweet. So, it's just Todd and me this time.

There are lots of options for romantic couple getaways, and I spot a few in the Canary Islands. One has its own hot tub and mini pool with an incredible view. I glance up at my husband and have the overwhelming urge to go and put my arms around him, nibble his ear and initiate sex. He'd be up for it. We're always both up for it. Probably another reason we get on so well: our sex drives match.

I paste the link into the Word document I always use to keep holiday research together, but my laptop screen goes black. It's plugged in, so it can't be the battery. The screen turns red. A spinning wheel in the centre indicates something is happening. Perhaps it just crashed? I probably should get a new one, it's pretty old. Just as I'm about to switch it off and on again, a black notification with white text pops up to fill the screen.

It reads:

Oops! Your data has been encrypted. To get it back, send £75,000 in bitcoin here.

I stab at the keys and tap the touchpad. But nothing happens. The screen stays the same.

'Todd!'

He turns to me. 'What's up?'

'My laptop has gone nuts. Look.'

We both stand and edge around the model to meet in the middle. He reads the screen. 'What's all that about?'

'I must've been hacked. Crap. Years and years of photos are on that laptop. And loads of documents and important stuff.'

'Seventy-five grand to get it back? That's a huge number,' Todd says.

'I'm going to turn it off and on again. See if that helps.'

Todd watches as I switch off the power button, count to ten and turn it back on. The laptop whirs to life. 'Oh, it looks normal,' I say as I put in my password and the home screen displays.

'Phew,' Todd replies.

I click on my Photos folder, but the *Oops!* notification pops up again.

'Dammit,' I say. My heart sinks. 'I can't lose all those photos. Of you, of Seth, of my bees. My best mead recipe is saved on here.'

Todd chews at his lip, thinking. 'Didn't you tell me that Lily is studying computer science? She might be able to help.'

'Yes!' I kiss my husband's cheek. 'Great idea.'

I unplug my laptop, and we barrel down the stairs and across the garden terrace to the main house. Seth and Lily are in Seth's telly room with the door closed. By the sounds of it, they're playing a video game.

I put my laptop on the dining table and knock on the door. 'Guys? Can I come in?'

'Sure, Mum,' Seth replies.

I open the door. They're both sitting on the edge of the sofa, eyes glued to the telly, hands gripping the controllers, fingers going crazy.

Seth presses pause. They turn to look at me.

'I was wondering if you might be able to help me, Lily,' I say hopefully.

She points to herself and looks pleasantly surprised. 'Yeah, sure! How can I help?'

I beckon them into the dining area and point at my laptop. 'I think I've been hacked or something. Check out the screen.'

They both move closer and look.

'Seventy-five grand,' Seth exclaims.

'Ransomware,' Lily says, pulling out the chair in front of my laptop to sit and look closer at the screen. 'Your laptop's been infected by malicious software that holds your data hostage and demands a ransom. You can still use the laptop, but just can't access files – sometimes all of them, sometimes a select few.'

'We don't have seventy-five thousand pounds to pay it,' I say.

Lily pushes her fringe off her forehead. 'Most of the time, even if you pay you don't get access to your data back.'

'Can you help?' I ask desperately.

'I can certainly give it a go,' she says excitedly. 'Seth, please could you get my bag?'

'Yep.' Seth bounds into the telly room and comes out holding her rucksack. He hands it to her and she pulls out her laptop. It's battered and clearly well used with faded stickers all over it. She opens it and places it next to mine.

'Have you switched it off and on again?' Lily asks me.

'Yes.'

She nods, taps a few things on her laptop, and it springs to life. She opens a Word document and types some notes.

'Is there anything I can do to help?' I ask.

She thinks for a minute. 'Could you make me a coffee, please?'

'I'll do it,' Seth says and jogs to the kitchen area.

Lily pulls out her mobile phone from the pocket of her rucksack. 'Do you mind if I take photos of your screen and what I do? I want to make notes and maybe write it up into a case study for uni.'

'Of course,' I reply.

'Thanks.' She finds a scrunchie in her bag and ties her hair back. 'Right, let's get to work!' She takes a photo of my laptop screen and writes some notes on the Word document on her laptop.

Seth brings over her coffee. The smell so late in the day turns my stomach. I only usually have coffee first thing in the morning.

'Do you need me?' he asks Lily.

'No, all good here,' she replies without looking at him, too focused on the two laptops.

'I'm going to go back and finish the game,' he says.

'Sure thing,' she replies.

Todd, who has been leaning on his forearms on the kitchen island, says, 'Good luck, Lily.'

She gives him a thumbs up as he walks through to the lounge and switches on the football channel. But I hover, anxiously wringing my hands. All those photos.

'When was the last time you did a backup?' Lily asks.

'Umm... never.'

She nods. 'We might lose all your data.'

'Bollocks,' I reply through gritted teeth.

She holds up her hand. 'I'm going to do everything I can to make sure that doesn't happen though.'

'Thank you so much.'

She takes a sip of coffee. 'And do you remember clicking on anything, like a link in an email, where you might have downloaded this onto your laptop?'

I rack my brains. 'Nope. I don't remember clicking on anything dodgy.'

She types a few things, brings up another screen on her laptop and types some more. I continue to loiter at the end of the dining table.

She glances up at me. 'This might take a while.'

She's too sweet to say, *go away, you're distracting me*, but I get the hint.

'I'll be upstairs. Call me if you need me for anything,' I say.

But she doesn't reply, too busy tapping away on her laptop and snapping photos of her screen. She hums to herself as I head upstairs to our bedroom. I pull out my choir music and wander the room singing the new song that we started learning last night. I'm part of a local choir that meets every Wednesday. I love it. But I've never performed publicly with them, even though they perform regularly, all around Southampton and sometimes further afield. I can't risk a photo being taken and used somewhere openly or my face being recognised by the wrong person in the crowd.

We're learning *The Addams Family* theme tune, just in time for Halloween in a couple of weeks. Last year, we learnt *Ghostbusters*, and the year before was Michael Jackson's *Thriller*. My choirmaster likes to tie what we learn into public holidays and festivities.

I'm a soprano. I read my part on the sheet music and belt it out, attempting to quash my nerves about my infected laptop by singing at the top of my voice. I find singing to be an amazing stress reliever. But I can't shake the feeling that I'll never see all those precious photos and all my important documents again.

I practically shout the lyrics and can hear my voice going hoarse from overdoing it. But after the fifth time round, Seth shouts up the stairs.

'Mum! Lily has fixed it!'

I rush down the stairs and into the kitchen. Lily stands between Todd and Seth. She's elated. She beckons me to her. 'Come see.'

My laptop shows my home screen. She taps the back of the chair, and I take a seat.

'Just double-check, but I think everything is the same as before.'

I click a few things and open a few documents, and it does all appear to be unchanged. 'Wow, you're a genius, Lily.'

'It's the kind of thing I find really exciting. It's like a game of hide and seek – I work out what kind of access they have, make sure there are no back doors, and then boot them out.'

'Thank you so much.' I stand and hug her.

She accepts it happily. 'It was a great experience for me. I noticed that your anti-malware software is out of date. Which is likely why your machine was infected. I have a spare licence on my account. Would you like me to add it for you? Otherwise you might keep getting reinfected.'

'Yes, please. That's very kind of you.'

Lily sits back down in front of the two laptops.

'Do I need to put it on my laptop, do you think?' Todd asks Lily.

'Nah, Dad, didn't Gavin get yours set up with the IT peeps at the club?' Seth asks.

'Ah, yes, you're right,' Todd replies.

Gavin is Todd's shared PA who works at Southampton Football Club and helps a few of the retired players with managing their diaries and dealing with fan mail and so on. Even though Todd purchased the laptop, the club helped him set it up.

'I put all the stuff on mine,' Seth says, 'when I got my new laptop for uni. I should've checked your licence at the same time, Mum. Sorry about that.'

'Not a problem. Lily has saved the day.'

I squeeze her shoulder gratefully, and she looks up at me, cheeks flushing. She turns back to the laptops.

'There you are,' she says after typing a few more things. 'All done. You shouldn't have any malicious attackers on your laptop again.'

. . .

On Saturday lunchtime, Todd and I are sitting at the kitchen island eating lunch: salad drizzled with my homemade honey mustard dressing.

The front door opens and closes, and Seth and Lily come into the kitchen. Lily is in tears, and Seth's face is tight, his muscles tense, obviously distressed. It rends my entire being in two to see him like that. I put my cutlery down, alarmed.

'What's happened?' Todd asks.

Lily tries to speak but can't get the words out through sobs.

Seth puts his arm around her and pulls her into his chest. 'It's Lily's house. It's got a pest infestation—'

'Rats,' Lily cuts in and shudders.

'They've been getting in through a gap in a rotten window frame in the basement,' Seth continues. 'There are droppings and holes in the floorboards.'

'And we've got to move out for who knows how long while the landlord deals with it. But I've got nowhere to go because the others are breaking their tenancy agreement to move in together...' Lily trails off, distraught.

Seth rubs her shoulder. 'She lives with three students from the year above. She didn't apply until quite late, and by that point all the halls of residence were full. This was the only thing she could find at short notice. But they're not getting on.'

Through sobs, Lily says, 'They told me I was weird and wasn't fitting in with them. They do drama and art and are obsessed with taking pictures for social media and doing stuff that I'm just not interested in. They told me it wasn't working out and that they're going to find a three-bedroom place. The landlord has agreed they can end the contract early because of the rats, so I have to leave as well.'

My heart goes out to Lily. I know only too well from my childhood what it's like living with people who don't get you. I was always told I was strange. I was always the odd one out. I left home at sixteen.

Lily wipes her eyes with the cuffs of her sleeves. 'I checked with uni, and there are still no rooms in halls available, there aren't any other student houses that are advertising a room, and I can't afford to get anywhere on my own...'

'And if she can't find somewhere to live then she might have to move back to her aunt's,' Seth says.

Lily sobs again. 'In Inverness!'

Seth's face crumples further. Inverness is pretty much the other end of the UK, a ten-hour drive away, at least.

Lily's voice rises in pitch. 'I'll have to leave uni. Maybe transfer to one up there. Ohhh!'

She looks up at Seth.

He takes her hand. His voice rising in tone and desperation to match Lily's. 'I'll transfer up there with you. And if I can't get into another uni, then I'll jack it in and find a job. There must be something I can do in Scotland.'

'No,' Lily wails. 'You can't give up your degree. You love it.'

'I will, for you,' he replies, his eyes welling up.

'Steady now, let's not make any rash decisions,' I say.

Todd and I glance at each other. He's thinking exactly what I'm thinking, I can tell. He dips his chin at me.

Seth and Lily look at us.

'Lily can stay here until she gets herself sorted,' I say. 'It'll be no problem at all. I'm sure a room will come free in halls at some point soon – there's always a few people who drop out.'

Seth's face immediately lights up. 'You're sure?'

Todd says, 'Absolutely.'

Lily blinks away her tears and sniffs. 'Really?'

I laugh. 'Yes.'

Lily jogs around the kitchen island and clasps me tight. Seth follows, encircling us and Todd with his arms and squeezing us all in together.

'Thank you so much,' Lily says. 'I'll be the perfect house

guest, I promise. I'll be super quiet. And I'll do chores and anything you need doing.'

Seth breaks off the embrace and takes hold of Lily's hand, pulling her towards the door. 'Come on, let's go and get your stuff right now and move you in.'

He turns back to grin at us. Then the whirlwind is out the front door and gone again.

'I'm happy that he's happy,' Todd says, and he finishes the last few mouthfuls of his lunch.

'Me too,' I reply.

It'll be nice to have another woman around the house. It'll be like having a daughter. Todd and I tried for a second baby, but discovered that Todd can't have children. After considering other routes, we decided we were happy – and blessed – to be a family of three. Seth has always been a wonderful son, but I've always wondered what it would be like to have a daughter.

'Do you want some help with the bees this afternoon?' Todd asks.

'Yes, please. I washed our suits so they're shiny and white again.'

'Excellent,' he says.

After work on Monday, I'm pottering in my veg patch as the light fades. Todd isn't due home for another hour. Seth and Lily were out when I got in, so I got changed into my garden gear and headed straight out for some fresh air and dirt under my nails before it got too dark.

While I'm on my knees harvesting leeks, the sound of sobbing reaches me.

I get to my feet.

'Oh!' Lily exclaims, jumping in surprise. 'I'm sorry, I didn't think anyone was home yet.' She quickly swipes tears from her cheeks and attempts to rally herself. 'Seth's still at uni, so I walked back. And just fancied a little moment in your lovely garden.'

'Are you okay?' I step out of the dirt and onto the path where she's standing. I instinctively want to hug her, to soothe, to make better.

'Yes.' Her lips form a tight line.

'Sure?' I gently probe.

Her resolve cracks, and she hunches in on herself, palms flying up to hide her face. 'It's so silly,' she says through sobs. 'I don't know why I'm so upset... You must think I cry all the time.'

I put my arm gently around her shoulders. 'What's happened? You don't need to tell me if you don't want to.'

She sniffs. 'We did a test last week in one of my modules, and I got the results back today...' The tears come thicker and faster.

Rubbing her shoulder, I say, 'Take your time. Just breathe.'

She takes a breath. 'I didn't do as well as I thought I would. I was so sure I'd smash it.'

I hold her tighter. 'I can understand why you're upset. It's always disappointing when things don't quite turn out how we were expecting. You're not being silly at all. You're passionate about what you do and want to do your best. I get that.'

'I do.' She cries noisily. 'I should've done better.'

'When the next test comes around perhaps you can revise more, or study the subject with a study group, or even ask your lecturer for help if things aren't clear?'

'Yes, I probably should've prepped more.' She turns her body into mine and puts her arms around me, resting her head on me. I hug her back.

We stand in the embrace for a few moments. I've never held another woman close like this for this long. I was never cuddled as a child, never had any affection from my mother or grand-mother, never really had any close friends growing up. I've hugged Todd and Seth like this, of course. And have given brief hugs to Simon and to others, but this is something different.

It fires up my maternal, nurturing nature and feels wonderful.

Eventually, Lily pulls away. 'Thank you,' she says.

'You're welcome. You'll be all right.'

She takes a step away, and a wistful look crosses her features. 'I really miss my mum. I haven't had a hug like that in a long time.'

We take each other in, and I thrum contentedly.

'Come on,' I say. 'Let's go and get a cup of tea.'

'Or maybe some mead?' Lily replies, perking up.

I pick up my gardening things and follow her into the house. She fits in so perfectly. It's like she was always meant to be here.

CHAPTER SEVEN

18 YEARS AGO

DAILY TIMES
Wednesday 5 July 2006

GRANDPA MURDER LATEST: ARREST MADE AFTER FINGERPRINT MATCH

Ocean Village local arrested on suspicion of murder

Just days after the body of 69-year-old Jerry Ward was found at his house in Freemantle, Southampton, an arrest has been made. The suspect was apprehended in the upmarket Ocean Village area of Southampton on Tuesday 4 July following a fingerprint match.

Detective Chief Inspector Rohan Bhatia said: 'We are very thankful to everyone who called in with information relating to this case. We follow up on all avenues of enquiry, but on this occasion a fingerprint found at the scene was matched with one we held on file and led us to this particular suspect. We are now conducting extensive interviews and forensic investigations.'

CHAPTER EIGHT

'You look like Gamora from *Guardians of the Galaxy*,' Lily says with a chuckle.

'And you look like someone out of *Avatar*,' I reply. We both laugh and pull funny faces at each other.

It's Tuesday mid-morning, and we're sprawled on the large sofa in the lounge. After exfoliating our faces, Lily has a blue-coloured 'blueberry' face mask on, and I've chosen a green 'avocado' one. Lily found a screensaver of a crackling fire for the telly, and we've lit all the scented candles, the room now filled with a delightful fragrance of mulberry and fig.

She found a 'spa music' playlist on Spotify which plays from her laptop. It's a gloomy and rainy day outside, but we're cosy inside with mugs of hot lemon juice and honey steaming on the coffee table in front of us.

Seth is in lectures all day today, and Todd is in London again recording a guest appearance on a popular football podcast. Then he's going for dinner and to stay overnight with his friend, an ex-football player and the person Todd does most of his charity fitness challenges with. They're going to research and plan their challenge for next year. Lily doesn't have any lectures on a Tuesday, and I don't work today, so when she came down a few minutes before 11 a.m. suggesting a self-care session, I happily said yes.

Lily picks up the now-empty face mask sachets. 'My aunt sent me these in the post. I've no idea where she gets them from. They're always crazy colours and flavours. We don't have much in common, and I didn't particularly like living with her, but we did enjoy doing face masks together every now and then, and she'd treat me to a spa day once in a while. It's not really my thing, but occasionally I like to do it.'

'I rarely pamper myself, so this is fun,' I reply and blow on my drink to cool it.

'I'm so pleased you said yes. Another way for me to say thank you for having me to stay.'

'It's no problem at all. You've been a delight.'

She smiles. It's true – she has been a delightful house guest. Polite, friendly, tidy. She and Seth made a roast dinner together on Sunday and cleared up afterwards, which was fabulous. Seth is happier than ever having Lily here, which is also fabulous.

'Todd and I booked a holiday last night for January. It's the first time without Seth. Do you want to see where we're going?' I ask.

'Oooh, yes. Let's have a look.'

I slide my laptop off the coffee table and click a few things to bring up the website for the five-star hotel in Fuerteventura.

While I'm finding the right page for the room we booked, she asks, 'How long are you going for?'

'Two weeks. I can't wait to just chill on a sunlounger by the pool.'

The page loads, and I'm about to hand it to Lily when my laptop dings, and a notification pops up in the bottom right.

It's red and flashing and ominous.

'Oh no,' I say and show Lily my screen. 'I think I've been reinfected.'

The notification stops flashing, and she reads it. 'Nope, the account I set you up with is doing its job and scanning the dark web for your details. That's one of the features, among other things.'

I rest the laptop on my knee and look at it properly. It reads:

ALERT

Danger – we monitor and scan the dark web for your name and personal details as a standard feature. Your name and home address have been found on a potentially dangerous site on the dark web.

CLICK HERE to take action now.

I hover my mouse arrow over the link but then pause. I know not to just click on random pop-ups, even if this is from legit software.

Lily notices my hesitation. 'You've probably been sent an email as well.'

I press the cross at the top, and the pop-up disappears. I open my emails. And at the top of my inbox is an email from the anti-malware software. I open it. And it tells me the same thing as the notification – I need to take urgent action: my name and address is on the dark web.

My muscles stiffen. I have a vague understanding of the dark web from watching movies and TV shows. 'What on earth is my name and address doing on the dark web? That can't be good, can it?'

'The dark web keeps internet activity anonymous, and you need specific software to access it. It's used for some good, such as avoiding government censorship in countries with non-existent freedom of speech, but – yeah – it's mostly used by criminals and those carrying out illegal activities online,' Lily explains passionately. This is most definitely her *thing*.

'Crap,' I say as my heart thunders.

But Lily's exhilarated. 'We had a lecture on the dark web the other week. Your details are probably there due to hackers stealing private information through big company data breaches or phishing scams or a whole load of other things. It's most likely either a password has been linked to your email address or maybe your financial information. Possibly someone has stolen your credit card details and put them on a website for everyone to use.'

'How long do you think my details might've been on there for?'

Lily scratches the side of her nose, trying not to take off too much blue cream. 'Who knows. Days, weeks, months, years. The new software has run a scan since we installed it and found your details. Have you had any money taken? Or receipts or invoices for things you've not bought or applied for?'

'No. But the alert only said my name and address, not my bank details.'

'That's because I only added in your name and address when I set it up. I don't know your bank details.'

'Of course.'

'Have you noticed anything weird with any of your subscriptions? Like, if you've got Spotify, have you noticed songs played that you've never heard of? Or movies favourited or things like that?'

'No.'

Lily wiggles her mouth and nose to prevent the mask from drying too tight. 'Then hopefully it's nothing.'

But I have a worried knot forming in my chest. 'If you received this alert, what would you do?'

Lily's eyes brighten. She interlaces her fingers and stretches them out in front of her, as if preparing for a strenuous bit of activity. 'Right, first thing I think we should do is wash this stuff off our faces.'

Once we're face mask-free, I set up my laptop on the kitchen island, and we perch next to each other on stools. Lily tells me to check all my bank and credit card accounts for any suspicious or unknown activity (there's none), cancel my debit and credit cards and order new ones (easy), change all my passwords and use different passwords for everything (I have to write all the new ones down), log all devices out from everything and log in with the new passwords everywhere (a hassle), check emails for anything unusual (nothing) and make sure all my software is up to date to prevent any backdoor entry to my laptop (which Lily does in a few minutes).

'Anything else?' I ask her, feeling much better about the entire situation.

She taps her finger to her lips, thinking. 'You could look at the email and see what actions the anti-malware software suggests?'

'Good idea.' I open and read the email. 'We've done everything it says to do and more.'

Lily looks pleased.

'Crisis averted! Thank you, computer ninja.' I clap appreciatively at her, and she takes a little bow. 'Right, shall we finish our pamper session? We can mix a small amount of my honey with face cream to slather on our skin.'

We slip off our stools and head into the lounge, settling ourselves on the sofa once again. Lily presses play on the spa playlist.

My mobile rings and makes us both jump. I pick up my phone. An unknown number flashes on the screen. 'Hmm, not sure who this is. I'll take it in the other room.'

Lily nods and picks up her laptop, skipping the track we're listening to.

I head into the kitchen, pulling the door closed with my foot in case it's a private call. I lean against the kitchen island and answer. 'Hello?'

'Hi, is that Mrs Jennifer James?'

The voice is calm and friendly, but I don't recognise it. It doesn't sound like a scam caller. I get enough of those at work to recognise the signs. 'Who is this?'

'My name is Kiah Wong. I'm a documentary maker.'

The name doesn't ring any bells, but then I wouldn't know the name of any documentary maker unless it was Louis Theroux, so that's hardly surprising. Why on earth is this Kiah Wong calling me?

'What kind of documentary?' I ask suspiciously, fully expecting her to be a full-blown Todd James superfan trying to get to him through his wife. 'Is it about football?'

'Err, no.'

I can almost hear her shaking her head and frowning through the phone, as if football is a subject that is far, far beneath her.

She continues, 'I'm making a documentary about the dark web. About a very *specific* part of it.'

My body tenses – this must have something to do with my details being on there. But how does she know about that?

She adds, 'I'd like to talk to you face to face about something urgent.'

She sounds genuine and matter-of-fact, but I'm not in the habit of meeting up with strangers. I prefer to keep a low profile. I like to socialise with my husband, son or best friend, and that's it. And I only engage with a select few trusted people, like my choir group and colleagues. I don't seek out new friends or happily open up and share my life story with complete unknowns. Of course, I'm chatty and friendly when I'm on reception, but that's not deep conversation, that's about the weather or traffic or what drink I can get them while they wait.

'Could you give me some more information over the phone, please?'

'Mrs James, I'll be completely honest with you, it's not safe talking over the phone. It really is best if we meet up somewhere very public and very busy – the more people around, the better.'

Not safe talking on the phone? What is this woman on about? I'll ask Todd to delegate to the media team at his club, and they'll make this go away. 'Can I take your contact details, and I'll talk to my husband—'

She cuts me off abruptly. 'I don't think that's wise.' I hear her take a breath, and her tone softens. 'Listen, I don't want to alarm you, but it's imperative that I talk to you. Life-or-death urgent, if you get my meaning. And it's best if you don't mention it to your husband just yet.'

Life-or-death urgent? Have my credit card details been used for something absolutely awful that hasn't appeared on my statements yet? But why not just tell me? What's with all the secrecy? 'I'm really not up for meeting you. I have no idea who you are. If there's something you need to tell me then let's discuss it now.'

'Look, I know this is crazy me calling you out of the blue. But you need to trust me. Please,' she pleads, 'please trust me on this. We need to meet in person ASAP.'

Trust. That's a complex concept that I certainly don't have with this random person on the other end of my phone. 'How did you get my phone number?'

'I'll explain everything when we meet.'

'Listen, Kiah,' I say firmly. 'You're going to need to give me something concrete right now. Otherwise, I'm hanging up and blocking you so you can't contact me again.'

She sighs. 'Okay. As part of my job, I often work with sources. You've got corporate whistle-blowers, hackers, ex-criminals. People who have suddenly grown a conscience and shouldn't be talking to me for whatever reason. For my current documentary, I've been working with an anonymous activist hacker. They run regular scans of the dark web for certain *specific* activity and tip me off. They found some things about you and gave me your mobile number.'

'Things?' I probe.

But Kiah isn't relenting. 'I'll explain more in person. It really is *very* important.'

Is Todd or Seth in danger somehow? If my details are on the dark web, are theirs too? 'Does this have anything to do with my family?'

'No. Well, yes.' She pauses a moment. 'It's highly possible,' she adds ominously.

I tell Kiah Wong that I'll get back to her, write down her contact details on the pad we keep attached to the fridge to use for the shopping list and hang up. I grab my laptop and open a browser, googling her name.

A LinkedIn profile comes up, and I read through. She's a credible documentary maker with a few credits for the BBC under her belt, as well as some other production companies whose names I don't recognise.

I click into her website. There's a professional shot of a young woman, a slight smile on her serious face. Kiah doesn't look much older than early twenties. But some people just have baby faces, don't they? A detailed About Me page gives a timeline of her career from university to date. She's older than she looks, around twenty-five, based on the date that she finished her degree. She's done a lot in a short space of time. I click into the top link. It's a documentary about sex trafficking that she worked on as a researcher. Her name is listed in the credits on the website of the production company. Back on her website, I click through to the BBC link and see she's listed as a producer on the credits of a documentary about illegal cigarette smuggling into the UK.

She appears legit. The little worried knot from earlier reappears and blooms into a panic-laced, tangled lump in my chest. What could she want to talk to me about? Why has she singled me out?

My phone bleeps with a message. It's from Kiah, once again pleading for me to meet her, telling me it's very urgent.

I tap out a reply agreeing to meet her. Although I prefer to keep myself to myself, I need to know what this is all about. I need to make sure Todd and Seth aren't in any trouble. Kiah replies with a time and place to meet.

Lily heads into the kitchen and towards the sink with her empty water bottle. She clocks my furrowed brow and immediately looks concerned. 'Everything okay, Jen? You look really shaken up.'

I debate whether or not to tell Lily. But what's the harm? I need to talk to someone about this, and Kiah told me not to talk to my husband. He'll likely have his phone off anyway because he'll be in the middle of recording the podcast. 'I've just had a very strange call from a documentary maker. She wants to meet me. She says it's to do with the dark web and it's very urgent.'

'Whoa. Sounds intense,' Lily replies, curiosity brimming.

'I'm going to meet her. In an hour.' I fold my arms and stare off into space. I can't quite believe I agreed to the meeting.

Lily comes over to stand next to me and puts her hand on my shoulder. 'Do you want me to come with you? For support?'

CHAPTER NINE

We arrive early at the Muffin Society café in Westquay shopping centre. It's a busy part of Southampton city centre, and I can understand why Kiah Wong suggested here. It's heaving with shoppers, professionals buying coffees and lunch, parents with strollers and groups of students avoiding the rain.

The café has plenty of tables dotted along the walkway, but Kiah specifically asked for us to sit inside, at a table nowhere near the window that overlooks the rest of the shopping centre. I don't see her so take a table at the back of the bustling café. We order coffees, and Lily orders a carrot cake. With my cards cancelled, I pay with cash. I always keep a large sum in my wallet. Just in case. It's a habit from the time before that I've not got out of.

I'm pleased Lily's here. I don't have any close friends, apart from Simon, and her presence is comforting. I asked her earlier not to mention anything to Seth just yet, until we know more details. She agreed.

Kiah Wong arrives at the same time as our coffees and Lily's cake. I recognise her from her website and give her a wave. She spots me immediately – we're the only people sitting at the back of the café.

'Mrs James?'

'Yes.'

She thrusts out her hand for me to shake. 'Kiah Wong.'

Kiah looks even younger in person. Her round face is framed by poker-straight black hair that has been pulled back into a low bun but is escaping in wisps around her hairline. She has brown eyes, naturally red lips and a straight nose. She's wearing a small amount of make-up, very professional. Her baby face doesn't match her tall, slim figure, and she's dressed in a smart navy suit with white shirt and black, low-heeled boots. She has an air of seriousness and maturity that also belies her youthful appearance. She carries herself as if she's twice her age.

She's surprised to see I'm sitting with someone else. She leans in to me. 'Is this your daughter? Can you trust her?'

'Yes—' I'm about to say that yes, I can trust her but no, she's not my daughter, but Kiah cuts me off.

She shoves her hand towards Lily. 'Kiah,' she says.

'Lily.' Lily shakes Kiah's hand. Lily glances at me, as if to say, *shall I tell her we're not related*? But the moment passes because Kiah's not alone.

Two film crew are with her. One with a handheld camera on his shoulder, and the other with a large microphone in one hand and a bag with various wires and smaller microphones in the other.

Kiah perches on the edge of the seat, looking around nervously. A clang of coffee cups from the counter makes her jump. She's twitchy, and it makes me twitchy.

I only picked a table with three seats so the two others stand over us. One looks around for a spare chair.

She gestures to them. 'This is Neil and Bobby. We'd like to

film this interaction. Is that okay with you?' Kiah asks the question, but it's clear she's not expecting an objection.

Neil, the one with the handheld camera, places it on the table to go and grab a chair he's spotted.

'Absolutely not,' I say. 'I do not agree to this meeting being filmed.'

I don't want my face all over the telly. For eighteen years I've done my best to remain under the radar, with no social media or publicity of any kind. Seth once secretly entered me for a beekeeping TV show, and I freaked out to the point that he agreed never to do anything like that again. Todd is the only famous one in this family, thank you very much. This documentary will probably be very respectable and credible, but I can't risk it.

Kiah holds up her hands in a placatory gesture. 'It's only for the documentary. We might not even use it.'

Neil returns with the chair, sits and fiddles with his camera. The sound guy sorts out a microphone.

I stand up. 'I said no. This meeting is over.'

Lily shoves a forkful of cake into her mouth and stands too.

Kiah gets up from her chair, her cheeks colouring, looking flustered. 'It's okay. We won't film. Please, Mrs James, sit.' She gestures to Neil and Bobby. 'Guys, please go and wait outside. We're not filming this.'

They grunt and sigh and heave their equipment up and weave their way through the café to the exit. Only when they're out the door do I sit again. Lily plonks herself down and picks up her fork.

'You can call me Jen,' I say to Kiah, to clear the air. It's obvious from her scowl that she doesn't hear 'no' often.

Kiah sits too. She pulls a small device out of her handbag. 'Can I record you and just use the audio?'

'No,' I say emphatically, irritated now.

Kiah's eyebrows shoot up, but she recovers herself and

smiles gently. 'Sure, no worries.' She picks up the device and puts it back in her handbag.

'Please put your handbag on the floor,' I say. I'm not taking the risk that she's still recording.

She puts the bag by her feet. It's highly unlikely to pick up my voice with all the noise of the café.

Kiah sweeps her eyes around the place. Satisfied no one is listening or looking our way, she leans in to me.

In a whisper, eyes darting everywhere, Kiah says, 'I'm making a documentary about certain elements of the dark web. Certain dangerous elements.'

I nod. I scan the café too; I can't help it. Everyone is going about their business. We're completely inconspicuous tucked at the back of this popular eatery.

Lily is fixated on Kiah, eating her cake without looking at it, but Kiah maintains eye contact with me and pretty much ignores my 'daughter'.

Kiah relaxes somewhat. 'I feel compelled to tell you something. I just wouldn't be able to live with myself if I didn't.'

'Go on,' I say.

'I'm sorry, but your name and address is on a murder-for-hire website on the dark web.' Kiah gives me a sad look as if she's just told me that my son has died.

'Whoa,' Lily says.

But I'm not overwhelmed with shock, I'm sceptical. 'What exactly does that mean?'

Kiah reaches out and touches my hand. 'It means someone wants you dead. Someone has paid money and ordered a hitman to kill you. It means there's a hit out on you and your life is in danger.'

Lily drops her fork on the plate with a clatter. A chunk of cake flies off, but she doesn't notice.

I pull my hand away and frown. Then I laugh, I can't help it, it's so utterly ridiculous.

'Is this some kind of joke? Did Seth put you up to this?' I turn to Lily. 'Are you in on it?'

But Lily gapes and slowly shakes her head.

Kiah fixes me with a look so heavy with solemnity that my laughter shrivels to a crisp.

I blink at her. She blinks back patiently, waiting for me to catch up.

'You're serious, aren't you?'

'Absolutely serious. This is no joke.' She holds eye contact for a beat too long. 'I'm sorry. I wish this wasn't real.'

I look away and skim the café again. Panic swills, washes against my chest, flushing away my scepticism. 'Is a contract killer about to leap out at me? Is that why you're so twitchy? You know it could happen at any minute? It could be anyone in here, holding a knife or about to poison my drink or something.' I push my half-drunk coffee away and shunt my chair back. It makes a loud scraping noise. 'I need to get out of here. I need to go home!'

'Calm down,' Kiah says and places her hand on my shoulder. 'You're freaking out. That's why I opted for this place – it's busy. Nothing will happen here.'

'We need to call 999, right now!' I fish in my handbag for my phone. Then come to my senses. I don't want anything to do with the police if I can help it.

'It's okay, we're already working with the authorities on this. It was the first thing we did when the hacker contacted me.' Kiah gestures for me to pull my chair in again. I do.

She continues, 'Yours was the only British name, the rest are in the US. We got in touch with the UK's National Crime Agency, the NCA. I have a contact there.'

'The NCA,' Lily says in awe. 'I'd love to work there one day...'

I blink at her, unable to form words. This is far more serious than I thought. I don't want the authorities looking into me. I don't want to be the only British name, to be spotlighted. I'm happy with my quiet, steady, idyllic life. This is very bad.

Kiah continues, 'We're pretty sure the murder-for-hire site is run by Hungarian gangsters. It's called "We Take Care Of Your Problem". You'll need to download some software to access the dark web if you want to check it out. People go there to order a hit on someone and pay in bitcoin. All highly illegal.'

'Right,' I say, attempting to process that. Contract killers, assassins, guns for hire, hitmen – they're all part of the movies, aren't they? But this is real life. My life. It's very surreal.

Kiah's serious expression becomes even more intense.

'But here's the thing,' she says, 'and this is what you should be very worried about – someone has paid bitcoin to the tune of fifty thousand US dollars to have you killed.'

'Fifty thousand dollars,' I repeat.

Kiah nods. 'That's about forty thousand pounds. A lot of money. The most someone has ever paid for a hit on that site, according to the data the hacker has provided us with.' Kiah grasps my hand to ensure I look at her. 'Someone wants you dead, Jen. Very dead.'

'Very dead,' I echo.

'Fuuuck,' Lily whispers.

'That's why I wanted to tell you face to face, so you'd understand the seriousness of it. Your life is in danger.'

A baby cries out. All three of us jump.

Kiah scans the café again. 'And unfortunately the Hungarians are onto me. I've had death threats, and strange things have happened recently. They don't want their website or identities revealed in my documentary. They make absurd sums of money from it. They're criminals. They'd do anything to stay in business. That's why I'm so anxious.'

'Death threats?'

'Yes, but you don't need to worry about me. You need to worry about yourself. I've had death threats before. It comes with this line of work, unfortunately.' She leans down to pick up her bag. 'I'm just going to get my phone out. I'd like you to speak to my contact at the NCA. He'll verify all this and will reassure you they're taking this seriously.'

'No, that's okay,' I blurt before thinking about it.

Kiah looks surprised. 'You don't want to speak to him?'

I backtrack, fast. I have to hope the authorities won't look into me too deeply and won't make a song and dance about me being a famous footballer's wife. Hopefully they're too busy looking into Hungarian gangsters. 'I mean, yes, sure, if it isn't too much trouble for him. Don't want to bother him...'

'Not at all. His name is Hadley Perry. His contact details are in my phone.'

I pull out my mobile and open a browser. I search for Hadley Perry and NCA. There's not much about him, but a news story on the *Guardian* quotes him in an article about cybercrime. And there are a few other mentions. It's understandable that his details aren't strewn across the internet for every cybercriminal to see.

She shows me her phone's screen. 'This is his office landline number. His extension is four three eight. I've also got his mobile number if he's not at his desk.'

She hands me her phone, and I press dial.

The number rings once, and a recorded message plays to inform me I'm through to the National Crime Agency and to ask me to hold for the main switchboard or to use the extension of the person I want. I press four, three, eight and the hash key as instructed. It rings and rings, but there's no answer, and it doesn't switch to an answerphone. I hang up. 'Not answering. What's his mobile?'

I hand back Kiah's phone, and she taps a few things before giving it back to me. The screen says Hadley Perry and a mobile number. I press dial.

After two rings, I hear a brusque, 'Hello? Hadley Perry here.'

'Hi, Mr Perry. My name is Mrs Jennifer James. I'm here with Kiah Wong. I'm calling about the hire-a-hitman site on the dark web.'

'Ah, yes. So Kiah contacted you.'

'She did. I just wanted to hear from you what's happening.'

He sighs. 'Of course. Give me one moment to go somewhere private.'

There's a rustle, the sound of footsteps, and I hear a car door open and shut.

'Right,' he says. 'It's a complex case. We're working with the Hungarian authorities as well as those in the US, including the FBI and other agencies around the world. We're looking to get the site pulled down and track who's behind it. But it takes time. Kiah's source has proved very helpful in providing critically important data. Please be assured we have a number of people working on this. I'll keep in touch with Kiah, and she can keep you informed. Okay, Mrs James?'

'Um, yes.'

'Excellent. Get my mobile number from Kiah. Do call me in an emergency.'

'Will do.' But I know I won't. I'll never contact him again, if I can help it.

'Any other questions?'

'Um, no.'

'Right. Goodbye then.' He rings off.

I slowly lower the phone. My hands shake so much that Kiah's mobile falls from my grip. She catches it and places it on the table.

My mouth opens and closes, shock snuffing out my ability to speak.

'Are you okay?' Kiah asks.

I swallow hard. Someone wants me dead. Has paid a huge

sum to make it happen. That bombshell explodes within, rattling my bones. I pick up my mobile with trembling hands. 'I need to call my husband. I need to speak to Todd.'

'No.' Kiah snatches my mobile out of my hand, holding it away from me. 'You can't.'

I gawp at her. Lily gasps.

Kiah hands me back my phone. 'I'm sorry. But please listen to me before you make that call.' She gently places her palm over my hand. 'Please,' she pleads.

'Go on,' I say.

'I started with you because I'm based in the UK, but I'm slowly trying to contact everyone in the US too. I'm telling you this like I'll tell everyone else. You need to understand that it'll be someone very close to you – spouse, child, ex-partners, ex-colleagues, business relationships or friendships or family connections turned sour, that kind of thing.'

I put my phone on the table.

She continues, 'Truly, I feel awful having to tell you this, but it's usually the spouse. It's highly likely to be your husband.'

'Todd? Never.' I shake my head adamantly. Not my perfect husband.

Kiah gives me a sympathetic look. 'I suggest you don't tell anyone, but investigate yourself who it could be. Please do me a favour and don't immediately discount your spouse.'

I don't reply.

She continues, 'I know this must be a terrible shock, but I can help you. The NCA and police too if you find evidence that a crime has been committed or is about to be.'

The camera operator, Neil, snakes through the café towards us. 'We'd better go,' he says, looking at his watch.

Kiah nods and gathers her things. 'Call me night or day. You've got my mobile number. I'll help no matter what. I'll be in touch when I know more, but I need to go now. I can't be out in the open for too long.'

She stands, pushes her chair under the table and adds, 'You need to think long and hard about this, Jen. Who in your life wants you dead?'

The question pulses through me. *Who?* flashes before my eyes over and over. *Who? Who? Who?*

She takes a few steps and turns back. 'Be careful. Take precautions. There's a hitman after you.'

'Fuuuck,' Lily says for a second time and stares at me open-mouthed.

I'm pinned to my chair. I watch as Kiah and her crew go through the door, huddle closely together and head down the busy walkway out of sight. The café spins around me as if swept up in a tornado.

A hitman after me, Mrs Jennifer James. A devoted mother and wife. A part-time receptionist. A keen beekeeper, chorister and vegetable grower. A lover of houseplants. To the world, I'm an unremarkable forty-four-year-old. Out of 67 million people in the UK, I'm the one with the hit out on them.

Lily pulls her laptop from her bag – Seth was right when he said she takes it everywhere – and opens a browser. I watch as she googles 'hitman dark web' and clicks into a few articles. We both scan them. They confirm what Kiah said. Lily opens a link, and we read about a woman in France who paid for a hit on her ex-husband being brought to justice, as well as a Canadian man who wanted his fiancée killed because he suspected her of cheating. The article states that there are a few sites that have been brought down, but many are still operating.

I gulp. 'What Kiah said is true.'

'Yes,' Lily says simply. 'Do you want me to download that software so we can take a look at the website itself?'

'Is it safe?'

'Yeah. It's just software. I'll scan it first to make sure it's not trojan malware, and then we can take a look. And I'll delete it straight after. I'm curious. Aren't you?'

She has that excited look in her eyes again.

'Go on, then,' I say.

She pulls her laptop to her and taps away. I watch her fingers work. She pauses and drums her fingertips on the table. 'It's just downloading,' she tells me. A few seconds later she's tapping away again.

'Whoa,' she says, and she turns her screen to me.

It's the homepage of We Take Care Of Your Problem. We look at each other for a beat and back to the screen. She clicks into a few pages, including the payment page and the testimonials page.

She tuts. 'These are reviews from people who are happy with the hits they've ordered. That's so awful.'

My stomach flips. 'Close it down and delete the software. I don't need to see anymore.'

She does just that. After it's done, she closes the lid of her laptop and slides it back into her rucksack.

I continue, 'I have to believe Kiah, because what's the alternative? I choose not to, swan around as if that meeting never happened and turn myself into a sitting duck? I could get bumped off the moment I leave this café because I haven't taken any precautions to protect myself. Not a chance. I am not leaving Seth without a mother.'

Lily takes a long breath. Her mouth opens to say something but closes again. It's clear she has no idea what to say.

I continue, 'How do I keep myself safe? All I can think about is having a target on my back, a big flashing beacon with a sign that says "hitman strike here"!'

Am I safer here where there's a lot of people around? Or in my house where I can lock all the doors? Everything in me screams: *go home*. I always feel safe there.

'Let's get back,' I say.

I jump up and dart from the café, Lily rushing to keep up. I walk closely behind a group of young mums and veer towards the first car park payment machine I see. There's a queue three people deep. Lily stands next to me. I wait a few paces away from the person in front and get anxious when someone behind gets too close. Will they pull a knife and stab me in the back before sprinting out? I glance over my shoulder – it's a young couple snogging and very into each other. Not a danger.

A hundred different ways to die run through my mind – stabbing, strangulation, sniper from a distance, gunman from close range, hit over the head, suffocation, poisoning, beaten to a bloody pulp...

I take in Lily, who fidgets and bites her nails, and panic – will they target her because she's with me?

I pay for the car park. The act of finding change in my purse pulls me from my horrific murder visions. We race to my car. It's in a multi-storey car park that throngs with people visiting the shops and city centre. I unlock the car but waver. Car bomb?

'Lily, stop,' I shout before she can open the door.

I assess our surroundings and decide that no one could've planted one without being seen. And we've only been gone about an hour – surely not enough time to do anything? My insides swirl with indecision.

A large bang reverberates through the car park. I duck, my heart exploding. But I'm not hurt. The bang goes off again and then sputters. It's just a car backfiring. Someone laughs in the distance.

Get home! my brain yells. I check under the car but can't see anything suspicious.

'Let's go,' I say to Lily. She pulls the handle of the passenger side.

I open the car door, get in, take a deep breath, scrunch up my eyes and start the engine.

It fires up as usual.

'Phew. Still alive, not blown to smithereens like Michael

Corleone's poor Sicilian wife in *The Godfather.*' I attempt a joke, but Lily looks like she might vomit. She hugs her arms around herself.

I drive home like a maniac: too fast, too erratic. Could someone ram me off the road? Kill me and Lily by making me swerve into a tree or a lamp post or something? I scrutinise the cars around me for any driver looking my way, acting suspiciously. The traffic in Southampton is a nightmare, and we crawl along. A ten-minute journey feels like ten hours.

When I finally pull up to the house and open the gates with my remote, my bowels turn to water. I park the car, run into the house and straight to the downstairs loo.

As I'm sitting on the toilet, nausea forces the coffee back up. I snatch up the wastepaper bin and vomit.

I finish up and wash my hands, running cool water over my wrists for a moment. I need to calm down, to think. I'm safe here. No contract killer is about to spring out at me.

I wash out the bin in the shower and leave it upside down to dry. Then I head to the kitchen.

Lily sits on one of the kitchen island stools, her laptop open. She closes the lid when she sees me. I pull out a stool and sit, dazed, staring into space.

What the hell do I do now?

'Do you want a cup of tea?' Lily asks, her voice shaky.

'Yes, please.'

I need to work out who has hired a hitman to kill me, and what I'm going to do about it. And having a cup of tea is as good a place to start as any.

CHAPTER TEN

18 YEARS AGO

DAILY TIMES

Friday 7 July 2006

WOMAN CHARGED WITH MURDER OF SOUTHAMPTON GRANDPA

Natalie Owens accused of murdering Jerry Ward in Freemantle on 1 July

A 21-year-old woman has been charged with the murder of Jerry Ward. Natalie Owens is accused of murdering the 69-year-old retired grandfather on Saturday 1 July in the Freemantle area of Southampton.

Owens was arrested three days after the murder following a fingerprint match before being charged yesterday.

A Southampton native, Owens was known to the police due to a shoplifting incident three years previously. Owens had been renting an apartment in Ocean Village at the time of her arrest and was a glamour and promotional model, appearing in men's magazine *Nuts* and working as a ring girl at high-profile boxing matches.

Owens remained tight-lipped in front of the crowd of media and photographers while being transferred by the police.

She has been remanded in custody and will appear at Southampton Crown Court on Monday 10 July.

CHAPTER ELEVEN

For hours I haven't moved from the stool around the kitchen island. My brain is taking its time to process what I learnt this morning. All my energy has been directed there and not into moving.

Stillness. That's what I've needed.

But I need to get up and switch on the light. I'm sitting in darkness, and it's ridiculous. I also need to make some dinner. I didn't eat any lunch, even though Lily made me a sandwich. I just couldn't get it down. Now, though, my stomach grumbles.

I'm alone in the house. Todd is in London overnight. Seth went straight from uni to his best mate's house to stay over and play video games, and Lily is in Bournemouth at a gig with her friend and then staying overnight at her friend's boyfriend's flat. Lily insisted she cancel and stay with me or call Seth to get him to come home, but I said no. I didn't want to disrupt their evenings and also felt it was safer for them if they weren't in the house or anywhere near me.

I made Lily promise she wouldn't tell Seth about the hire-a-hitman news or about our meeting with Kiah because I wanted to tell him, and Todd, in my own time. I could see she was conflicted by this request – it's clear she and Seth tell each other everything. She chewed her lips but reluctantly agreed.

'Come on,' I tell myself out loud and slip off the stool, turning on the light and making myself some toast with peanut butter. Even with the knowledge that I've got a hit out on me, a mark on my head, that I'm a walking dead woman, I need to eat, to function.

Who could want me dead?

I should call Todd; I know I should. I'm itching to pick up my phone and unload the crazy meeting from earlier. But Kiah's warning rings in my mind. And experiences from my past, from the-time-before-Todd, give me pause.

What if it is him? What if my beloved husband of sixteen years and partner of eighteen wants me dead?

I just can't believe it.

We're as close now as the day we met. We'll be together forever; I have no doubt about it.

But who else could it be? Kiah said sometimes it's the children. But I can't believe it would be Seth. We share a very strong mother-son bond. Yes, Todd and I haven't told him that Todd isn't his biological father, but Seth is completely unaware of that fact. And if he found out, would he want me dead because of it? He's a forgiving boy. It would upset him, but I'm certain he'd get over it.

I eat my toast slowly. The house is unbearably quiet, but I don't put on any music or a podcast or an audiobook. It would mask the sound of an intruder. I listen for any little noise, just in case.

What else did Kiah say? People want other people dead because of relationships that have turned sour. I don't have any relationships that are rotten to the core, I'm sure of it.

An early night. That's what I need. It's only 8.45 p.m., but I'm exhausted. I walk around the entire house checking all the doors and windows are locked and the lights are off before going upstairs. We have windows on three sides of our vast bedroom. I close the curtains but on the third set of windows something catches my eye.

This window faces the lane and the gates. The gates are closed. Lily's friend came to pick her up earlier in her car, waiting on the lane, and Lily used the code to open the gates. They automatically close.

I stare fixedly at the gates and see it again – movement. There's someone there. Standing right by our gates looking in at our property, up at our house. They're dressed all in black with a baseball cap on and a hood up over the top of it so I can't see a face.

They can't see me. I always close the curtains before I switch on the lights. I'm not sure why, a habit from childhood, maybe? Todd is the other way around – he turns on the lights and then closes the curtains. We joke with each other about it.

I've never seen anyone hanging around by our gates before. This property is at the end of a lane and is very private. The lane goes no further. There's dense woodland beyond and behind our grounds. I've always loved the private setting, but now it feels too remote. The trees cast too many shadows. Our nearest neighbours are a little way away up the lane.

This person is very definitely watching the house.

My pulse hammers. It has to be the contract killer scoping out the place, searching for a way in, checking to see if I'm at home.

I pick up my phone and call Todd. I know Kiah said not to, but what else am I meant to do? I'm certain it's not him. But he doesn't answer. Too busy chinwagging with his mate about fitness challenges, no doubt. I call Seth. No answer. I debate whether to call Lily, but honestly, what could she do? It would take her an hour to get here from Bournemouth.

The person reaches out and gives the gates a little nudge, testing if they'll open on their own. They won't. This is the only security feature we have. High fences and bushes all around our boundary and high metal gates that only open with the code or remotely from an app. Maybe we should've invested in CCTV or one of those doorbell cameras, but this house, this area, has always been so safe, so out of the way. Not even Todd's most passionate fans bother coming here to catch a glimpse of their hero.

What am I supposed to do? Call the police? What would they even do? This person isn't doing anything, just acting suspiciously. Would the police drive by to check? Doubtful. And the last thing I want to do is waste police time, especially as Todd's best friend, Rohan, who's been in the police for nearly thirty years and steadily worked his way up to the top position, complains frequently about time wasters and not having enough officers to send out on wild goose chases.

Rohan is older than Todd and is like his big brother. They've known each other since living on the same estate as children and kicking a football around in the park. Todd thinks that's why he got so good at football – from a young age he used to play with the older kids. Rohan was the first friend that Todd introduced me to a few weeks after our first date. Rohan knows me as Todd's wife, and I don't want to give him any reason to delve deeper than that.

And the less I have to do with the police, the better.

Who else is there? I don't exactly have a brimming contacts list.

The person disappears into the shadows, and I can no longer see them. Ice shoots through me. Where have they gone? Have they found a way in? Got past the gates? Are they going to break into the house?

I hold my breath. All is still. But that doesn't mean that someone isn't breaking in *right now*, isn't stealthily creeping about my home in the darkness.

I strain to listen. Absolute silence.

There's nothing – not even the sound of a neighbour's car, or an owl, or the wind swishing through the treetops. Usually, I find silence peaceful and calming. But now it's eerie.

I'm frozen to the spot. If the hitman is out there watching for movement in the windows, they'd immediately see the curtains closing. I creep slowly away from the window and pin myself flat against the wall, facing the bed.

The sumptuous bedsheets and top-of-the-range mattress, which usually feel so comforting, so relaxing and cosy, now look obscene. A vision of Todd coming home tomorrow to find his wife's dead body sprawled across the marital bed, the now-dry blood a stark smudge against the white sheets, fills my mind, and I know I need to move.

This is a big house with big rooms. It has always been my most cherished sanctuary and safe space. But someone could be inside, and I might not hear them. A crushing feeling of being very small in a huge space takes my breath away. I'm rattling around in this dark house on my own. I don't feel safe now.

I'll be damned if I'm making this easy for a killer. I sprint from the bedroom and switch on the hallway light. I run from room to room on the first floor switching on all the lights. We never leave on lights if we can help it. We're a very environmentally conscious family, especially with Seth's passion for conservation. But tonight, needs must.

Panting, heart racing, I peer down the stairs to the ground-floor hallway.

Silent.

All the hair follicles on the back of my head itch with the notion that I'm being watched. I spin, but the hallway is empty. I'm about to charge across the landing to kick open Seth's bedroom door, but I stop myself. There's no one in there. I would've heard or seen them when I switched on his light.

This is absurd. My composure is unravelling. I can't be here on my own.

I know who'll help me. I find my phone.

Simon answers on the second ring. My best friend has always told me he's a night owl. He's in the IT department and has flexible hours. He always rolls in about 11 a.m. By that point, I've been on reception since 9 a.m. so I look forward to seeing him. We always have a little chat. And usually have lunch together at 1 p.m.

I attempt to explain that Todd is in London, that I'm alone, that there's a person hanging around outside, but my voice is so shaky, I stutter and stumble over words.

'You sound absolutely terrified, Jen. I'm coming over right now,' Simon says.

'I'll come to yours,' I say. I have to get out of the house, away from the person outside about to kill me. I can't risk bringing Simon here and him getting caught up in any attempt on my life.

'No problem,' he replies.

'I'll be right over.'

We hang up, and I head down the stairs, turning on all the lights, and grab my car keys. But I put them back. I don't want to take my car. What if someone jumps out at me when I'm getting into it on the driveway? Or tries something while I'm waiting for the gates to open? Or rams me when I'm on the lane so I have to pull over, and then *bang bang bang*, and I've been shot in the head.

I feel far too jittery to drive. And I'd have to find a parking space on the roads around Simon's building and walk in the dark to his front door. No. Much better to get dropped off right outside.

I book a taxi on the app on my phone. Thankfully it'll be here in ten minutes. I spend that time watching as the taxi dot on the app gets closer and, as it nears the house, I press the button to open the gates. It drives right up to the front door, which suits me fine. It has the name of the taxi firm emblazoned down the side of the car, so I know it's genuine. I lock the front door and run to the taxi, jumping into the back seat.

I'm relieved when the driver is a woman. I immediately feel safer.

She confirms the destination and sets off. I slouch on the back seat, scanning the lane for the contract killer as she pulls out of our driveway. But they're gone. Or are they hiding? Or following? I look out the rear window.

'Everything all right?' the driver asks.

'Did you see anyone watching my house when you arrived?'

'Nah, don't think so, but then, I wasn't looking.'

'And do you think anyone could be following us?'

The driver looks in both her side mirrors and in the rear-view mirror. 'Nope.'

'Okay, good.' I let out a long breath and relax a little.

Within ten minutes, we're at Simon's flat. He comes out the front door to greet me from the taxi, which I'm grateful for. He gives me a big hug and leads me inside.

'You've never been inside my flat before,' he says excitedly. He's out of breath, as if he's just sprinted down the stairs. 'Welcome.'

It's true. I've only ever dropped him off or shared taxis back from work parties, and so on. Most of our interaction is at work, in our lunch breaks, or occasionally after work at a quiet pub. He's only ever been over to mine a handful of times. He and Todd don't particularly get on. Simon clams up when Todd's around – possibly because of Todd's fame, but I'm not really sure – and I prefer Simon's company when it's just the two of us.

'Are you okay? Can I get you a drink? A cup of tea, or something stronger?' Simon asks as we enter his flat and he directs me towards his open-plan lounge-kitchen-dining area.

'A chamomile tea would be lovely, thanks.' It'll help steady my nerves. And I know he'll have it; it's his favourite.

Simon gestures for me to sit on the sofa in his lounge. I take off my jacket and sit. He glides around his kitchen making my drink.

I study his flat. It's neat and orderly but overflowing with knick-knacks, houseplants and pictures on the wall. It's cosy, and I immediately relax.

He arrives with a mug of chamomile tea, placing it on the coffee table in front of me. He picks up a few plants from around the room and sets them down next to my drink. 'Look how well all these plant babies are doing.'

Over the years, I've lost count of the cuttings and propagated plants I've given to Simon.

He motions to each. 'Spider plant, pilea and peace lily all thriving. Aloe vera took a while to get going, but look at it now.' He picks up a lush aloe vera plant and twirls it for me to see. 'All cared for with so much *love*.' He emphasises the last word and looks at me pointedly.

I'm not quite sure what he's getting at, but his intense gaze becomes uncomfortable so I look away.

He sits down next to me, slightly too close, and tilts his head to indicate he's listening. 'Sorry, you're not here to talk plants. Tell me what's going on.'

'There was someone watching the house. It was terrifying. I had to get out of there.'

His forehead creases with concern. 'Who would be watching the house?'

I debate how to tell him about the hire-a-hitman thing. I know Kiah told me not to tell anyone, but he's my best friend. But he's a bit... off. His eyes are glazed as if he's not quite seeing me. It's late; he's probably tired.

He fills the pause by asking, 'Is he watching and listening to you in the house? You said he's away in London, so did you need an excuse to come here that would be plausible?'

I have absolutely no idea what he's talking about. I blink at him, baffled.

'You don't need to pretend while you're here.' He bends, swipes his glass off the coffee table, takes a swig and places it back.

Pretend?

In response to my mystified silence, he holds up his hands. 'Sorry, sorry... I won't mention it again.'

It's then I notice the nearly empty bottle of whisky on the table.

He follows the line of my gaze and says, 'I'm celebrating.'

Have I forgotten some special occasion? I know it's not his birthday.

He notices my blank face and says with a big grin, 'You know why.' He grabs the whisky bottle, glugs straight from it and holds it up to me like some kind of toast.

I rack my brains, but there's nothing. 'Please enlighten me. What are you celebrating?'

He places the bottle back on the table with a flourish and turns to me. He's giddy with excitement, it bounces off him in waves. He clenches his mouth shut but practically vibrates attempting to contain whatever it is that's buzzing inside him.

He blurts, 'I've waited patiently for eighteen years, and then *boom* out of nowhere your email this morning, and now you're here. Really here.'

'What email?'

Simon mimes zipping his mouth closed and throwing away the key. 'Okay, sorry. I'm getting ahead of myself.' He attempts to regain control by adjusting how he's sitting. 'Please, tell me more about this person outside your house.'

I can tell by his tone that he doesn't really believe me and thinks we're playing some kind of game. He's very drunk.

'I don't know what to do,' I say, but he's not paying attention. Normally, he's a great listener and always gives me good advice.

He moves closer to me and puts an arm around my shoulder. 'It'll be okay, I promise. We'll make this all okay.'

Confused by his bizarre behaviour, I let him hug me. I've never seen him like this before: sozzled and making no sense. I don't like it.

He inhales deeply, and I get the unpleasant sensation that he's sniffing my hair. His finger finds my chin, and he lifts my face up to his. 'I feel the same way, Jen. I didn't think it would happen so soon, but I'm ready. I've been ready since the moment we first met. It's always been you.' He moves to kiss me.

I spring up from the sofa. 'Simon, no! We're friends. What's got into you? What about Miranda?'

My reaction smacks the excitement clean off his face. It's replaced with confusion just as deep as my own.

'This is what you want... I've dumped Miranda. She was furious, but I don't give a monkey's about that bitch anymore.'

'You've split up with Miranda?'

'Yes, of course...' He gestures at me. 'Because of your email this morning...' he stutters.

'I never sent you an email this morning.'

Simon gives me an incredulous look.

His disbelief riles me up. 'Show me this email,' I demand.

He picks up his phone and taps a few things to find his emails. He scrolls through. 'It should be right here... maybe I deleted it by accident...' He looks up at me, a frown smearing his features. 'I can't find it. That's so weird...'

'Because you're making it up.' I gather my jacket and handbag.

He slumps on the sofa. 'I've ruined everything, haven't I? I should've done what you said. But then you came here, and I thought it was the start of us... I love you too, Jen. Don't leave, please,' he begs.

Whoa.

I bundle out of the flat. He wails behind me, too intoxicated to get off his sofa to follow me.

This is the first time he's not been a good friend to me. We met eighteen years ago when I first started on reception and immediately hit it off. Soon after, we went on a date, which I wasn't really up for but said yes to because I didn't want to upset him. There was no chemistry between us. I told him, and he agreed. A few days later, I met Todd.

After that one failed date, there's never been the teeniest hint that he's had anything other than platonic feelings for me.

But he's *in love* with me.

Shocked, I stumble in the stairwell, slip down a few stairs and grab the banister to prevent myself from tumbling all the way down.

Why has this come out now? Today of all days?

He said he didn't think it would happen 'so soon'. He must've been expecting me to take longer to discover the We Take Care Of Your Problem order. Perhaps he planned to cancel it when I blamed Todd and fell into his arms.

He certainly has the IT know-how to get on the dark web and use bitcoin. He's been telling me for the past few years that he's saved a lot of money, wanting to buy a bigger house at some point. But maybe he's spent it on this?

And why is he lying about me sending him an email? Was that to throw me off the scent somehow?

But his scheme has gone tits up.

So, what is his plan B?

Maybe now he won't cancel the hit. Love makes you do crazy things, doesn't it? If he can't have me then no one can.

Panic rises, and the air in my lungs twists sharply.

I thought I could trust my best friend. But Kiah was right, I really can't trust anyone. It's unbearable.

Alone on the street, I need to make a decision. And fast. Option one: hyperventilate and go to pieces. Or option two: calm down and handle this.

I book another taxi on the app. It says it's fifteen minutes away. It's a chilly night, and Simon's street is empty. I edge back into the shadows and hang around by the window of a ground-floor flat that still has light creeping out from around the curtains and the sound of a TV blaring from inside. If anyone approaches me now, I'll bang on the window, and the occupants will hopefully hear me and look out and come to my aid if necessary.

By going home am I willingly walking into the hands of a hitman? About to get murdered by the person lurking outside the gates, waiting for the perfect opportunity to jump me? I shudder.

The taxi arrives, and I scurry from the shadows and jump in the back.

It's a gruff male driver this time, and he grunts at me, 'Where to, love?'

I tell him the name of a cheap city centre hotel in a busy area that should take cash. And pray it has an empty room.

Tonight is not going to be my last night on this earth. Not. A. Chance. I'm a fighter. And there's plenty of fight left in me yet.

CHAPTER TWELVE

After a fitful night's sleep in a tiny hotel room with a lumpy bed, I get a taxi back to the house first thing on Wednesday morning. It's daylight, and there's nobody hanging around. The taxi driver pulls up right outside the front door.

The house appears untouched. Gives off its usual welcoming, homely, safe vibes. Inside, I shout hello but no one is home yet. I plug in my phone to charge. The battery died soon after I got into the hotel room last night. I turn off all the lights, shower, get ready and drive into work.

I arrive at work at 8.40 a.m., parking in my usual spot and scrutinising the car park for any suspicious loiterers before I get out. I hurry into the office and set up the reception area to my liking. I job-share with Penny, and she likes the chair and screen at a certain height, which is far too low for me. I adjust and raise everything up and get comfortable.

I pull out my mobile.

Todd has messaged to say he's on the train on the way back from London, will be going into the radio station for a meeting before heading home and will pick up some bits for dinner because he fancies fajitas. He tells me he'll probably be home about three-ish.

I rarely make personal calls when I'm at work, but I have an overwhelming need to hear his voice. It's still early and doesn't get busy until after 9 a.m., so I phone him.

'Hello? Jen?' Todd answers, surprised. He probably thinks it's an emergency.

'I just wanted to tell you, I can't wait to see you and eat Mexican food,' I say.

'Right,' he replies. 'Good.'

We say our goodbyes and hang up.

Seth has messaged me asking if I've seen his green hoodie because it's not in his room. I reply to say that it's probably on his ironing pile because he put it in the wash last week. He must've got home and everything must be fine. He responds with a thumbs up.

There are also multiple messages from Simon. Sent last night after my battery died. The first says:

I'm so, so sorry.

I skim the rest. They all follow a similar vein. I don't reply.

What is he saying sorry for? For the hit that's about to happen? For the end of my life that he's paid for? Or just for being a drunken, rambling mess last night?

I call Kiah.

She answers with a sleepy, 'Hello?'

'Kiah, it's Jennifer James. I'm sorry to get in touch this early, but you did say to contact you night or day if I needed anything.'

'I did,' she replies, her voice immediately sharper, her interest piqued.

'I know you're in the middle of investigating all this and there might be confidential stuff, but is there anything else you could share with me about my details on that murder-for-hire website? Anything that might give me a clue as to who it is?'

'I'll check with Hadley and ask my source. Leave it with me.'

We hang up.

Checking my work emails, I see one from Simon's boss letting me know Simon's called in sick and to forward any calls for him through to his colleague. Simon clearly doesn't want to see me today. That's fine with me. I don't want to be near him, either.

People start arriving for work, the busy time between 8.50 a.m. and 9.30 a.m. Usually, everyone says hi to me as they walk past. But today I notice people aren't saying hi, Clare gives me side-eye and Tobias completely blanks me. But then I'm not being my usual chatty, smiley self, so maybe they're responding in kind to that.

Could someone at work want me gone? Kiah did say that it can sometimes be colleagues holding grudges, but who'd hold a grudge against me? Penny started about a year ago and has always said she'd like this job full-time if I ever decided to leave, but she's never pushed the matter and seems quite happy doing two and a half days per week. The half-day on Thursday afternoon is shared with me. We're meant to spend the time together handing over tasks and keeping each other updated, but that takes us about an hour and the rest of the time we chat easily.

My gut churns with it all, and I visit the loo what feels like a hundred times. But the hitman won't try anything in broad daylight, will they? Or in a busy city centre office block? I'm at the front of the building, by the large entrance doors, greeting people as they come in. Our offices are over two floors – it's a busy, well-run charity. We manage two women's shelters, one in Southampton and one in Portsmouth, and they're currently planning to open a third in Bournemouth after funding was secured recently.

Generally, I love welcoming people to our lovely charity. I also answer the phone and put through calls to relevant colleagues or filter them if the caller sounds like they're sales, or scammers, or vague and after something.

But today I feel uncomfortable. We're on the busy road from Southampton Central train station through to the city centre. It has a steady flow of buses, pedestrians, cyclists and traffic. There's tinted glass, so I can see out but no one can see in. There's a café opposite with seats outside. I realise that anyone sitting there can see straight into my reception area whenever the door opens and watch me come and go – this is the main entrance.

I fidget and sweat in my office swivel chair. I really just want to go home. It's safer there, away from this busy world, where anyone could be a killer, could be a hired hitman paid to take me down.

And that's when I see them: on the other side of the road, a person dressed all in black with their hood up over a baseball cap. They slowly walk past and stare straight at my building. My heart beats out of my chest. I can't see their face. Is it the same person who was watching the house last night? It must be.

What if they come in the door? What do I do? There's a panic button under my desk in case of emergencies that alerts the people in the nearest office that I need help. I've never used it, but the idea is that they'll all come running into reception to assist me and someone is designated to call the police. How long would that take though? If that person over the road came in and raised a gun at me, I'd just about have time to push the button before they fired. My colleagues would all run in, and I'd be bleeding out or dead, and the shooter would be long gone. Run in, shoot, run out.

But the person in black walks past. I watch their back until I can't see them anymore. Gone. I sort through the post, one of my tasks every morning, and glance up. I drop the letters on the floor. The person is back, sauntering past the café, as if debating whether to get something. They stop, turn and get out their phone. I swear they snap a photo of the front of my building.

It's the contract killer. They've not found a way to get to me at home so have come after me at work.

The phone rings. I answer, fumble when transferring and cut off the call. Oops. My brain is disengaged from what my fingers are doing, too busy panicking that I'm about to die any moment now.

The person goes into the café, comes out with a coffee and sits at one of the tables. They stare at my building as they slowly drink, occasionally looking down at their phone. Although I know they can't see in through the tinted glass, just in case someone opens the door, I slide down my chair and hunker behind the reception desk as much as I dare before I look like I'm asleep on the job.

The door flying open makes me jump. The person is still sat across the street. Stood in front of me is a woman. It takes me a moment to place her.

'Er, hi, Miranda,' I say as professionally and politely as possible, sitting up a bit straighter.

Miranda is livid. Her entire body tense, her jaw set and nostrils flared. She glares at me.

'Simon isn't in today,' I say quickly. He dumped her yesterday. She's clearly here to confront him.

She jerks her chin at me. 'Where's the other one? Penny?'

'Penny doesn't work on Wednesdays. And if she did, she'd tell you the same thing,' I say. Miranda thinks I'm covering for my best friend, that he's asked me not to let her near him.

Miranda gets closer to my desk and leans over threateningly. I realise she wasn't questioning my honesty but was checking if I was alone on reception, checking if Penny would be arriving back any time soon.

My hand moves towards the panic button.

The internal door swings open and chatter from my colleagues in the next room makes her pause whatever she was planning. She edges back and quickly exits the front door, jogging down the street.

My breaths come short and sharp as I push my swivel chair back and put my head between my knees.

'Are you feeling okay, Jen?' my boss, Syreeta, asks as she strides through reception on her way out.

I slowly sit upright, pushing aside all thoughts of Menacing Miranda, and take in Syreeta. She's been my boss for the past six years. I like her. She's a great boss. I think she thinks that I'm a great employee. But – oh crap – is it her?

No. Stop this, Jen. Why would Syreeta want you dead?

'Er, well, not really.' Do I confide in her? I don't feel like I can trust anyone, and it's making my skin crawl.

She waves her assistant on. 'You go ahead. I'll be one sec.' She turns to me. 'Jen, you really don't look too great.'

I fan my face. I'm sweating. My cheeks are on fire. I edge down even further on my chair as her assistant opens and closes the door. That exchange with Miranda has not helped my frame of mind today one bit.

Syreeta looks concerned. 'Head home if you're feeling rotten. See if Penny will come in today.'

I nod, and she heads out after her assistant. The person dressed in black is gone. I check up and down the street but can't see them. Are they waiting by my car? I wish I'd seen which way they went.

I don't finish until 5 p.m., so if they are by my car, perhaps they won't wait that long? Perhaps someone will see them and chase them off thinking they're about to steal a vehicle, or something. I just want to go home. I message Penny.

I fret and sweat until Penny comes in at ten to one.

'Hey,' she says in her chipper manner, and we hug.

'Pen, will you walk me to my car, please? It's just out the back,' I ask as I log off and collect my handbag.

Penny frowns momentarily at the odd request but then nods. 'Of course, sugarplum. Let's go.'

If it's Penny who wants me dead to take over this job full-time, then hopefully I've caught her off guard, and she's not going to try anything right now like alerting the hitman to my whereabouts or holding me down so a killer can get me. No. Whoever ordered this hit wouldn't want to be anywhere near me when it happens – that's the whole point, isn't it, to keep their hands completely clean by hiring someone else to do the dirty work.

Penny walks me to my car, chatting about her weekend – raucous, as usual. She's the host at a comedy club on Friday and Saturday nights, and after the acts it turns into a nightclub. Penny DJs until the time I'm just about waking up in the morning. I wonder how she has the energy, but I guess she's about ten years younger than me. It's hard to tell. She's a proud goth, and her heavy black eye make-up, black shaggy hair and unfailingly black attire doesn't give anything away. Her tales usually have me howling with laughter – she works being a goth into her comedy routine in a hilarious, self-deprecating fashion – but today I'm mute, distracted.

Penny notices. 'You're, like, really ill, aren't you?'

'Yes,' I reply. I don't think I've ever lied to Penny, and it floods me with guilt.

'Feel better soon.' She gives me a peck on the cheek and skips back to reception.

I drive home quickly. I just want to get back, to lock myself in, to feel safe.

As I get through the front door, my phone pings with a message. I lock the door and look. It's Kiah.

The hacker has more information. They're trying to get hold of some of the messages the person who ordered the hit sent to the hire-a-hitman site. They've got hold of one message so far. More will hopefully follow. I'll send you the screenshot now.

A few seconds pass, and a screenshot of what looks like an instant chat conversation on the We Take Care Of Your Problem website comes through. I read the message exchange:

Fedup24: It's been eighteen fucking years. Not waiting any longer. Get it done ASAP.

Wetakecareofyourproblem: Understood.

Who the hell is Fedup24? Kiah messages:

Does Fedup24 ring any bells with you? The number twenty-four, perhaps?

I reply in the negative. A few moments pass before Kiah responds:

If I were you, I'd think long and hard about what happened eighteen years ago.

I plonk down on the sofa in the lounge. I can't stop thinking about what happened eighteen years ago. It was a pivotal year in my life. A turning point.

I thought my life pre-Todd was firmly in the past, never to be dragged up again. It's been nearly twenty years, and I've been so careful. I was sure it was buried. But it's not, is it. It's risen up from the depths to bite me.

Fear ripples beneath my skin.

I've been thinking about this all wrong, suspecting all the people in my life *now*. But I should've been looking at those who plagued it *before*.

A lot happened in 2006. I try to think about it in order.

My boyfriend, the man who I thought I loved, the man who I thought loved me – Damian – had beaten me again. This time it was half to death. He was sick of Seth crying. 'Make the damn baby shut up,' he kept yelling at me. I attempted to soothe Seth, to shush him, but he had colic. He was only a few weeks old. I told Damian it was normal for a baby to cry, that he'd just have to get used to it for a little while.

But he flew into a rage and beat me. And then he went for Seth. And that was it.

I left Damian and took Seth. Left everyone I'd ever known without so much as a word. I wasn't bothered about my family, about my parents and older brother, about my grandparents and aunts and uncles and so many cousins. I'd never fitted in; I'd always been overlooked. My brother was the apple of my parents' eyes. My younger cousins monopolised my grandparents' time. I didn't shout loud enough, so I received no attention whatsoever.

I left my family, but they wouldn't have cared. They loved Damian and took his side when I confided in my mother that he was hurting me. She told me I was making it all up. 'Lovely Damian wouldn't do that,' she'd said to me. 'You're attention-seeking. It's disgusting.' They enjoyed leeching off him. He had a decent-paying job and gave them regular handouts.

Damian got my bully of a brother a job at his friend's garage, even though I'd told Damian that one of my brother's favourite pastimes when we were growing up was to make me cry: pulling my hair, pinching, kicking me in the shins. My parents never stopped him. Once he gave me a black eye by throwing a toy at my head. My mother brushed it off when my school enquired: just a bit of rough-and-tumble play, just kids being kids. Damian would tell me my brother was a 'top bloke'. That I was the one with the problem.

Ever since I can remember, my mother suffered abuse from my father. He especially hated it when she laughed – for some reason, my mother being happy pissed him off the most. *Rein it in.* She lived in denial. She wouldn't leave. She couldn't accept that her daughter wasn't also going to put up with it for the rest of her life. The men in that family were always treated like the meat – the best part. The women and kids were the veg and gravy, the trimmings – only around to worship, take care of and be the punching bags for the men.

They'd all been so pleased that I'd had a son – another male to add to the clan, to fawn over. I had to get Seth away from that poison.

And I didn't have any friends left by then. Damian had scared them all away.

It was easy to hide in a big city. I went straight to a Southampton women's shelter. They gave us a room; they didn't ask any questions. One look at my bruised face, the baby in my arms, the lack of any luggage and the small amount of cash in a plastic bag told them all they needed to know.

After a few weeks, they gave me a job. The same job I still have today. I met Simon at work, and we became firm friends. Not long after, I met Todd at the charity event. Seth was being babysat by one of the other women at the shelter where we were staying. I was upfront with Todd that I had a baby, but it hadn't put him off at all. We fell in love almost instantly, and he immediately took Seth on as if he was his own. It was a blessing after what we had escaped from.

I told Todd and Seth that my parents died in a car crash shortly before I met Todd and that I had no siblings and no other family. I told them my father was an only child of only children who'd passed away, and my mother had lost touch with her family in Greece when she came to England and hadn't spoken to them in decades. I said that Milton Keynes held too many memories of my parents and made me sad and that I never wanted to go back there.

When I met Todd, I was already estranged from my family with absolutely no plans to reconnect. It was easier to tell a lie that they were all gone. It stopped any probing or chance that Seth might get curious one day and want to meet them. They were all dead to me, so they might as well be dead to my son and husband too.

It's for the best. All my family are still alive. Probably. I haven't been in touch with them for eighteen years. They're gone. For good.

But I did something truly awful in 2006. Something I'll never forgive myself for. I did it to get away from Damian once and for all. I didn't want to do it. But it was the only way. It should haunt me, but I push it to the back of my mind. As far as I'm concerned, it never happened. I started a new life and shut the old one away for good.

A flash of blood smeared everywhere streaks across my vision. The smell of it scrapes at my nostrils. My hands are slick with it, the wetness heavy on my skin. The drip, drip as it spills from a wound.

Trembles hit me from head to toe. I tap my forehead, say, 'get out'. I summon Seth's face to the front of my mind and fixate on it.

If I hadn't done what I'd done then he'd be dead. Damian would've killed him.

I visualise putting the memory of that dreadful evening in a box and shoving it to the back of my mind. I can't let it break out and befuddle me. I need all my wits about me.

I've never told Todd about Damian or what happened.

About the terrible thing I had to do. I'll take that secret to my grave.

But my past must've caught up with me. I'll give Todd a watered-down version of events. I know he'll help me. There's nothing he wouldn't do for me.

CHAPTER THIRTEEN

The noise of a car coming up the gravel driveway snaps me to attention. I hurry to the window in the kitchen and see it's our gardener and not a We Take Care Of Your Problem contract killer. He always comes on a Wednesday afternoon. I'm not usually here though. I'm usually at work.

I watch as he goes about unloading a few tools from his truck and gets to work. It's soothing to have another person here. He's been doing our garden for almost a decade. He's trustworthy. He whistles as he prunes a tree.

I get changed out of my work clothes and wait in the kitchen for Todd to get home.

Around three, a taxi pulls up, and Todd gets out. He says hello to the gardener, and they have a brief chat before Todd lets himself in the front door and immediately comes through to the kitchen to put the bag of fajita ingredients down.

'Oh,' he says as he sees me. 'What are you doing home?' He looks closely at me. 'Are you ill?' It's very rare for me not to be at work on Mondays, Wednesdays and Thursdays, unless we're on holiday. I'm never off sick.

'Yes, not feeling too great,' I reply.

He immediately comes over to hug me and kiss my cheek.

But I pull away. 'Don't get too close, whatever I've got might be catching.'

'I don't care,' he says and hugs and kisses my cheek anyway.

He switches the radio on and unpacks the shopping bag. He chats amiably about his day yesterday, his evening with his friend, his meeting at the radio station.

I study him carefully. He's acting in exactly the same way as he usually does. In fact, he's in a great mood. It confirms my certainty that he's not responsible.

'I'm not going to choir practice later,' I say.

He stops what he's doing and turns to look at me. 'Oh dear, you must be really poorly. Are you sure you fancy fajitas for dinner?'

It's unheard of, unless we are away, for me to miss a Wednesday night choir practice. I love going so much.

'I was thinking we could curl up on the sofa with a movie tonight?' I plan to tell him about my past then, when we're both relaxed and can focus. When Seth and Lily are out or upstairs or in the telly room.

After dinner, we're cuddled up together under a blanket. Todd has put on a gentle murder mystery series. Halfway through our meal, Seth and Lily came in, said hello and went out again, so it's just us in the house.

Now's my moment. 'Todd, something happened that I need to tell you about...' I start but my phone pings.

'Hmm?' he says, deeply invested in the show on the telly.

'One sec,' I say and look at my phone.

It's a message from Kiah about the person who ordered the hit. I shift on the sofa to make sure Todd can't see my screen.

'Comfortable?' he asks, readjusting his arms around me.

'Yes, sorry, leg was going dead.'

He kisses the top of my head, and his eyes go back to the telly.

Kiah's text says:

I have more messages from the hacker. Let me know when it's a good time for me to send them.

I tap out a reply:

Ready now.

Screenshots pop into my WhatsApp.

My skin prickles. It's more of the conversation between Fedup24 and We Take Care Of Your Problem. In a series of messages, Fedup24 has written:

She works Mon, Weds, Thurs 9 a.m.–5 p.m. at Rosewood Women's Shelters Charity. Drives in and parks in nearby car park. Numberplate BH18 GVP.

She'll be alone at home on evening of Tuesday 22 October, everyone out the house.

DO IT THEN. Don't want to wait any longer.

Code to front gate is 0747.

I must tense at the exact same moment as something jumpy happens on the TV show that Todd is watching because he says, 'Didn't see that coming, did we?'

'Hmm,' I reply.

But I've got no idea what's going on in the drama on the telly. I'm stuck in a drama of my own.

Who knows our diaries that precisely other than us? Todd goes away randomly and sometimes at the last minute. How could all this information be found out about us, about me? Has someone been watching us for a long time? Spying on us from afar and somehow finding out our front gate code and whereabouts? Has someone close to me been bribed to hand over that information? But who?

The only people other than me who know all that information are Todd, Seth and Lily. Well, the cleaner and gardener also know the gate code, but they don't know our diaries. They wouldn't have known I'd be on my own on Tuesday night. Oh, and Todd's best mate, Rohan, knows the gate code but he's the chief constable of the local police constabulary, so I doubt he's using dark web murder-for-hire websites.

Todd snorts. 'Way too obvious,' he says, a comment on the plot of the mystery he's watching.

Another screenshot comes through. It shows the end of the previous message with the gate code, and under it says:

> But better to get through the broken fence panel at the end of the garden near the beehives, entering from the woodland. Won't be spotted. Get to woodland through a path at end of the lane.

An itchy, creeping sensation starts at my feet and works its way up my body. Realisation hits me like an avalanche. All the points where Todd's body touches mine burn. I want to jerk away like I've just been seared by a hot dish from the oven.

It's him. My husband. It can only be Todd. My rock of eighteen years wants me dead.

He shifts his arm around me. No longer a comfort, now it's too heavy, crushing, suffocating.

Todd and I are the only ones who know about the broken fence panel. We noticed it on Saturday when we were sorting out the bees. It must've been blown over by the wind. We talked about getting it fixed. We didn't mention it to Seth or Lily, because why would we? They're teenagers with zero interest in something like that. I was going to get it repaired but hadn't got round to it yet.

Todd knew I'd be alone last night, Tuesday 22 October. Both Lily and Seth had told us their plans for that evening days in advance, and he'd booked in to see his friend the week before when he confirmed the London podcast appearance. He gave out our code to the front gate so the hitman could let themselves in but suggested going through the broken fence. There was someone outside last night. Were they just waiting for the right time to pounce? Maybe when they disappeared from view, they'd gone into the woodland searching for the downed panel.

Thank goodness I left and went to Simon's. They must've thought I was out for the night and gave up waiting, changed their plan because I'd done something unexpected.

Is that why Todd sounded surprised when I called him from work this morning? Was he expecting me to be dead?

The blood crystallises in my veins. Will Todd let the hitman into our house to do it tonight?

Something inside ruptures.

'Got to run, not feeling too great.' Phone in hand, I bolt up from Todd's embrace and dash to the door.

'Jen?' Todd says behind me. He mutes the telly.

Over my shoulder, I say, 'Upset stomach.'

'Can I get you something?'

'No, I'll be okay. I'll sleep in the guest room tonight and use that en suite. Just in case I'm up and down all night.'

'Okay, my love. Shout if you need anything.'

'Will do,' I say, closing the door and sprinting up the stairs.

In the guest room, I head straight to the en suite and lock myself in.

I pace the room, looking at my phone. I should've grabbed my charger out of the bedroom. I put my phone down on the sink unit to conserve the battery.

Think, Jen, think.

Should I go somewhere tonight? But I have no friends or family. My only real friend is Simon, and after last night I don't want to go back there again.

Should I go to the police? But Todd's best friend runs the local police, and what would I tell them – there's no emergency. There's not even any evidence that it's definitely Todd who has committed a crime. They'd think I was crazy. And I don't like the police, try to avoid them at all costs.

My phone lights up with an incoming call.

'Hi, Kiah,' I answer in a whisper, covering my mouth. Todd is downstairs and not likely to hear me, but I can't take any chances.

'Hi, I've just had some news. Is now a good time?' she talks rapidly, clearly excited.

'Yes, go on.'

'The murder-for-hire site on the dark web is a scam. It's a fake website, but people think they're genuinely ordering a hit. The website takes their money, and then nothing happens.'

'A scam?' I repeat.

'Yep. The customers who have paid to have someone murdered aren't exactly going to complain to anyone when the hitman doesn't materialise, are they? It's a clever con.'

'That means there isn't a hitman after me.' Sweet relief coats my tongue like a spoonful of honey.

'Yes. But listen to me. Hoax or not, the *intent* is definitely real.'

My mouth turns sour. 'I'm still in danger?'

'Afraid so. There's been a few cases where people whose

names have been on these sites have been murdered by the person willing to hire the hitman in the first place. There was a case recently in the US. A woman was murdered by her husband after he'd paid money to a murder-for-hire site on the dark web and nothing happened. He lost patience and did it himself. As I said, the intent is very real, even if the site is a scam.'

My entire being jolts. I feel light-headed, peculiar, as if the blood pumping in my veins has suddenly decided to change direction. I lean against the wall, prop myself up against the bath, hold the sink cabinet – anything to keep me upright.

'I think it's my husband.'

'Really?' Kiah exhales loudly. 'That figures. Sadly, it's often the spouse.'

'And I think he was expecting it to be done last night when I was alone in the house.'

'Are you safe now?'

I look around the locked bathroom. 'I think so.'

'Try and find some evidence, okay? I need to talk to Hadley Perry at NCA. Speak soon.' She rings off.

At 10.50 p.m., I hear the sound of the lounge door swishing open and shut. Todd is coming upstairs. Is he coming to kill me? Has he lost patience waiting for the site to deliver on his order and, realising it's not going to happen any time soon, he's going to do it himself? I check the lock is definitely on and hold my breath.

His feet pad across the carpet. 'Jen? Are you okay? Can I come in?' The bathroom door handle moves as he attempts to let himself in.

'No!' I cry. 'I've got a very upset stomach. You really don't want to come in. I'm on the loo.'

The handle springs back. 'Oh, right. What do you think has caused that?'

'I've got no idea.'

'Do you need anything?'

'No, I'm fine. You go to bed. Hopefully, I'll feel better in the morning.'

'I'm up early tomorrow to do a twenty-mile training run, and after I'll go straight into the club for a meeting with Gavin. I'll shower and get changed there.'

'Okay,' I reply.

'And in the afternoon, I've got a charity thing with that Eastleigh concrete company. So I won't be back until about six-ish.'

He always does this – runs through the following day's schedule with me. We've always kept each other informed of what we're up to. And Todd's week varies depending on appearances and other things he's got booked in.

'Hope it goes well,' I squeak. It breaks my heart that he's acting so normal.

'I won't wake you up in the morning. Love you. Feel better soon.'

There's a pause. He's expecting me to reply with 'I love you', as usual, but I can't even force myself to say it. His footsteps pad away.

In case he's listening, I flush a few times and pour water down the toilet to make it sound as if I'm vomiting. He can't know that I'm on to him.

He'd have to smash down the bathroom door to get to me. And that's pretty incriminating for the police, isn't it? He'd want to get away with it – that's why he was willing to pay for a hitman in the first place.

I make a seat out of the towels and attempt to get comfortable on the cold tiled floor. I have to remain alert. A locked bathroom still isn't safe. If Todd wants to get in, he will. What could I use as a weapon? I pull a vase of dried flowers off the windowsill and ditch the dried flowers.

Clutching the vase, I sit perfectly still and listen. Todd

usually falls asleep as soon as his head hits the pillow, but I wait to make certain.

The front door opens and closes, and Seth and Lily's hushed voices drift up. There's no way Todd will try anything with them in the house – they're witnesses, and he wouldn't risk it.

I'm safe. For now.

CHAPTER FOURTEEN

Find some incriminating evidence. That's what Kiah said. And that's what I've been thinking about all night locked in the guest room en suite. I need absolute proof.

I hear Todd get up at 5 a.m. to go for his run.

At 7 a.m., I send a message to Syreeta to say I'm still not well and won't be in today. She replies almost instantly saying she didn't think I looked good yesterday and that I should take as long as I need off. She says she'll message Penny to see if she can cover today. I feel guilty. I never call in sick.

But I think my husband wants me dead. And could kill me at any moment. If that doesn't warrant a sick day, then I don't know what does.

Seth and Lily get up and head out around 8.30 a.m. I count to one hundred, just to make sure they don't return, and leave the bathroom.

Todd's office is the first port of call. I need to get into Todd's laptop to see if it's definitely him. There must be something incriminating: the messages or payments or something. Maybe I could check his bank account to see if he's paid out $50,000 recently. We have our own accounts and a joint account for the house and shared things.

The door to the outbuilding has a code to open it rather than a key. It's 0747, the same as the gates. I stab in the numbers, head through the gym and up the stairs. I feel like I'm betraying a sacred bond of trust as I step into Todd's office.

My heart breaks all over again as I take in his railway model and all his gear. How could he do this to me? How could he want me dead? We're so in love. Tears spring to my eyes, but I fight them back. I have to get this done.

I open his laptop lid and hope it will spring to life. It doesn't. I rub my finger over the touchpad, but nothing happens. I press the power button, and it flicks on. And requests a password. I've never needed Todd's laptop password so have never asked him for it. He'd readily give it to me. Just like I'd tell him my passwords if he ever asked.

I type in my name followed by the number one. It doesn't work. I try various combinations of my name, Seth's name, my date of birth, his date of birth, his middle name, but nothing works.

How the hell am I meant to get into his laptop?

The trill of a mobile phone startles me. Has Todd forgotten his phone? No. It's not his usual ringtone. I follow the sound, and wedged between the back of the sofa and the wall is a cheap, basic mobile phone. Not a smartphone. Just for calls and texts.

The name flashing on the phone is Gemma.

Who on earth is Gemma?

The call rings off. A few seconds later the phone bleeps with a text message.

It shows briefly on the home screen, just enough time for me to read it:

Tuesday night blew my mind. Can't wait to be with you again. Gem xxx

I collapse in a heap. Was Todd with this Gemma on Tuesday night when he told me he was with his friend planning charitable fitness events? Is he having an affair?

That thought is such a shock that I have to lie back on the carpet for a minute and take some very deep breaths.

I decide to call this Gemma.

I press the digits for our dates of birth and other random numbers, but can't guess the PIN code.

Aargh! I pocket the phone and bring Todd's laptop and charger back to the main house with me.

Hours later, at around 2 p.m., Lily gets home. She has morning lectures on a Thursday and gets the bus home after because Seth is there all day. I wait for her in the kitchen.

'Hi,' I say.

'Hi,' she replies. 'You're not in work today?'

'Not feeling too good so called in sick.'

'Sorry, Jen. I hope you're okay?'

'I'll be fine. Have you had lunch? Can I make you something?'

She shakes her head. 'Thank you, but I had a salad at uni. There's a decent salad bar in the food hall. The rest of the options aren't so great.' She makes herself a glass of squash. 'Can I get you something? If you're not feeling well?'

'No. I'm okay, thanks.' I lift up a debit card. 'New card came in the post.'

'Excellent,' she says. She points towards the hallway and moves in that direction. 'I'm going to head upstairs and crack on with a lab exercise we've got to do for tomorrow.'

'Lily, I need your help.'

She stops, swallows and turns back to me. 'Something to do with the dark web stuff, right?'

'Yes.' I point to the mobile phone and the laptop on the kitchen island. 'Can you help me get into these? It's Todd's laptop and secret mobile phone.'

Her eyes widen.

'Please, Lily. I think it's Todd. I think he's having an affair.'

'I'm so sorry. This is so awful.' She wrings her hands. Chews her lips. 'I've not said anything to Seth. And it's really eating me up.'

'Thank you for not saying anything. Will you help me with this?'

'You're asking me to hack into someone's laptop without their permission. That's illegal.'

'Please, Lily,' I beg. 'You're my only hope.'

She fidgets and looks anywhere but at me. Reluctantly, she nods. She heads towards the front door and comes back with her rucksack. She pulls out her laptop and puts it on the kitchen island. She takes a seat next to me and pulls Todd's laptop closer to her.

She points to the phone. 'Can't help you with that. Phone hacking stuff is a second-year module.'

'No problem, the laptop will be enough. Thank you.'

She powers up Todd's laptop and wakes up her own. 'There's a tool that can be used to crack passwords...' she says, but she's talking to herself more than to me. Her face isn't excited. It looks concerned.

She types a few things and takes a sip of her squash. 'This might take a while depending on how complex the password is.'

Her laptop dings a second later. 'Wow. That was quick. The password is SouthamptonFC7.'

Of course. His beloved football club and the number of his shirt.

Lily types the password into his laptop, and it immediately opens onto his home screen. 'What are you looking for on here?'

'Can you do a search for the name "Gemma"?'

'Yep.' She types, and we watch as the screen shows a search in progress.

It stops and displays a list. She scans it. 'Looks like there's a folder and also quite a few emails.'

'Let's look at the emails first.'

She nods and navigates into the inbox. She turns the laptop to me. I scroll through the inbox and see hundreds of emails from a Gemma Murray to Todd spanning years. I click into the sent items and see Todd has emailed Gemma Murray hundreds of times. I open a random email from him to her. It reads:

> Soon, my love. It's complicated, but I'll get rid of her, I promise. She won't go easily. This has to be done right. I don't want to lose my son. Be patient, my Gem. I love you, T xxx

'Fuuuck,' Lily says over my shoulder.

I didn't realise she was reading it too. I look up at her, and she edges back.

She cups her cheeks with her hands. 'I can't believe he's cheating on you. You two seem so solid.'

I want to curl up into a little ball and die. But I don't. I open a few more emails. More of the same. A lot of sex talk. A lot of gushing lovey-dovey stuff. A lot of telling each other what an amazing time they had together. I bet if I checked dates, it would be when Todd had told me he was in London. Maybe she lives there? And that's where he stays when he tells me he's at a hotel or with his friend.

I close down the email app and turn the laptop back to Lily. 'Let's have a look in the folder.'

'It's hidden in some unused services folders.' She clicks a few things and brings it up. She turns the laptop back to me.

'I'm going to the loo.' She gets off her stool and heads out of the room.

I open Todd's 'Gemma' folder.

It's full of photos and videos. The photos show them together at restaurants, bars, around famous landmarks in London. Confirming my suspicion that she lives there. They look so happy. There are eight videos. I click into one.

It's a sex video of the two of them. Obviously shot in a hotel room.

Lily walks back in the room just as Gemma groans and shouts, *Yes, Todd!* and Todd grunts.

'Ew.' She stops dead in her tracks and covers her ears by screwing her palms into them.

I press stop. I don't bother looking at the other seven. I can guess exactly what they are – more of the same. I close the folder and memorise where on the system it's located in case I need to find it again.

I wave at Lily so she uncovers her ears. 'Could we search for a bitcoin payment or reference code or something similar? I don't know how all that works, but Kiah said the $50,000 payment was using bitcoin.'

'Sure.' Lily perches once again on the stool and types a few things and hits the enter button. 'Just running a search. Let's see what comes up.'

There's an awkward moment where we look at each other, and I feel like I should break the silence but don't know what to say. This poor teenager has just helped her boyfriend's mother discover that his father is cheating and has probably hired a contract killer to bump her off. Small talk doesn't feel quite appropriate.

Lily shifts in her seat and clears her throat. 'So intense...' she begins.

But a ding from the laptop saves her. She looks at the screen and types a few things. 'Found a bitcoin payment. Only one. For $50,000. There's a reference code.'

I message Kiah. Within minutes she's replied with another screenshot. I show my phone to Lily. 'Is that the same reference code?'

Lily types away, pauses, scratches the top of her head, makes sure what she's typing is the same as what is on the screenshot.

She freezes, her fingers poised over the keyboard, and cocks her head.

'Anything?' I ask.

'Yeah. The bitcoin payment reference matches what is on the hire-a-hitman site. Here, look.' She turns Todd's laptop so I can see the screen.

I don't really understand what I'm looking at – a black screen with white writing, split into two. I squint and wrinkle my nose. 'I'm not sure what that's telling me.'

'This' – she points out a long reference code on the left of the screen – 'matches this.' She points out the same code on the right of the screen. 'It's definitely him. He made this payment.'

'Conclusive proof it's my husband,' I stammer.

'Uh-huh,' she replies miserably. She looks close to tears.

Todd wants me dead. I spring up, pace a little and lean against the island. My breath comes short and shallow.

Lily stares at me as all the colour drains from her face. Her breathing becomes laboured.

'Are you okay, Lily?' I ask.

'What about Seth? Does Todd want him dead, too? What about me? Are we safe in the house with Todd? Oh god... *oh god...*'

She begins to hyperventilate.

I put my arm around her shoulders and press her into my side. 'Deep breaths. That's it.' Lily's panting calms. 'Todd adores Seth and won't do anything to hurt either of you. He's after me. That's it. I'll sort this out. I won't let him hurt you. You're both safe here.'

I pick up my phone. 'I'll let Kiah know that we found evidence so she can pass it on to her NCA contact. Perhaps they'll come and seize his laptop. Maybe arrest Todd.'

Lily's eyes go wide. 'Right, I'm just going to wipe all traces that I've been on this machine – that could land me in *a lot* of trouble. You'll just need to say you knew or guessed his password, okay? And that I had nothing whatsoever to do with it, *okay*?'

I nod my agreement. 'I promise you won't get into any trouble, Lily.'

Lily taps a few things, clears Todd's screen and powers off his laptop.

'I'm going upstairs. I need to chill before attempting that homework,' Lily says, rubbing her face. She still looks slightly panicked.

'Okay. Thank you,' I say quietly, still reeling with the absolute confirmation that my husband paid all that money to kill me because he's having an affair.

Lily picks up her laptop, rucksack and glass of squash and heads upstairs to Seth's bedroom.

What do I do now?

I told Lily I'd contact Kiah. But I can't. I place my phone back on the table. I can't go to the NCA. I can't risk them digging into my history. I can't have them asking for DNA samples and then linking it to a crime committed eighteen years ago. Uncovering who I really am, what I did. And besides, what did Kiah's contact say – that I was a tiny part of a massive international operation, that he's working with the FBI and agencies around the world. That it'll take weeks, months, possibly even years to bring people to justice. I'll probably be dead by then.

And I can't go to my local police, goodness no. All the officers know their boss's best mate is legendary footie star Todd James. Todd has made personal appearances at most of their Christmas parties for the past decade or so, had his photo taken with them or signed shirts for their kids. How could I tell one of them that Todd James wants to murder me, his wife? They'd be dubious from the off: *Pretty Boy wants to bump off his wife? Nah, he's such a top bloke.* And they might look deeper into my past, and then I'd be put away. Taken from Seth forever.

I have to think of another way. One that doesn't involve any police whatsoever.

Disappear and start again. I've done it once: started over, left one life completely behind. I escaped from Damian because I was certain he was close to murdering me and our baby.

Could I start again from scratch? No. I can't just leave Todd and take Seth. Seth is an adult now. And he loves his father and loves his life. How could I get him to give all that up? His girlfriend, his friends, his university place, his PondGuy social media, his entire identity.

I could never up and leave Seth. Never. He's my entire world.

What if I told Seth that his father wants his mother dead – would he believe me? It would destroy him. He'd never survive a revelation like that, he's a sensitive boy.

How long can I go on for? Knowing my husband is about to murder me any minute. It's torture. How can I live a happy life knowing every day might be the day I get murdered. I did that with Damian. And I'm never doing that again. It could go on for years.

No, there's only one solution I can see.

CHAPTER FIFTEEN

18 YEARS AGO

DAILY TIMES

TUESDAY 11 JULY 2006

SOUTHAMPTON WOMAN PLEADS NOT GUILTY TO MURDER CHARGE

Natalie Owens denied bail and will stay in prison until her trial

Natalie Owens entered a not guilty plea to the charge of murdering Jerry Ward on 1 July at Southampton Crown Court yesterday.

Due to the violence of the crime, Owens was not granted bail and will be remanded in custody until her trial. The date of which has now been set for 6 December 2006, at Southampton Crown Court.

Senior reporter's opinion:

The brutal murder of Southampton grandfather Jerry Ward has gripped the nation. Firstly, the gruesome nature of the crime – a throat slit with a kitchen knife – and secondly, the details of the multiple stab wounds inflicted in the moments before he died and in the moments after death. But Natalie Owens, the 21-year-old woman charged with his murder, insists she's innocent.

Ahead of the trial, speculation about just what motivated a young woman to murder has reached fever pitch with amateur sleuths, columnists and even celebrities weighing in.

Was Natalie's attack random and an impulsive, spur-of-the-moment decision? Or was it premeditated with Jerry Ward targeted specifically? If Jerry was targeted, why him? No conclusive links between the pair have been established, with the police remaining tight-lipped on the matter.

A few questions have prompted endless debate – if the police hadn't caught her, would she have murdered again? If that fingerprint hadn't been found, would Natalie Owens have gone on to be a serial killer?

We await the trial and the answers it will provide.

CHAPTER SIXTEEN

At around six, exactly when Todd said he'd get home, he gets home.

He comes through to the kitchen and sees me stood next to the dining table. 'How are you feeling, my love?'

He heads towards me with his arms outstretched for a hug, but I hold my hand up to stop him. 'I'm calling a family meeting. Right now, before we start on dinner.'

He nods, drops his arms and heads straight to the dining table. I call up the stairs to Seth and Lily and tell them to come down for a family meeting. Seth got home at around half four and headed straight up to his bedroom. I've not seen or heard Lily since she went upstairs earlier.

I've already put Todd's secret mobile phone and his laptop on the dining table. Todd doesn't even look at them, scrolling through his phone.

Seth and Lily arrive. Lily looks worried, stuffing her hands in the front pocket of her oversized hoodie. Seth puts his arm around her and guides her to the dining table. 'It's all right, we've always had family meetings when there's something important to discuss. It's nothing to worry about.'

She nods, and they sit at the table.

'Would anyone like a drink before we start?' I ask and flick the kettle on.

'Chocolate protein shake, please,' Todd says.

Seth and Lily gesture in the negative.

Seth stands and heads towards the cupboards. 'Actually, I fancy some crisps. Anyone want a packet?'

We all decline. As Seth is rifling in the cupboard for the crisps he wants, Todd stands and heads over.

'I'm peckish too,' he says. 'Think I'll get some nuts.'

I sort a cup of tea for me and grab a bottle of milkshake from the fridge and head to the dining table just as Seth and Todd sit back down.

Todd is next to me and Seth is opposite. Lily sits next to Seth and across from Todd. She chews her lips.

Todd unscrews the bottle cap and takes a swig, while Seth munches on some strong-smelling cheese and onion crisps.

I sit, clasping my hands in front of me. This plan has to work. It's life or death. It's the only thing I can think of to save my skin. 'I've called this meeting because I've discovered that Todd is having an affair.'

Todd spits out his mouthful of milkshake in shock. It sprays across the table, all over his bowl of nuts. He doesn't attempt to clean it up. He turns to stare at me.

'What?' Seth says, gobsmacked. He drops the packet of crisps on the table.

The atmosphere in the room freezes.

'There's more,' I continue. 'I've also discovered that Todd has paid money to hire a hitman to kill me so that he can be with his mistress. He's been seeing her secretly for years.'

Todd is speechless. Seth flicks his attention between me and Todd, utterly flabbergasted. Lily stares at her hands in her lap.

'Hired a hitman?' Seth asks slowly, as if the gravity of that is taking a while to settle in his mind.

I push on. 'I don't want to involve the police. I'd like us to work this out together.' I turn to face Todd and look him in the eye. He's still staring at me, mouth gaping wide.

'Todd, I will happily get a divorce. With no fuss. I won't come after any of your money, or this house or anything of yours. We'll separate quickly and cleanly. You can be with Gemma. And I'll live, there'll be no need to end my life. I can move out tonight if you wish.'

I've planned this out – I'll go to the shelter run by my work to stay for a few days. I don't have much money that isn't Todd's money. But I'll make it work with my part-time salary.

Todd finally finds his voice. 'I'm not having an affair. I have no idea who Gemma is. I'm not trying to get you killed. I haven't a clue how I'd even go about hiring a hitman. And I don't want a divorce. I love you. You're my soulmate.' He goes to hold my hand, but I pull it away.

'I have proof, Todd. Evidence. You don't need to deny it. Let's all be adults and talk about this openly.'

'What kind of proof?' Todd asks.

I pick up the phone. 'This is your secret mobile. I didn't go into work today and happened to hear it ringing in your office. It was Gemma. And Gemma messaged you about the amazing time you two had on Tuesday night. I'm assuming she lives in London and you see her when you go there. Put in the PIN code and let's read all the messages together.'

I hold the phone out to Todd, but he doesn't take it.

'I've never seen that phone before in my life. It's not mine,' he says.

Seth takes the phone from me and presses a button. The phone lights up. 'There's no PIN code, Mum. It's unlocked.'

I must've mistakenly thought it was locked earlier and didn't check it properly. Annoying, but never mind. 'Read out some of the text messages,' I tell Seth.

Seth presses a few buttons, and his face scrunches up. With disgust? With confusion?

He shows the phone to me. 'There's absolutely nothing on this phone. No messages, no contacts, no nothing. It looks like it's come straight out of the box.'

'What?' I snatch the phone back from him and look. He's right. What the hell has happened to that message I saw from Gemma? I slam the phone on the table and pull Todd's laptop towards me. I open the lid and type in the password. 'SouthamptonFC7,' I say out loud. 'I guessed it.'

Todd's face doesn't change. He's not worried that I 'guessed' his password.

I open his emails first. 'There are loads of emails between you and Gemma going back years.' I angle the laptop in the middle of the table so that all of us can see the screen.

I scroll through the inbox. But there are no emails from Gemma. I open the sent items – no emails to Gemma. Has he deleted them all somehow? But this laptop has been in my possession all day.

'What the hell...?' I mutter. 'There's a folder with photos of the happy couple and sex videos.'

Seth grimaces. 'Yuck.'

Todd's eyebrows knit together and his jaw drops halfway to the floor.

I navigate to the place in the system which has the 'Gemma' folder hidden in it. But the folder isn't there.

'Shit,' I say. How has everything just disappeared into thin air?

I grab my phone. 'A documentary maker contacted me because my details were on the dark web on this hire-a-hitman site. She's doing a documentary about it. Her name is Kiah Wong.'

I open WhatsApp to find all the messages we've sent one another and the screenshots. But the chat isn't there. Her contact details are no longer in my phone book. On Todd's laptop, I bring up a browser and google Kiah Wong. But her website, her social media channels, her credits on the BBC and other production company sites don't come up.

I jump up and pluck the notepad where I'd written her number from off the fridge, sit back down and call it off my mobile, putting it on speakerphone. The number won't dial. Instead, we hear the dead line tone.

It's like she never existed.

What. The. Fuck?

'I don't understand...' I mumble. Clutching at straws, I point at Todd, 'When I got back from that baby shower you were on your laptop and closed it so quickly when I walked in. You were messaging Gemma, weren't you? Or contacting the hitman. Admit it!'

Todd pales. 'What? No! I was researching holidays in the Maldives for January, wanted it to be a surprise...'

'Rubbish! Why not tell me?'

'Because you were so set on that place you'd found in Fuerteventura that I didn't even mention it, thought I'd save it for another time... A romantic wedding anniversary break or something.'

'Oh...' I falter.

Seth bursts out laughing. He points at me. 'Mum! What a wind-up! You really got us going there. Ha, ha, ha.' He points at Todd. 'Dad, your face! What a joke. And a week away from Halloween just to throw us off the scent. Brilliant.' He picks up his packet of crisps and continues eating them.

Todd nods slowly. His frown is replaced by a smile, which spreads across his face. 'Wow. You proper got us.' Todd takes a handful of milkshake-splattered nuts. 'I'll get started on dinner.'

Seth takes Lily's arm and edges back his chair.

'No,' I shout. 'This isn't a prank!' I gesture to Lily. 'Lily, tell them. Lily came with me to meet the documentary maker. She helped me find all the evidence – she saw it all.'

Todd and Seth both stare at Lily. She shrinks into herself and remains mute.

'Lily,' I insist. 'Tell them. It's okay.'

As quietly as a mouse, her eyes still on her hands in her lap, Lily says, 'I don't want to get involved in this.'

I stand and lean over the table. I have to get through to her. I wave in front of her face in an attempt to get her to look at me. 'Lily, I know I said not to say anything but now I want you to. Tell them the truth!'

Lily recoils, absolutely petrified.

'Whoa, Mum, chill. She doesn't want to get involved in your joke. Leave her out of it,' Seth says and shifts his body so he's between me and his girlfriend.

I attempt to edge round him. I just need to get her to look at me. 'Lily!'

'You're scaring her,' Seth says.

'Lily,' I bellow and attempt to grab her arm. 'Tell them!'

Seth blocks me.

'Enough, Jen,' Todd shouts. He slams his palm on the table with a bang. 'Leave the poor girl alone.'

We all go rigid. He's never raised his voice in this house. Has never shown any kind of anger. I stand back.

Lily sniffs back tears.

Seth gathers her up. 'We're going out.'

They hurry from the kitchen.

I stare towards the hallway.

Why won't she back me up? She was there with Kiah. She helped me find all the evidence!

'Seth,' I yell. 'Come back here. Just you.'

He trudges back, pulling his coat on and glaring daggers at me. 'What?'

'There's something not right here,' I say, but I can't articulate my gut feeling any further than that.

His cheeks colour, nostrils flare and jaw clenches. I've never seen him so incensed. 'There's something not right with *you*.' He stomps away from me and, a couple of seconds later, slams the front door.

Todd clears his throat, and I take him in. He slowly stands. He's upset. 'I know you were trying to be funny. But an affair? A hitman? A divorce? Jeez. Are you trying to give me a heart attack? I can't imagine my life without you.'

I gawp at him. Bewildered.

'I don't understand why Lily didn't back me up—'

He cuts me off. Something he never does. 'Stop with all this Lily stuff. Have you got it in for her? Are you jealous of her because Seth is obviously in love with her? Do you feel threatened because you're not the only woman in his life now?'

'What? No! She was right there with—'

He cuts me off again. 'Jen. You're being really weird tonight. Was that your plan, to make all that stuff up so Lily felt bad because you knew she wouldn't want to come in on your bizarre joke?'

I fold my arms. Remain mute. There's no point arguing with Todd when I'm not clear what I'm arguing about. Or what exactly just happened. Earlier, I was so certain about my plan, on what I had to do. But all of that has been blown to pieces.

Todd is crestfallen. He pauses a moment, and I can tell he's torn between comforting me and being angry with me. He opts for disappointed. He grabs the jar of honey-roasted nuts from the cupboard. 'I'm going to my office. You know I love you more than I love life itself. But please don't join me. I need some me time. I'll order a takeaway and eat it there. I think I'll sleep on the sofa in the office tonight too.'

He strides out.

Alone, I take stock.

It was all a hoax. There was no affair. No hitman. No documentary maker or NCA contact. It was all made up. And all traces of it have been deleted.

But what about those Todd and Gemma photos and videos that I saw? They were real, weren't they? But then I recall a Friday night movie we watched where someone had been blackmailed with fake photos that had been digitally spliced together. Deepfakes. Probably if I'd looked closer, I might've seen they weren't real. People get fooled by photoshopped images and AI-generated video all the time. And I got fooled, big time.

I can't believe I doubted all the people in my life who I love so much, all the people I trust.

But someone is screwing with me.

Lily is such a sweet, honest girl; I can't believe she wouldn't immediately have my back. She looked absolutely petrified earlier. Todd and Seth thought she was scared of *me*.

But perhaps someone is screwing with her too.

Whatever's going on, I'm going to get to the bottom of it.

CHAPTER SEVENTEEN

Seth and Lily returning at 2 a.m. wakes me up. Todd stuck to his word and is sleeping in his office. The bed feels empty without him. I listen to my son and his girlfriend come up the stairs and move around getting ready for bed. Then there's silence.

Am I jealous and feeling threatened by Lily? No. Lily is so perfect for Seth, and all I want is for him to be happy.

I wrap my dressing gown around me, put on my slippers and creep downstairs. In the lounge, I sit on the sofa and open my laptop.

I google 'Lily Hailstone'. Quite a few hits come up for Lily, mostly all her social media channels. These are all public; she clearly has nothing whatsoever to hide. I nose around her Instagram and TikTok. She doesn't post all that often, mostly food and drink, a pretty view or sunset, an occasional selfie showing a small part of her face – which, I note, Seth has liked with both his personal profile and his PondGuy profile. As far as I can tell, she mostly spends her time liking Seth's PondGuy posts and YouTube videos. She has a fair number of 'friends', and nothing appears strange about her social media presence.

I can't find much else about her, which is understandable – she's a teenager and most of her public online life is channelled into social media. I dig around a bit more and find a decade-old local newspaper article from a Basingstoke newspaper that mentions a school class raising money for charity with a Lily Hailstone noted as one of the children in the class. There's no photo, but this ties into Lily's mention that she lived in that area.

I don't find anything dodgy or suspicious.

Sighing, I put down my laptop.

The hairs on the back of my neck prickle, as if movement behind me has stirred a faint breeze. I have my back to the door, sitting on the sofa that looks out towards the garden. I take a deep breath and spin my head to look. Through the doorway I see the empty kitchen and, beyond, the doorway into the pitch-black hallway.

Something catches my eye. I'm not sure what. Is someone watching me?

I jump up and stomp through the kitchen to the hallway ready to catch them in the act. I switch on the light.

Nothing.

I shiver. It's just my imagination. I shake off the feeling and switch off the light.

It's 4 a.m., and I'm wide awake. It's pointless going back up to bed, so I head into the kitchen to make myself a chamomile tea with a spoonful of honey. The basic mobile phone that I found in Todd's office is still on the dining table. I pick it up and look at it.

Who planted this? Who has been in my home? Who could know all that information about my whereabouts and the code to get in the gate? Who would go to all the bother of this incredibly intricate planning to screw with me by setting up a hoax? I'm pretty certain that if my past had caught up with me, I'd be dead by now and not toyed with.

I put the phone back down and rub my confused forehead. A wave of exhaustion crashes and breaks over me. I perch on a stool around the kitchen island and sip my tea.

And that's when it pops into my head. A prank. On me. Todd, Seth and Lily are all in on it. We often prank each other, especially around Halloween. That's what Seth said to me last night. But he was acting, bluffing. They're winding *me* up, they must be. There's no other reason as to why Lily wouldn't tell them that she'd come with me to meet Kiah Wong or seen the evidence of Todd's affair for herself. They've roped her in on it.

I rest my head on the counter and close my eyes. I'll tell them tomorrow that I've rumbled them. We'll have a good laugh about it, and this will all be over.

A cough wakes me. I sit bolt upright, wiping away the drool.

'What are you doing, Mum? Did you sleep there? You look terrible,' Seth says. He bounces around the kitchen making breakfast for him and Lily. Lily stands in the doorway, looking at her feet, not able to look at me. Perhaps the poor girl is worried about what I might think because she didn't want to get involved with a family prank.

'Woke up early and couldn't sleep, so came down here. Must've nodded off.' I slide off the stool and stretch out my stiff body.

'Do you want a coffee?' he asks.

'Yes, please,' I reply.

Seth goes over to Lily to ask her too. She nods and says quietly, 'Just going in the telly room.' She glances at me. Seth kisses the top of her head. She shuffles into the telly room like a little mouse. The sound of the telly switching on is muted by the kettle boiling.

Lily's obvious discomfort puts me on edge. This is my home,

and I should feel comfortable here, but the dynamics have shifted after yesterday. I need to put this right.

'Seth...' I start but Todd's arrival in the kitchen, from the direction of his office and not from upstairs, stops me in my tracks.

Seth looks at Todd and frowns, also noticing where his dad has come in from. Todd has never slept in his office before. We've never had an argument where we've slept in separate rooms.

Todd comes to stand next to the sink, swerving me, not delivering a kiss or hug or any affection, which is completely wrong.

Seth flicks his eyes between us and decides the two of us need to talk without him about. He quickly puts a mug of coffee in front of me, then gathers his and Lily's mugs on a tray with two bowls, a packet of cereal and the milk and takes it all through to the telly room.

Right, I need to clear the air, tell Todd I'm on to their prank and it can stop, and then we can move on. I feel out of kilter in my own home, with my own people, and it's unnerving.

'Did you sleep okay?' I ask.

'Not really,' Todd replies unhappily, also keenly aware of the imbalance hanging in the air.

'Look, I've guessed—'

'Mum,' Seth's yell from the telly room cuts me off. 'Come here!'

Todd and I catch each other's eyes, both worried, and run to the telly room.

Seth and Lily are sitting on the sofa, eyes glued to the morning news. Seth turns to me. 'The local news is about to start, and it showed a photo of Simon. He's going to be on the news.'

'Simon?' I say, baffled. What is Simon doing on the local news?

'Yeah, your best mate Simon,' Seth says, as if I'm being particularly slow this morning.

There's a brief jingle, and the local news team's studio appears. They film in the same building as Todd's radio station; Seth and I have been in to see it.

The newsreader says: 'In breaking news, a Southampton man has been arrested following a tip-off. Simon Pitt worked for a women's shelters charity in the city for two decades, and it is thought during that time he used his position to groom, traffic, abuse and illegally film vulnerable women, forcing hundreds, and possibly thousands, into pornography, sex work or domestic servitude.'

The screen switches from the studio to footage of Simon being led out of his apartment building by police – the apartment building I was at a few days ago. The newsreader's voice continues over the top:

'Simon Pitt is thought to be the head of a powerful, international crime network that operated on the dark web. Police have seized his computers and will be employing the latest in digital forensics to uncover the extent of his illegal activity.'

'Whoa,' Seth says.

The screen cuts to a presenter standing outside Simon's building.

The newsreader says, 'Charlotte, I understand you're with a neighbour of the accused?'

The presenter says, 'Yes, Harry, I'm here with Simon Pitt's neighbour Everly Bonnet.' The camera zooms out and the presenter sticks a microphone in the woman's face.

'Everly, I understand you were friendly with Mr Pitt. What are your thoughts on his arrest?'

'Yes, we're on good terms. We've lived next to each other for almost ten years now. I've been over to his flat a few times. He seemed like such a normal, nice guy. I literally can't believe it. I mean, his flat is full of houseplants. You don't expect a criminal mastermind to have a passion for plants, do you? I'm in absolute shock, but I guess you never know what goes on behind closed doors.'

The presenter's voice continues as the footage cuts to a woman hustling her way through police and bystanders towards the front doors of the building, being intercepted by a police officer and then hurrying away. It's Miranda. 'Earlier, a woman believed to be Mr Pitt's ex-girlfriend attempted to enter his flat.'

'I have no comment,' Miranda snaps and swings her arm as if pushing away the camera. 'I have no idea what's going on. Leave me alone. I came to collect my belongings from his flat and there's police everywhere.' Miranda waves an empty box in front of her and pushes her way past the presenter and out of view of the camera.

The screen cuts back to the studio as they move on to the next local story, but I don't take any of it in. There's absolutely no way Simon is some mastermind criminal who hurts women. No way at all. I can't believe that a few days ago I doubted him and thought he might've paid for a hitman. Every part of my being tells me that this accusation isn't true.

Seth mutes the telly. Both he and Lily look up at me and Todd. All four of us are open-mouthed. I catch Lily's eye. I swear I see the briefest smirk cross her face.

Dark web.

A tip-off.

Computers.

That off feeling morphs into an absolute knowing.

'She did this,' I blurt and point at Lily. As soon as it's out of my mouth, I'm convinced. I'm not jumping to conclusions, not having a knee-jerk reaction that's way off the mark. I've hit the bullseye. In the very depths of my being, I *know*.

She winces and draws back from me.

'She did what?' Seth asks, reaching out and taking Lily's hand.

I thought they were pranking me, but there's no way Todd and Seth would bring my best friend into it. This has been done to upset me, I'm certain of it.

'She's planted stuff on Simon's computer and tipped off the police. She's the reason he's been arrested,' I shout.

Lily almost falls off the sofa. She wobbles and gets to her feet, eyeing the door ready to bolt. She's as white as a sheet. Seth stands and positions himself protectively between her and me.

'What a ridiculous thing to say, Mum. Why would Lily have anything to do with this? You're just upset because your best mate is evil and you didn't realise.' His voice is raised. He's angry at me. He's never angry at me.

'Simon is not evil. He's been set up. By her. Lily made up all that dark web stuff to mess with me, and now she's targeted my best mate.'

Seth gives me a look as if I've completely lost my mind. He puts his arm around Lily and barges past me, directing her as if he's a bodyguard making his way through fans with a celebrity.

They storm out of the kitchen.

I turn to Todd. He's still gaping.

'Lily's crazy! She's screwing with me and now my best friend. We need to stop her! We have to make a plan, right now. Get her away from Seth, out of this house–'

Todd holds up a hand to stop me mid-sentence. 'You, Jen, are the crazy one. You're spouting absolute nonsense. That sweet girl has done nothing but be a fantastic girlfriend to our son. She's a great house guest. She's helped you out without question. What is going on with you?'

He looks at me with such concern that I'm stumped and don't answer.

He softens. 'Simon's arrest must be a huge shock. You need

some time to process. As Seth said, Simon is evil and you didn't know – that has to be very jarring.' He gives me a pointed look. 'But you can't keep accusing people of things there's no way they've done.'

He's still upset about everything I accused him of yesterday. He clears his throat and adds, 'If you... umm... need to see a therapist to work through some things, then please book one and go. Today, if necessary. You're acting like a completely different person. Paranoid, and, well, delusional. I just want my Jen back, okay? I love you, and I'll support you through anything. You just need to take the first step.'

He pecks me quickly on the cheek. It has no warmth or love in it. It's perfunctory and forced.

He checks his watch. 'Need to get going. I've got a few re-records of tomorrow's show to make, and then I'm heading to the club to catch up with Gavin.'

Todd leaves the telly room.

I stand completely still as I hear movement upstairs and the front door opening and closing – all three of them leaving the house without shouting goodbye to me as normal. It sounds as if they're all hurrying, as if they can't wait to get out of here, to get away from me.

When the house is silent, I head into the dining area, pull out a seat and plonk myself in it.

What is going on with me? Am I losing my mind? Have I been making things up? Lily coming with me to meet Kiah Wong – was that all in my mind? Do I need help, like Todd suggested? He has only ever wanted the best for me. He wouldn't have said that unless he thought it would really help.

Paranoid and delusional. Yikes.

I stare into space.

The sound of my phone ringing slices through the silence.

I jump up and retrieve it from the kitchen island. It's work. I don't think work has ever called me on a Friday morning. It's not my usual day. There's never been any need. But we've never had a colleague arrested and on the morning news before, so I assume it's about that.

'Hello?' I answer.

'Jen, it's Penny!' She sounds frantic.

'Are you okay?' I ask.

'Have you heard about Simon?'

'Yes, we just saw it on the news.'

'I arrived at work not long ago, and there are police everywhere. They've seized all our tech – apparently, they have reason to believe that Simon's been storing bad stuff secretly on all our work computers. And they're interviewing people, starting with lovely Syreeta. They're making out like they've got something on her. As if she was working with Simon. As if we all had something to do with it. It's totally mental!'

'There's no way Syreeta would do anything illegal.'

'I know, right! But they're closing down charity operations until they've fully investigated.'

'What about all the women staying in the shelters?'

'Turfed out. They said they'd attempt to find them alternative accommodation, but we both know there's nowhere else for them to go if our shelters close.'

I shake my head sadly. 'Those poor women.'

'And our jobs are all on hold. After everyone here has been interviewed, we've been told to go home and not return until further notice. So don't come in on Monday. I've gotta go – a police officer is here to take our reception computer.'

She hangs up abruptly.

And I know what I need to do.

CHAPTER EIGHTEEN

18 YEARS AGO

DAILY TIMES
Thursday 7 December 2006

JERRY WARD MURDER TRIAL BEGINS AT SOUTHAMPTON CROWN COURT

Natalie Owens denies charges

A woman murdered retired grandfather Jerry Ward in Freemantle, Southampton, before thoroughly cleaning the victim's house in an attempt to remove all traces of evidence, a court heard today.

The trial of Natalie Owens, 21, who is charged with murdering the 69-year-old after meeting him in a pub and returning to his house on the evening of Saturday 1 July 2006, began yesterday (Wednesday 6 December) at Southampton Crown Court before judge Nicolas Riley. Owens denies a charge of murder.

Addressing the jury in his opening statement, the prosecuting barrister said the case 'concerns the death of an older man as a result of a knife wound to the throat' and involves significant pre- and post-death injuries 'inflicted by the defendant'.

He told the five women and seven men of the jury that through the course of the trial the prosecution would present witness evidence, play CCTV footage and submit forensic evidence.

Owens' defence counsel will then present evidence to the jury, with the trial expected to last for two weeks.

Owens denies charges of murdering Jerry Ward.

The trial continues.

CHAPTER NINETEEN

For some reason, Lily has got it in for me. I'm not paranoid or delusional or acting crazy. I'm perfectly sane and need to find out what she's up to. And fast. I'm usually a very good judge of character. But not this time. Lily and I are not friends. She orchestrated all that dark web stuff, she's put Simon in jail for something that there's absolutely no way he did, she's sabotaged my work's computers and messed with my beloved charity, and she's turning Todd and Seth against me.

What does she want? What will she do next?

I need to find some hard evidence that I can show Todd and Seth.

After showering and getting changed, I jump in my car and head straight to the nearest electrical retailer and buy myself another laptop and all the latest anti-malware software. I pay for the shop assistant to set the laptop up for me and make it as secure as possible. It will be my secret laptop. No one, and especially not Lily, will know about it. I then head to a café with Wi-Fi and log on.

She's infected my old laptop, I know it. And Todd's. And

probably Seth's too. I run the same Google search as I did earlier. But this time, I look closer at her social media. I click on all her friends. They all look about the right age. But you can buy friends and followers, can't you? I'm pretty sure I read that somewhere. Neither Instagram nor TikTok says when she first set it up, and I can't look at all her posts because I don't have an account. I debate setting up fake social media profiles and befriending her and her friends, but what will that prove? Not a lot.

No, she's too clever on computers. I need to watch her in person. She'll slip up and reveal something. She's human. It's bound to happen. I decide to return home.

As I near the front gate, I notice two things: a car parked across the entrance and someone attempting to scale the gate with one leg swung up and almost over.

I stop the car.

The person climbing the gate hears the car and jumps back down. They have their hood up and a scarf wrapped around the bottom half of their face.

My brain screams, *It's the hitman come to kill you!* I vomit the two matcha lattes I had at the café down myself in shock. But then remember there is no hitman.

So who the hell is this?

The person makes no attempt to run. They face me, plant their feet and cross their arms, as if squaring up to me. As if expecting violence. My heart pounds.

Shakily, I turn off the engine and open the car door. I stand and close the door. If I screamed, no one would hear. The neighbours are a way up the lane.

Instead, I pull myself together and shout with a forced fierceness. 'Hey! What are you up to?'

They flip back their hood and pull down the scarf. It's then I see the face.

'You sicked up on yourself,' Miranda observes.

I'm too stunned to reply. I just caught my best friend's ex-girlfriend attempting to scramble over my front gate.

Miranda points at the house and then at me. '*You* live here?'

I frown and shake my head. Of course she knows I live here. What else would she be doing here? The acrid smell of sick on my clothes makes me want to vomit again. 'Were you trying to break in?'

'No,' Miranda says with zero conviction.

'Has this got something to do with Simon's arrest?'

She blinks a few times. 'I don't give a shit about that bastard. He got what was coming to him.'

'You can't believe he did it?'

'We're all capable of doing fucked-up things. Even the most sweet-looking people. Nobody is who they appear.'

'Simon is innocent.'

She snorts with a fake laugh. 'Whatever. Like I said, I don't care about him anymore.'

My frown deepens. I don't believe her in the slightest. 'What do you want, then?'

She hesitates briefly, as if deciding what to say next. Then she shrugs and says, 'Nothing.' She strides towards her car. Starts the engine.

I stare as she turns the car around and mounts the neatly mown grass verge to get past my parked car on the lane. One tyre leaves a churned-up skid of mud, a jagged gash that might never go away.

'Don't ever come back here!' I shout loudly as she passes so she'll hear through the car window. 'If you do, I'll call the police.'

She glares at me from the other side of the glass.

I won't call the police, of course. But she doesn't know that.

As the car disappears up the lane, and I press in the code to the gate, my brain digests that bizarre interaction. Was she planning to snoop around my home to find something out about Simon? To find something out about me?

The gate swings open and I get back in my car and drive it in, watching in my rear-view mirror as the gates automatically close behind me.

I have more important things to think about than Miranda. First: get changed out of these sick-stained clothes. Second: Lily.

Later that evening, I sit in the lounge angled on the sofa so I can look through the door into the kitchen. Seth and Lily are in there, baking. They arrived back not long ago, went upstairs briefly and then headed into the kitchen with a full supermarket bag. Todd and I had already eaten dinner; Todd made a simple salmon meal. I sat in my usual spot around the kitchen island while he cooked.

I told him about catching Miranda. He suggested she was upset about Simon and not thinking straight. And that if she did something similar again then he'd speak to Rohan about the best course of action. That I shouldn't get involved unless absolutely necessary because he'd deal with it. I agreed. I wasn't really paying attention. Todd continued to talk to me, but none of it went in. I had been too busy listening out for Seth and Lily's return home.

Todd is still talking to me. He sits on the sofa next to me, but facing the telly. It's just a steady stream of words that go in one ear and out the other. I'm trying to work out what Lily and Seth are making. Seth had told me that they wanted the kitchen to themselves, and, well, I'm suspicious. They giggle and whisper, things clatter and the blender goes. I can hear the oven switch on.

Then the telly turns on. Todd has given up talking to me. I'm usually very attentive, I love listening to him and hearing his thoughts and conversing about all sorts. But not today. I need to keep my eye – and ear – on my son's girlfriend.

The waft of a cake of some sort cooking in the oven drifts into the lounge.

'Smells good,' Todd says to himself. He doesn't even look my way.

It does smell good. I love the house smelling like freshly baked cakes and biscuits. It's warm and homely. But it's Lily who has made this smell. And she doesn't belong here, doesn't belong in my kitchen, using my things and baking for my family. I don't trust what she cooks, or that her intentions are to nurture and show love by making delicious food. Lily is clearly very comfortable in my kitchen. And it makes me... uncomfortable. She's encroaching on my home, taking over.

There's more clattering and noise from the kitchen, and Seth and Lily move into the corner near the oven so I can't see them. I strain to look.

Todd stands, walks around the sofa and pushes the door so it's half open and blocking my view.

'What did you do that for?' I ask him.

'Leave them to it. They're adults and don't need to be watched. They're very capable of making food for themselves,' he says as he sits back down.

I observe him for a moment. He thinks I'm worried that they'll have an accident or something. How wrong he is.

There's more noise and murmurs, but I can't quite hear over the din of the football show Todd has put on with its fake laughter. I'm just debating whether to get up and reopen the door when it sweeps open, and Seth comes in holding a stack of small plates.

'Surprise,' he says with a big grin.

Lily follows him in holding a large plate of cupcakes.

Todd mutes the telly to look. 'Ooh, what are those?'

With a shy smile, Lily comes around the sofa to deposit the

cupcakes on the coffee table in front of us. 'Honey cupcakes with honey and vanilla icing. I hope you don't mind, I used your honey, Jen. Seth said it would be okay.'

'Of course it's okay,' Seth booms. He puts the small plates on the table next to the cupcakes and takes a seat on the second sofa and gestures for Lily to sit next to him.

I stare at the cakes – they look and smell incredible – and then stare at Lily. What stunt is she pulling here? Has she tampered with these cakes somehow? Are they poisoned? Or full of broken glass or choking hazards? But Seth has been with her the entire time. He would've seen her being sneaky, wouldn't he? But then she must've swapped that burner phone with the message from Gemma for one exactly the same with nothing on it right in front of our faces, stuffed it into her hoodie pocket when no one was looking. She's capable of anything.

There's an awkward pause as everyone waits for me to say something.

'Lily found the recipe online, Mum,' Seth breaks the silence, full of enthusiasm. 'Doesn't the icing look incredible. It's the first time she's ever piped icing like that.'

I cross my arms and press my lips together. Found the recipe on my old laptop, more like. I had it saved in my recipes folder to make one day. She's been snooping around in all my data and found it.

When I still don't speak, Lily ventures timidly, 'We wanted to cheer you up because you must be so upset about your best friend...'

She trails off as I glower at her some more. Her cheeks colour.

Seth jumps in, 'It was all Lily's idea.'

'That's very thoughtful,' Todd says.

'Right, let's dig in,' Seth says and lunges for the cakes.

But I put out my hand to stop him. 'The cook should get the

first taste,' I say looking pointedly at Lily. If she's done anything to these cakes then I want to watch her eat one.

She smiles sweetly. 'I hope they're okay...' She reaches out to pick one up, but I pull the plate towards me.

'Oh, let me pick,' I say.

Todd gives me a look as if to say, *that was a bit rude.*

Seth's eyes scrunch, as he says, his voice etched with annoyance, 'I'm sure they all taste the same.'

But I ignore them both. I'm doing this for their own good as well as mine. I pick one at random and pop it on a small plate and hand it to her.

With everyone watching, she pulls down the wrapper and takes a bite, her pretty little mouth opening wide to fit the cake and icing in.

'Well?' Seth asks eagerly.

She makes a little 'mmm' sound, her mouth still full, and beams at him.

'Pass us one, Mum,' he says, beckoning to me.

I pause for a few more seconds, watching as Lily swallows. When she doesn't keel over or choke, I pass one to Seth and one to Todd, and take one for myself. Todd and Seth both devour theirs, and Seth scoops up a second. I pretend to nibble at mine and put it down. This woman put Simon behind bars. Enjoying her baked goods does not sit right; it leaves a sour taste in my mouth.

Lily notices me put the untouched cake back on the table. Her shoulders droop and the corners of her mouth turn down.

'Are you not eating that?' Todd asks me.

I shake my head. 'Absolutely stuffed from dinner. I'll have one later or tomorrow.'

'Well, I think I'll have a second too.' Todd takes my plate and eats my rejected cupcake. 'These are incredible. Well done, Lily.'

She perks up at the compliment. 'Pleased you like them. Are you doing another charity challenge next year?'

'I am. I booked it this morning! We'll be trekking up Mount Kilimanjaro, but with a twist' – he rubs his hands together animatedly – 'because we plan to *run* it.'

'Exciting,' Lily says, nibbling daintily on her cake.

She must be monitoring his laptop too and saw that he booked it. That's why she's asked.

'You didn't tell me that,' I say curtly.

His mouth tightens. 'I did, earlier. But you weren't listening.'

Oh.

The atmosphere thickens unpleasantly. Lily cuts through it with a swift and adept change of topic. 'Seth was top of his class today for his latest assignment.' She rubs his leg and gazes at him proudly.

He nods. 'I think that calls for a third cupcake.' He picks up another cake and holds it in the air like a celebratory glass of bubbles.

'Congrats, son,' Todd says.

Seth looks to me expecting praise, but all the words have been sucked out of my mouth. Why didn't he tell me that himself? Why wasn't I the first to know? He always tells me everything. I feel overwhelmingly off balance.

Seth's jubilant mood falls when I don't say anything. He takes Lily's hand. 'We're off to the telly room. Need to beat this one at *Call of Duty*.'

He goes to stand, but I find my voice. 'No. I think we should have a family movie night. We've not had one in a while. And you can tell me more about this assignment while we decide which one and get it lined up.'

Seth looks at Lily, he's checking with *her*. She dips her chin in agreement.

My son tells me all about the essay and lab experiment he

set up to test for different variables in seawater while Todd switches the telly to the streaming services page. I'm not really paying Seth the attention he deserves because I'm so focused on Lily. She finishes off her cake and quietly puts the plate on the coffee table, watching what's happening on the telly. Seth stops talking, and there's a pause of a second or two before I realise he's not just taking a breath, he's finished.

I rip my focus straight back to him. 'That's wonderful. Well done.' But it sounds hollow.

He hears the insincerity loud and clear, sniffs, folds his arms and leans back on the sofa next to Lily.

'What shall we watch?' Todd asks, poised with the remote.

'I've got an idea,' Lily pipes up.

Seth's face immediately brightens. 'Oh, yeah? What?'

'It's an action comedy with The Rock. Meant to be very funny.' She tells Todd the name of the movie and the streaming service. He finds it and reads the short description.

'This looks perfect,' he says.

Lily beams.

'Spot-on choice,' Seth says. 'This is exactly the kind of movie we love to watch. It's like you've been a part of this family for years. You love this kind of thing, don't you, Mum?'

'Hmm,' I reply indifferently. *Part of the family? Pah!* Lily's no doubt looked through our browsing history to see what we watch. I don't believe that was a lucky guess.

Todd presses play on the movie, and everyone settles in and turns their eyes to the screen. Except I don't. I face the telly, but I watch Lily out of the corner of my eye. Seth puts his arm around her, and she snuggles into him. Todd puts his arm on the back of the sofa, an invitation to me to lean into his armpit like I usually do. But I ignore it. He leaves it there for a while, but when I don't move, he puts it down again and looks a little hurt. Instead, I put my legs up under me, lean away from my husband and into the side of the sofa to get a better view of her. I pick up a cushion and hug it into myself as if it can provide some kind of protection.

The three of them laugh at some opening joke. But I don't even hear it. Seth glances at me, looks away. Then Lily glances at me and catches me looking at her. Her entire body tenses, and she swiftly looks back to the telly.

Todd and Seth laugh at something else, but Lily doesn't. She squirms, knowing full well that I'm still watching her. Seth picks up on Lily's unease, and worry tinges his features. He barely smirks at any more jokes, obviously concerned about his girlfriend.

Eventually, Todd picks up on the prickly undercurrent. I attempt not to watch Lily, to watch The Rock in what is probably an excellent film, but I can't stop myself.

Everyone is tense and awkward, not relaxed and happy like every other movie night we've ever had as a family. Without Lily.

The moment the end credits roll, Seth jumps up, pulls Lily up and stomps out of the room with a brusque, 'We're going to bed.'

'Shouldn't we put the cupcakes away...?' Lily says.

'I'll do it. You head up.'

Lily hurries across the kitchen and up the stairs as Seth comes back into the room to pick up the plate with the remaining cupcakes and the smaller plates.

He doesn't look at me. He's angry with me, I can tell. It's not a situation I'm used to.

Then he straightens. 'You made that really weird, Mum. You need to chill out. Lily is cool. You're being a dick.' He storms out with the plates and sorts them in the kitchen.

I look at Todd. He shrugs. 'It's true. You barely even looked at the telly, you were fixated on that poor girl.'

'Fixated?'

'Something has really got you rattled, hasn't it? You've been acting weird for days.' He sighs. 'I'm going to bed. Coming?'

I follow him up, noting the kitchen is tidy, and that Seth and Lily cleaned up after themselves.

Todd and I get ready for bed in silence. I'm pleased he's decided to sleep here rather than in his office again, but he gets in the bed and immediately turns his back to me, giving me the cold shoulder. I want to discuss my suspicions about Lily. But the last time I tried he told me to book in with a therapist. So I keep shtum. It feels unnatural, unpleasant. We're usually so open with one another. Well, apart from those secrets from my past. But they're dead and buried. I don't know why I keep thinking about them recently. I have to open the void in my soul and throw them down there once again. I need to focus on the present danger.

Lily has pulled the wool over Todd and Seth's eyes. I have to make them see.

CHAPTER TWENTY

'You're up early,' Todd says cheerily as he enters the kitchen the next morning.

That's one thing I love about this family, we don't hold grudges. Todd comes immediately over to where I'm sitting at the kitchen island to hug and kiss me on the cheek. He smells freshly washed. I take in his scent, which always elicits such tender emotions in me. But today they're stunted, shoved aside by far more pressing matters.

There's someone in my house who doesn't belong. Who I need to get out.

It's a sunny, crisp, delightful Saturday in October, and I know precisely what Todd is going to say any minute now. And I know exactly how I'm going to reply.

He glances out of the window. And, as expected, he says, 'It's such a glorious day. Shall we go out on the boat, zip across the Solent to the Isle of Wight for some lunch? Have some quality time, just me and you. It'll be wonderful. We might not get too many more days like this until next spring.'

Todd has a powerboat, and I love going out on it with him. I love watching him being so passionate about his hobby. He probably feels the same about watching me get so passionate about my bees, and that's why he always offers to help.

We've had many a happy family sailing holiday over the years. Although Seth is busy doing his own thing these days, so he doesn't come out on day trips so much anymore.

Normally, I'd say yes to a boat day. Normally, it would be a given. Todd asks out of politeness but we both instinctively know what we'd be up to on a day like this one. And we both know we'd have a wonderful time – we always do, we love each other's company.

But not today.

'I think I'm going to potter about the house, do a few bits and pieces, sort out the prop station, harvest the veggie patch...' I trail off. 'But you crack on – it'll be fabulous on the water today.'

He looks surprised at my response, then disappointed. But it passes quickly. He kisses me again.

'Okey doke,' he replies.

'Shall I make you some breakfast?' I ask.

But I know what he'll say.

'No, thanks. I'll get something from Mabel's.'

Mabel's is the café near the marina where he keeps the boat. We always grab breakfast and a coffee from there on boat days.

'Hopefully they'll have those divine lemon curd Danishes again,' I say, remembering Todd's fondness for the pastries and his delight every time the café has them in.

He grins, raises his hand and crosses his fingers. 'I'll eat one for you if they do.' He gives me another kiss. 'Right, I'll be off. I'll be back in time for dinner.'

He exits the kitchen, roams around the house finding what he needs for a day on the water, then heads out the front door shouting a final, 'Bye, my love!' in my direction.

I hear the gates creak open, his car drive away and the gates closing again. Once I'm certain he's not returning, I take the glass lid off the cake stand that holds the remaining two cupcakes baked by Lily. They've been leering at me for hours. I throw them in the bin, take the black bag out and put it in the wheelie bin outside ready for the bin collection on Monday.

I head back inside and take up my position on the stool, elbows on the kitchen island.

It's still only 8 a.m. So now I wait and listen.

Just before midday, I hear movement from Seth's bedroom. Floorboards groan and there are distant voices in conversation. The pipes rumble as someone turns on the shower in the family bathroom.

I leave the note I wrote earlier on the edge of the counter where Seth will see it, grab my car keys and leave the house. I drive up the lane, onto the main road and immediately turn into an opposite lane. I do a three-point turn and park up so I can see the entrance to our lane but am hidden from view by another car parked in front.

The note reads: 'Dad's gone out on boat. I've gone to garden centre. Love you, Mum x'

He won't think twice about it. I have no idea about my son and Lily's plans today. But if they leave the house they have to come out of this lane, either on foot or in Seth's car. And I'll see. And I'll follow.

I'm determined to discover what Lily is up to. This is the only way.

About an hour later, Seth's white car comes up the lane and stops at the junction. He looks either way for traffic and pulls out. Lily is with him. They don't see me.

I follow them. It's not so hard. It's a busy day in the city, and they take a route that thankfully doesn't involve many traffic lights. I try to keep one or two cars between us at all times.

I wonder where they're off to. But Seth's indicating tells me:

the McDonald's drive thru. I follow them in but park in the car park and slouch down low. They don't even look my way. They appear to be in animated conversation. Lily is laughing. It looks as if Seth is singing. They go behind the back of the building in the drive thru queue to order. But they have to drive past me again to exit.

McDonald's must be a Lily thing. Seth has never been bothered about fast food. Even as a kid, he never begged us to take him there or considered it a treat. He was always happy when I made his favourite honey cake or honey-roasted nuts. And, as he grew up, he'd rather always pick food that hadn't travelled far or had been grown sustainably and locally. We get the majority of our meat and veg delivered from local free-range and organic farms. And I grow a lot too. Seth would always want to help me harvest crops. But not so much lately.

What other things has Lily influenced Seth on?

I hunch down even further in my seat as Seth's car comes around the corner. To my dismay, they park up in the car park a few spaces away from me. But luckily there are two cars between us. I watch surreptitiously as they polish off their food. The waft of fried food and old cooking oil through my window makes me nauseous and hungry in equal parts. I haven't eaten anything today, and now I'm regretting it.

It doesn't take long for them to finish their burgers. Lily jumps out of the car to put the rubbish in a nearby bin, and they set off again. I follow behind.

They head out of the city, and I wonder where they're off to next. It soon becomes clear as Seth heads towards the New Forest National Park and turns into the car park of his most favourite place in the forest. When he was a child, we used to come here a lot. There's a natural pond and boggy area, which Seth delighted in exploring.

I drive past the turning, pull over in a lay-by, count to ten, do a U-turn and head back. I drive in behind another car and park a little way away from Seth's car. They're already out and at the start of the path.

Seth has his backpack on, and Lily is carrying his tripod. They're off to film at the pond. Seth will be making his latest PondGuy video. My heart breaks ever so slightly – I used to help him carry his tripod to film at this spot. At other places too. But now he relies on Lily.

I jump out the car and follow behind them. I don't need to get too close; I know exactly which route they'll take and where they'll end up. The national park is busy today with walkers, cyclists and horse riders, so I doubt they'll notice there's someone behind them. I take in a long, deep breath – the earthy forest smell such a welcome contrast to the fast-food restaurant odour earlier.

I observe them from a distance. I have to admit, they're a cute couple. They laugh and look at each other often. Seth points things out, and Lily looks at where he's indicating and back up at him. He puts his hand around her shoulders and on her neck often. I'm certain if she wasn't clutching the tripod, they'd be holding hands.

Their behaviour reminds me of Todd and me. They appear truly in love. Lily looks utterly smitten. I want to be happy for Seth – my baby boy all grown up and in love. But I'm worried. Lily got Simon arrested. She faked all that dark web stuff. She's shut down the incredible charity that I work for. She's not sweet and loved-up. She's dangerous and unpredictable.

But still, guilt suddenly eats me up, and my palms go sweaty. I feel bad for invading Seth's privacy, for lying to both him and Todd about what I was up to today. That's not something I've ever done before.

Seth and Lily turn down a path that isn't well used. It's uneven, overgrown and can be very muddy. But it's the way to Seth's favourite spot near the pond. Most people do the loop on the gravel path, so I'm going to have to be careful not to get spotted because it's likely to be just us using this path, and maybe a New Forest pony or two.

I slow my pace, pause for a moment as if I'm debating which way to go and allow a dog walker with two bouncy Vizslas to pass me.

'George!' the dog walker shouts as one jumps up at me and licks my face. 'Sorry!'

I indicate it's fine, wipe the drool off my cheek and turn down the path. Up ahead I can see Seth and Lily as they turn a corner. For the briefest moment, Lily looks behind her. I freeze. Did she see me? Has she recognised me? Oh crap. But she turns back to Seth, a big smile on her face, and they carry on.

I slow right down, not wanting to get caught. The path opens onto the pond and looks like a dead end. But there's a route you can take around the pond, although very muddy. I know a spot where I can lurk and watch them. They'll be there a while if Seth is filming.

A few moments later, I turn the corner where they turned and can't see them ahead. There's nobody around, and suddenly the shadowy trees are eerie. The wind rustles through the canopy and chills me to the bone. I should be able to see them up ahead. Where the hell are they?

Has Lily done something to Seth? Dragged him off the path and into the dark shadows to hurt him, or kidnap him, or worse? Panic swills through my veins, and I charge along the path scanning either side, desperate for any glimpse of my son. I can't lose him, I can't. I love him more than anything in this world. It would destroy me.

I'm just about to yell out his name when a man jumps out in front of me and takes hold of my shoulders.

I shriek.

But I see his face. Seth.

'You scared the life out of me,' I say, catching my breath and clutching my chest, in an attempt to soothe my heaving lungs.

Lily scrambles from the bushes to stand next to my son. 'Oh my goodness, so sorry, Jen. Didn't mean to frighten you. Are you okay? That scream...' She looks concerned. She peers up at Seth. 'I said we shouldn't jump out at her.'

But Seth doesn't reply. He glowers at me.

Lily looks back to me and chews her lip. She's uncomfortable and upset and takes a small step back to allow Seth to handle his mother. I watch her, and she looks at her feet, adopting a meek and mild and non-confrontational manner.

'Mum!' Seth's harsh bark draws my attention immediately to him. 'What the hell are you doing here?'

I wasn't expecting to get discovered. Lily must've seen me when she looked back and told him. I say light-heartedly, 'Fancy seeing you here. Just wanted a little fresh air...'

But the look on his face tells me he's not buying it. Not one little bit. And I'm not surprised. Apart from a few whopping great lies that are well and truly buried, I don't tell my son little white lies. We're a very honest family with one another.

I glance at Lily and back to him. And he knows why I'm here.

He explodes. 'This is very, very fucking weird, Mum. It's like you're stalking Lily now, like you're obsessed with her. You need to sort out whatever this fucked-up crazy shit is. You. Need. To. Back. Off.'

I've never seen him so angry. It's clear I've crossed a line with my son that I've never even been close to before. I immediately hold up my hands to pacify him.

'I'm sorry, Seth,' I say, devastated that he's livid at me.

He points in the direction of the car park. 'Go home, right now. Never follow us again. Understand?'

'Yes, I understand. I love you. I'm going.' I back away quickly. I can't damage my relationship with Seth. 'I made a huge mistake. I'm sorry.' I pointedly look at Lily. 'I'm sorry, Lily.'

'It's okay,' she says kindly.

Seth puts his arm around her shoulder. 'Get home safe,' he says, and I know he means it. He loves me, and I've made him mad. He would never shout at me, at anyone, without good reason.

I hurry away and get in my car. As I'm reversing out of the space, I see Miranda in my rear-view mirror.

What the—?

I slam my foot on the brake and turn to look. But she's not behind the car, only the dog walker with the two bouncy dogs from earlier. My frazzled brain is messing with me.

I head in the direction of home. What a disaster.

Am I obsessed with Lily? Was that crazy stalking behaviour? What is going on with me? Am I falling to pieces because I'm jealous and feel threatened by her? Am I sad that my son has grown up and I'm losing him, and for some reason I'm directing that unease at his new girlfriend?

All the thoughts froth behind my eyes along with the vision of Seth's furious face. His incensed voice still rings in my ears.

I switch on the radio, and there's a clip of Todd bigging up his football show on Saturday mornings and telling listeners that they can listen again on the radio station's app. My husband's voice settles me, and I drive home feeling terrible and determined to call a therapist for some help.

Swallowing hard, I let myself in the front door and lock it. I take a deep breath to reset and gather myself to research therapists in Southampton.

But then I see it.

Lily's jacket on the hooks by the front door. Two pairs of her shoes on the rack next to my shoes, next to my family's shoes. They do not belong. She does not belong.

I'm not crazy. She met that faker pretending to be Kiah Wong with me. She must've switched out the burner phone and edited those sex videos so it looked like Todd with another woman. She got Simon arrested.

She is not the perfect first girlfriend for my darling boy.

My home has been invaded. She is a hostile alien attempting to take over.

I'm not going to stop. She has no idea who she's dealing with.

CHAPTER TWENTY-ONE

18 YEARS AGO

DAILY TIMES

Friday 8 December 2006

JERRY WARD MURDER: FORENSICS EVIDENCE PRESENTED

Natalie Owens is standing trial accused of his murder

Just one fingerprint at the victim's house places Natalie Owens firmly at the scene of the crime, a police expert has told the jury.

Since the trial at Southampton Crown Court began on Wednesday, the court has been shown CCTV footage of the accused, Natalie Owens, 21, with the victim, Jerry Ward, leaving the Jockey Arms pub around two hours before his estimated time of death. They have also heard from witnesses at the pub who saw the pair together.

However, until now, there had been no evidence presented that indicated Owens had been present at Ward's house.

Jurors heard from a police expert that the brutal nature of the crime would've seen Ward's blood everywhere, and, at the very least, some forensic evidence left by Owens. However, the house had been thoroughly cleaned, even eradicating most of Ward's fingerprints around his own home.

But, in the clean-up, one piece of evidence was missed: a fingerprint was found on the floor near the body and later confirmed to belong to Owens.

The court later heard from Owens' defence counsel that the fingerprint does not prove Owens committed the murder or that she was present at Ward's house later in the evening at his estimated time of death. The fingerprint only proves that she, at some point and not necessarily on the night of the murder, had been in his house.

The prosecution has closed its case. Owens' defence barrister confirmed Owens will be giving evidence and that witnesses will be called on Monday.

The trial continues.

CHAPTER TWENTY-TWO

The first thing Seth does when they get home on Saturday night is call a family meeting.

Lily doesn't attend.

Seth tells his dad all about me following them into the forest, while I sit mute and guilty. There's nothing I can say to make things better.

Seth's anger sizzles off him. And the heat of Todd's displeasure is only a notch or two lower.

I apologise profusely and tell a whopper of a fib. 'I won't do it again.' And then another. 'I'm going to get some help because I'm dealing with emotions about Seth growing up that I can't handle and I'm channelling that strange energy into a fixation with Lily.'

Todd runs a hand through his hair and looks appeased. Seth marches off upstairs to his girlfriend.

Late on Sunday morning, Seth comes downstairs and barely acknowledges me.

'Did you sleep well?' I ask.

He shrugs off my question, still in a mood. He makes a quick breakfast for two and takes it back up to his room.

It's a drizzly, miserable day.

'I'm going to clean the house from top to bottom,' I announce to Todd across the dining table.

He flicks down a corner of the newspaper he's holding – he only ever reads the Sunday papers, mostly to feast on all the in-depth football sections – and peers at me over the top.

'Can I help?'

He's a thorough cleaner, and we always help each other with chores. Usually, I'd say yes. It's just another way we gel – we're a team when it comes to things like that. But not today.

'No, thanks. I want to do it.'

He nods, slightly rejected, and gathers up the pile of papers. 'Going to finish these in the office and get cracking on the rest of those model trees.'

I smile as he passes me, wait until he's out of the door then jump up and grab the cleaning things.

I don't really want to clean, but it means I have an excuse to stay in the house, to be upstairs, to hang around. I listen and surreptitiously watch. If Lily ventures out of the bedroom, or if one or both of them leave the house, I'll know immediately.

Seth comes down at lunch and fixes them food to take back upstairs.

Todd also emerges from his office around 2 p.m. and makes us both a sandwich.

'Shall we do a top-up shop this afternoon?' He asks as he peers in the kitchen cupboards, making a list of nearly empty items and anything we're missing. 'Need some more bread flour.'

'You go, I've got my mind set on finishing the cleaning. Not too much to do now,' I reply, attempting to not make a big deal of declining something that I'd normally do with him.

The slightly rejected look from earlier amplifies, and Todd's shoulders sag. He shrugs, says, 'Fine,' in a way that he tries to make sound like he's not bothered. But he's undoubtedly *extremely* bothered after learning about my following-Seth-and-Lily-into-the-forest escapade, and now I don't want to do stuff with him that I usually do with him, even if it is just going to the supermarket.

He heads out. I keep 'cleaning'. And spying from afar.

When he gets back, he makes bread and a roast dinner. Seth comes down to make up two plates.

'Why don't you and Lily come and eat dinner with us?' I ask lightly, pretending I don't care either way. 'She's not left your room all day.'

Seth glares at me. 'Because you properly freaked her out yesterday and she feels uncomfortable now around you. She doesn't like conflict or drama.'

'I'm completely over it,' I say.

He sighs. 'She just needs a few days.'

Guilt at lying to Seth plucks at my heartstrings all evening, but I know it's for the best. He doesn't need to know that I won't stop until I confirm my suspicions that she's not to be trusted.

First thing on Monday morning, Todd leaves for a breakfast meeting with a producer for a 'football in the noughties' documentary, and I call my boss Syreeta. I usually work on Mondays, but after Friday's events I don't know if I have a job to go to. She doesn't answer.

I call Penny. 'Hey, Pen. Sorry to call so early, but I tried Syreeta and she didn't pick up. Just wondering if I should go in today?'

'No point, sugarplum.' Penny's voice hitches with sadness. 'Syreeta was taken in for questioning. All the computers were seized, and the police are still going through them. Going to take a long time, apparently, because there's a lot of data to sift through.'

She sobs, and I soothe her.

'We're jobless,' she wails. 'And all those poor women turfed out of the shelters and on the streets with nowhere to stay. It's so awful.' She sobs some more.

'It is,' I reply. And I'm going to sort it out, I add silently. I know who is responsible and am working on taking her down. 'Any news on Simon?'

'Still in prison. They kept him for longer while going through his computer. They charged him yesterday. I can't believe it.'

'I can't either,' I reply. 'I know he didn't do it.'

Penny snuffles. 'The evidence is damning...'

I hear noise from upstairs. 'I'll speak to you soon. Gotta go.'

We ring off, and I sprint out of the house.

About an hour and a half later, Lily appears at the end of the lane on foot, turns left and walks in the direction of the university, her rucksack on her back. I'm parked up in the road opposite again, waiting for her. I know she has lectures on a Monday morning and that Seth doesn't so she walks in. She could get a bus, but she told us she prefers the fresh air.

I jump out the car, lock it and follow her at a distance. It's about a fifty-minute walk into the main uni campus and, thankfully, mostly down two long and straight roads, making it easy to follow her from a long way behind.

Once we turn onto the main road into Southampton city centre, she pulls her hood up. It's a drizzly day again but not raining. But as soon as I hit the road too, I understand. It's busy and not a particularly pleasant walk. Cars whizz past, the roar almost deafening, and the fumes burn my nose and get stuck at the back of my throat. I pull my hood up too.

It's also a great way to hide. I don't want anyone I know to see me walking down this road – it would be noticed and innocently reported back to Todd or Seth. It's not the kind of road you take a leisurely stroll down if you can help it.

Lily keeps up a steady pace, turns off the main road and heads towards the university's main campus. I'm not entirely sure what I plan to do while she's in lectures. Maybe I'll just head home. On reflection, this probably wasn't the smartest move, and I need to think of something else.

As she gets closer to the university gates, I hang back. I'm just about to turn around and head home when she does something unexpected. She walks straight past the gates and keeps going past the campus. There's probably another entrance to her building.

I keep following.

She walks further away from the university buildings and in the direction of the city. Not a nice part of the city. And not a part where there are any university buildings.

Where is she going?

She takes a turn, and I hurry to get nearer to her. This is not a long, straight road, unfortunately, and she's making lots of turns. Sweat beads and dampens my clothes unpleasantly. She looks back over her shoulder to cross the road, and I duck behind a bus shelter.

Oh bollocks, did she see me?

She'll immediately tell Seth, and he'll be furious. He's still angry with me about Saturday, and he's never been angry like that with me before. If he discovered I was following Lily again, what would he do? Never talk to me again? I shudder at the thought. That would destroy me. I chance a quick glance from behind the shelter. Lily hasn't seen me and continues on. I count to five and trail her.

She enters a rough housing estate in an area called Bevois,

which I know, from conversations with Todd's best mate, is a part of Southampton that the police will only enter in groups of three or more. And yet she strides in, full of confidence, not looking at her phone for directions, knowing precisely where she's going. She passes burnt-out, smashed-up cars, upended supermarket trolleys, overgrown gardens, dumped electrical items and abandoned mattresses covered in stains. A distinct smell of cannabis permeates the place.

What the hell is she doing here? Is she visiting someone?

The tall, intimidating apartment blocks tower over me, and my skin prickles as if I'm being watched by many eyes. Lily walks straight up the broken pathway to the door of an apartment block. There's a large man stood in the doorway, arms crossed, hood up, snarl on his face. The muscular dog by his feet lunges at Lily, snapping and barking.

But she doesn't flinch. She holds out her hand for the dog to sniff, and it stands down, tail wagging. The man gives her a nod and shifts out of her way so she can get to the door. She pulls out keys from her bag and lets herself in. He goes back to his position blocking the door.

They know each other.

The man notices me and stares. I'm exposed on the other side of the road, dawdling. An unknown. The dog barks as I rotate and hurry back the way I came in. There's no way I'm going deeper into this estate, it's no doubt a rabbit warren, and I'd need my phone to find the way out – a sure sign of an outsider, an easy target.

I take note of the name of the road and, as soon as I'm back on a main road, jump on the next bus heading towards the university. I sit and open my Google Maps app, putting in the name of the road and using Google Earth to find the apartment block. It's Bevois Mansions, Block 3. Although the building is as far from a mansion as any building could get. And as far from the glamorous place the French-looking name implies – it's pronounced 'bee-vis'. And, as Todd told me when I first moved to the city, anyone saying 'bev-wah' would likely get the piss ripped out of them and possibly a smack in the face.

That man in the doorway knew her. Who else does she know? There are all kinds of shady people living in this part of town. She let herself in with her own keys. Is she going to her own flat? Does she have a relative that she's not told us about who lives there, and so has a set of keys to come and go? Has she been going there instead of lectures this entire time? Is she even a student?

My mind boggles.

I get off the bus at the main university campus and head straight in the main doors to the reception desk. I know the way from attending an open day with Seth before he started here. There's a big, echoey foyer with a busy stream of students coming and going. I shrink into myself – I can't let anyone see me who might tell Seth.

I hurry to the reception desk and lean into it in an odd way, turning my back to the main flow of students in an attempt to hide my face.

A very smiley receptionist says, 'Hi, can I help you?'

I glance either side of me and whisper, 'I need to talk to someone privately about the welfare of a student. It's urgent.'

The receptionist's eyes widen, and she nods. She makes a call, saying quietly, 'Somebody needs to talk about student welfare. Urgently, privately.' She puts down the handset and says to me, 'Danny will be with you soon.' She points to a little waiting area beside the desk and out of view of the main route into the building. 'Please, take a seat.'

I gladly take a seat and make sure I've got my back to the doors.

Danny appears moments later and holds out his hand to me, introducing himself as a student welfare support officer who should be able to help. He has a laptop under one arm. He asks my name.

'I'd rather go somewhere private, please,' I reply.

'Of course.' He directs me down a corridor off the entrance foyer and into a poky, stuffy, windowless room with a table and four chairs in the middle. There are framed photos of way-too-happy-looking students, large posters of famous artworks, as well as a shelf full of fake plants in colourful pots. They've tried to make the room feel homely, but it's claustrophobic.

I take a seat, and Danny takes one opposite, putting his laptop on the table.

'My name is Mrs Jennifer James. My son is Seth James. He's a student here. His girlfriend is also a student here, and I'm very concerned about her. She's currently living with us. And I'd like to speak with her lead tutor about a few things, please.'

Danny smiles. 'You can talk to me, and I will pass on the message.' He opens his laptop.

'No, thank you. I want to speak to them myself.'

His smile tightens. I'm being difficult.

I continue, 'I'm certain you would be very discreet, but this is private and important, and I know dear Lily wouldn't want everyone to know her business. This is a delicate situation as it is.' I stress the word 'delicate'.

Danny nods. He taps a few things on his laptop. 'Please can I see some ID, Mrs James?'

I pull out my driving licence. He looks at it carefully and hands it back.

'And your son is Seth James, correct?'

'Yes, that's it.'

He taps some more and reads the screen. 'What is Seth studying and what year is he in?'

'First year, studying zoology.'

Danny nods, satisfied. 'Right, what is the name of the student you are concerned about?'

'Lily Hailstone.'

He taps a few more things. 'Here we are...'

My heart sinks. She *is* a student.

Perhaps a uni friend lives in Bevois Mansions and Lily went to hers to study this morning. Perhaps it's a regular Monday morning thing, which is why that man and his dog know her. Maybe she has a set of keys because the buzzer doesn't work, and her friend lives on the top floor and there's no lift so doesn't want to walk down to let Lily in. A thousand innocent scenarios whizz through my mind.

Danny frowns. 'No, wait. I typed the wrong thing. Lily Hailstone, you say? Not Halston?'

'Hailstone, like the... er... weather event.'

His frown deepens. 'We don't have a student with that name registered.'

'Could she be registered under a different name?'

He shrugs. 'It's possible.'

'Could you just try Hailstone?'

He types and shakes his head. 'There are no Hailstones. It's an unusual surname.'

I continue, more urgently, 'Try Lily?'

He looks up from the screen to scrutinise me. Heat rises to my cheeks, and I suddenly feel all flustered. He's doubting me. I struggle in the small space to take off my large winter coat.

'Mrs James, there will be hundreds, if not thousands, of Lilys attending the university. If you don't have the student's name, then for privacy reasons, I cannot help you any further.'

'Could you look up Lilys in the first year studying computer science with modules in artificial intelligence and cybersecurity?' I ask.

'No,' he says immediately, closing his laptop lid and folding his arms.

I fan my hot face. I have to get him to check. I have to know for sure whether or not Lily – or whatever her name is – attends this university.

I swallow back the guilt for being pushy and lean across the table. 'I'm very concerned for Lily's welfare. She's possibly registered under another name and hasn't told it to us. If she harms herself or something worse happens, then I will personally blame the university, and *you*, for not helping at this point.'

Danny's face pales.

I continue, 'And I will let the *Daily Times* know that this university does not care about the welfare of its students and could've prevented an incident and chose not to, even after I visited them to bring it to their attention.'

He baulks at my threat and opens his laptop up again. He types a few things. 'Three Lilys in first year doing computer science.' He turns his laptop so we can both see it.

I look at the screen. It's a database. He clicks on a few things so three photos of smiling students come up.

'None of them are my Lily.' There's an awkward pause. I continue, 'She might be using a different first name. Can I see all the students in first year computer science, please?'

He shakes his head. 'No. That's an absolute breach of privacy. If you want to talk to the newspaper, then do, but I'm not showing you the faces of every student on that course.'

I pull out my phone and find Seth's WhatsApp profile picture. I show it to Danny. 'That's my son and that's her. Blonde. Female. You look through the photos.'

'There are two hundred-odd students on that course.'

I blink at him, as if to say, *so?* He blinks back, as if to say, *not a chance.*

'You will be helping a student in need. Please, just look,' I say, softer now.

He sighs resignedly and pulls his laptop towards him. He gestures for me to show him the photo again. He peers at it and then at his screen. He types a few things and clicks regularly. I assume he's looking through photos.

After about five minutes, he says, 'No one who looks like the girl in that photo is on this course.'

Lily isn't studying computer science. She doesn't go to university. She's lied to Seth, to all of us.

'Could your system have been hacked?' I blurt.

'What? Absolutely not. We have the highest level of security across all our technology and some of the world's leading lecturers in cybersecurity here.' He appears affronted that I even asked.

As I think it through, it makes no sense for Lily to wipe herself off the system. She would've added herself to the database if she thought anyone would be looking into her. It would support her lies. But perhaps this is a network she's not been able to hack into.

Abruptly, I stand. 'Thank you for your help, Danny.' I make for the door.

'Mrs James,' Danny says sternly behind me. 'What is going on?'

'I made a mistake, sorry. It's *Bournemouth* University she goes to. Forget I was even here!' I fake-laugh and scarper down the corridor, leaving Danny exasperated behind me. I wrestle my coat on and burst through into the main entrance foyer, swinging past the reception desk and flying down the stairs.

And straight into... Seth.

He's just come through the doors and is chatting animatedly to a friend. I swerve, missing my son by inches, tug up my hood and sprint to exit the building.

I brace myself for his voice, his shout, to hear the word 'Mum' flung at my back, but it doesn't come. I risk a glance back. Through the glass doors, I can see him still chatting with his friend, disappearing into the belly of the building. He has lectures on Monday afternoons and sometimes comes in early to study.

My heart bangs painfully as I get in a taxi waiting at the taxi rank and give my home address. After a few deep breaths to steady myself, a rush of adrenaline courses through me, and I punch the air discreetly so the taxi driver doesn't see.

I finally have proof that Lily is a liar. I feel elated, validated. But the joy soon fades.

Who the hell is she? And what does she want?

CHAPTER TWENTY-THREE

I decide to make this as pleasant and drama-free as possible.

Last night, in front of Todd and Seth, I asked Lily if she fancied a girly pamper session in the morning as my way of saying sorry for following them and being strange recently. I blamed it on my hormones and wittered on about how much I love Seth and how it's really hit me that he's all grown up now and how I haven't reacted well, *blah blah blah*.

All three of them lapped it up.

But I'm ready to confront Lily with the evidence that she doesn't go to the same university as Seth and that she visits an address in a rougher-than-rough part of the city frequently enough that the locals know her. I won't make a scene, just present it, ask for her explanation and tell her to leave. And, bish-bash-bosh, she'll move out, it'll all be over and I'll have my family back.

Todd and Seth both headed out early this morning. And at 10 a.m., the time we agreed last night, I'm waiting in the lounge for Lily.

Right on time, she wanders in clutching a couple of sheet face masks.

'Hi,' she says timidly, holding up the packets. Her sweet smile grates now I know she keeps secrets.

'Morning.' I stand and walk around the sofa to face her. I'm quite a bit taller, and peering down at her bolsters my resolve. 'Lily, I know you don't go to Southampton University. And I know that you spend time at an address in the city, in a block of flats called Bevois Mansions.'

Her eyes widen. She brings the hand not holding the packets up to cover her mouth, as if in shock.

I push on, keeping my body language calm and my voice reasonable and steady. 'You've been lying to us. And I have a strong suspicion that you manufactured all that dark web stuff, that you instigated Simon's arrest and the closure of my charity. I'm on to you. What do you have to say for yourself?'

Lily shakes her head, eyes bulging, hand still covering her mouth. 'I have no idea what you're talking about…' she mumbles from behind her hand.

'Oh, come on,' I insist, not falling again for her cute-girl act. 'Why are you lying? What are you doing here?'

Her hand slowly falls away from her mouth. She looks horrified.

But the façade slides off.

Her eyes narrow, and her mouth twists into a smug smirk. 'You want to know why I'm here?' she asks, her voice sharp and glare steely. 'I'll tell you. I'm here to make *you* suffer.' Her face screws up in disgust as she points at my chest.

I knew there was something not right with her, but this complete U-turn from angel to demon throws me off guard. I feel unsteady, as if blasted by a fifty-mile-per-hour gust of wind.

She snorts. 'I knew you were following me yesterday. I was wondering how long it would take you to work it out.'

'Why are you doing this?' I say, a little less sure of myself than moments earlier.

'You'll find out soon enough,' she replies.

We both pause as the front door opens and closes.

A second later, Seth's voice echoes through the house. 'I'm home! Lectures cancelled because the lecturer's off sick. Lily? Mum? Is there a spare face mask for me?'

We hear him padding through the hallway towards the kitchen.

As quick as a flash, Lily throws the two sheet mask packets at the coffee table with one hand and punches herself in the face with the other.

She hits herself so hard that tears come to her eyes and an angry red mark immediately blemishes her cheek.

'Seth,' she wails, turns on her heel and runs into the kitchen just as he appears in the doorway. 'Help me!'

They run to each other, and Lily falls into Seth's arms, bawling and hysterical.

Seth looks up and sees me stunned and speechless in the lounge doorway. 'What the hell happened?' he demands.

'Your mum hit me,' Lily squeals before I can say anything. She shows him her cheek. 'She slapped me so hard.' She's crying and snotty and oh-so believable.

Seth examines her face and glares at me. 'Fucking hell, Mum.'

Words finally find my tongue. 'She punched herself in the face! I didn't touch her.'

'What a load of bullshit,' Seth yells at me. He guides Lily out of the kitchen, shouting over his shoulder, 'I'm calling Dad. He needs to come home. This is a family emergency. You've lost the plot.'

They head up the stairs, and Seth's bedroom door slams shut.

I sink to my knees. Shock and fear hang around my neck like a dead weight. Who is this woman?

. . .

Todd comes flying through the front door twenty minutes later. He shouts up the stairs for Seth and rushes through the kitchen into the lounge, where I'm still slumped on the floor. He gently helps me up.

'Are you okay?' he asks. 'You look like you've seen a ghost.'

He walks me through to the kitchen, and we come face to face with Seth and Lily. Seth has a protective arm around Lily and angles himself in front of her, shielding her from me. Her cheek is bright red.

Todd puts a hand on my shoulder, but also motions to Seth to imply calm. 'Right,' he says as if he's a judge in a courtroom. 'What on earth happened?'

'Mum slapped Lily in the face for no reason,' Seth declares. Lily clearly feeding him lies the entire time they've been in his bedroom.

Todd looks at me, encouraging me to speak.

'Absolutely not true,' I say as calmly as I can. 'She hit herself, just as Seth came in the front door.'

Seth screws up his face and shakes his head in disbelief. 'Why would she do that?'

'Because she's a liar, and I caught her out in a lie. She's manipulating you both into taking her side.'

Seth looks like he might explode, but Todd takes a step forward and holds up his hands in a pacifying gesture. Seth's body language deflates as he understands his father is attempting to keep the peace.

Todd turns to me. 'What do you think Lily is lying about, Jen?'

'Lily doesn't go to Southampton University. She spends her time at an apartment in Bevois.'

Seth's look says, *what a load of twaddle*. Lily keeps her gaze on her feet, stays silent and meek.

Todd says, 'Seth, go and get your laptop. Lily, you can stay here for a moment.' Lily clings to Seth in panic. Todd adds, reassuringly, 'You'll be fine, I promise. I won't let anything happen to you.'

Won't let anything happen to *her*? What about *me*?

She nods and unclutches Seth so he can run upstairs and grab his laptop. He's back in seconds and puts the laptop on the counter. He types a few things and shows me a page from the university website that appears to show Lily Hailstone as one of the students.

He points to it. 'See, Mum. Of course she goes to uni. An address in Bevois? What are you going on about?'

'That's fake. She's infected all our laptops. She's planted that page on the university's site so you'll see it.' I debate momentarily whether to go and get my secret new laptop, but I don't. I don't want Lily to know I have that and infect it like she has all the others in this household.

'Don't be ridiculous,' Seth replies.

'I don't think that's right,' Todd says, frowning at me.

Neither of them believes me. Desperately, I say, 'I went in to the uni yesterday and asked them to find her details on their system. And guess what – they couldn't. Lily Hailstone is not a student. She's up to something. And she's in our house. She needs to leave!'

'Up to something? Like what exactly?' Todd says, edging closer to Seth and Lily. Three against one.

'She told me she wants to make me suffer. She wants to do me harm.'

Seth exhales noisily.

Todd asks, 'Why does Lily want to do you harm?'

'I don't know,' I shout back, frustrated.

Todd comes over and puts his arm around me. It's not in a supportive way, it feels as if he's doing it out of pity. 'Lily,' he says, 'can you explain what happened, please?'

Seth moves to one side so we can all see sweet and innocent

Lily. I can see right through her act, but Seth and Todd are entranced.

She clears her throat. 'It all happened so fast. I really didn't see it coming and wasn't expecting it. One minute we were laughing, and the next, *bam*, she slapped me.'

'Lies,' I shout.

Lily shrinks into herself.

I continue, 'I'm terrified of what she might do next. Of being in the house with her.'

'Lily is terrified of being anywhere near you,' Seth counters.

'Let's all just calm it down a notch or two,' Todd says.

'I'm so sorry I've caused all this upset,' Lily says. 'I'll move out as soon as I can find somewhere.' She looks sad.

'No, you can stay here for as long as you like, Lily,' Todd says gently, as if talking to a toddler. 'Jen is just having a funny turn. It'll pass soon.' He turns to me. 'Won't it, darling.'

He says it in such a way that it's an order and not a question. It grinds my gears. How can he be so sucked in by this stranger and not fully supportive of his wife?

I scowl at Lily.

Todd and Seth both stare at me.

Lily, aware that mine are the only eyes on her, breaks character for the briefest second and sticks her tongue out at me like a petulant child.

'She needs to leave. Right now,' I bellow.

'If she leaves, then so do I,' Seth shouts back. 'We wanted to tell you in a happier moment, but we're engaged. So, wherever she goes, I go too.'

'Engaged? Are you kidding me? Seth, no!' I lunge for my son, for Lily. I don't know why, but maybe to shake some sense into them.

But Todd grabs me and holds me back. 'Calm down, Jen.'

'I love her. I don't need your permission,' Seth says. A note of defiance punctuates his tone.

Lily clings to Seth, glances at me and back up at Seth's face. She says softly, 'Let's go outside for some air. We all need to calm down. And the sun's out.'

Seth nods, and they head out the back door and into the garden.

I watch their backs, seething. *Engaged!*

'Our son cannot marry that lying bitch,' I tell Todd.

He grips my shoulders and turns me to face him. 'What is up with you? This is very out of character. Violence? I suggested you see someone, but you haven't and you're getting worse. I don't want to force you, but enough's enough. We're getting you help, today. I'll organise it. I'll get Gavin to find someone discreet and well-respected. And I'll come with you. Okay?'

But Lily's piercing scream from outside skewers the conversation.

We look at each other as our brains process the noise.

Has she murdered Seth? *My boy!* I dash from the kitchen. Todd follows.

'Mummm,' Seth bellows.

They're at the end of the garden, near my three beehives.

Todd and I arrive there in seconds, panting. Something is very, very wrong.

Lily is crying silently.

Seth points.

My eyes follow his finger to the grass around the bottom of my hives.

And that's when I pinpoint what's off – there's no activity, no movement, no buzzing of happy bees going about their business.

My hives, always so brimming with life, are still. The bodies of thousands of bees are littered on and beneath the hives.

My soul cracks, and I let out a pained groan. My pets... I

loved them like people love cats or dogs. I stare at the harrowing scene.

'Oh, Jen,' Todd says and goes to put his arm around me. But I shake him off.

Lily is grizzling, saying something about how sad it is because the world needs more bees and not less.

'Lily wanted to look at the bees...' Seth says quietly, respectfully.

I bet she fucking did.

She did this. I know it. But I don't say it.

I can feel everyone's sad eyes on me. Two sets of eyes are genuinely sad for me. The third pair is laughing at me.

'Maybe they got a disease...' Seth says, sorrow tingeing his voice.

I take one last look at the piles of dead insects, turn and stomp back into the house, refusing to look at any of them, refusing to say anything. I head straight up to my bedroom, straight into my en suite bathroom and lock the door.

My glorious, beautiful bees did not get a disease. They got slaughtered by Lily Hailstone, or whatever the hell her real name is.

Their deaths will not be in vain. I'll make sure of that.

CHAPTER TWENTY-FOUR

18 YEARS AGO

DAILY TIMES

Tuesday 12 December 2006

NEW EVIDENCE IN JERRY WARD MURDER TRIAL CASTS DOUBT

Was there a second person?

Jurors hearing new evidence in the trial of a woman accused of murdering Jerry Ward were today told that forensic tests may indicate that a second person was involved in the murder.

The court previously heard that a fingerprint belonging to Natalie Owens, 21, was found near the victim's body. The prosecution argued that this placed her at the scene of the crime and strongly indicated her guilt. However, the defence maintained that the presence of Owens' fingerprint was not conclusive proof that she murdered Ward.

A single strand of hair was also found at the scene and has not been identified. It does not belong to Owens or to anyone who was known to have visited Ward, including his family members and friends.

Owens' defence counsel has told the jury that this supports Owens' claim that she met Ward at the pub and had gone back to his house briefly but left before the murder was committed. 'He was very much alive the last time I saw him,' she said when on the witness stand yesterday, before maintaining her innocence.

The defence's closing statement reiterated that the single fingerprint does not prove Owens murdered Ward, it only proves that she was at his house earlier in the day. They insist she left before the murderer arrived and that she had nothing to do with Ward's death.

However, the prosecution's closing statement argued that: Owens was seen with Ward just hours before his death; there was no evidence that Owens left Ward's home when she claims; and she could not provide an alibi for her whereabouts later that night. The prosecution also reiterated that the speculated timings for events that evening did not appear to support Owens' claim.

Jurors have been told by the judge that they must decide on the evidence whether Owens was the person who cut the throat of the victim causing his death. A verdict is due later in the week.

Senior reporter's opinion:

In the explosive final days of the Jerry Ward trial, we speculate on what happened to the Southampton grandfather:

Could Owens have murdered Jerry Ward alongside a second person and be keeping quiet as to their identity for some reason?

Or could Owens have been a willing – or unwilling – accessory to murder, assisting this second person but not taking part?

Or did Owens in fact leave Ward moments before a second person arrived at his house and murdered him, and had no knowledge as to Ward's fate – as she has claimed?

On the witness stand yesterday Owens was volatile and angry, not endearing herself to the judge or the jurors. Towards the end, she shouted incomprehensibly and was escorted out of the court by her counsel and by police officers, cutting short her evidence.

We wait with bated breath for the jury's verdict. But one thing is for certain – we may never know what truly happened that night.

CHAPTER TWENTY-FIVE

Gentle tapping on the bathroom door brings me out of my grief stupor. I've been locked in the bathroom all day. Devastated. Angry. Not able to face anyone.

Earlier, Todd attempted to coax me out, to get me to talk to him through the door, to ask if he could bring me up some lunch, but I wouldn't respond. I've been sitting very still, with my back against the bath, my chin resting on my knees and my arms hugging myself. Processing. Mourning. Accepting. Planning. I've needed quiet. Todd gave up and told me he was going back to work, that he'd be home late and that he loved me. He left hours ago.

And now, my son is trying.

'Mum,' Seth's hushed voice comes through the door. 'Are you okay in there? I'm so sorry about your bees. Really, really sad. Can I get you some food? Or something to drink?'

He pauses, in case I might reply. But I don't. I'm still not ready to talk.

He continues, 'I'm heading out to my study group. Lily is going to stay in my room, okay? She's really upset about everything so please don't go near her. Mum? Will you promise me you won't do anything and you'll leave her alone?'

I don't speak. I'm not going to make a promise to Seth that I'm going to break the moment he steps off the property. I'd like to promise him that I'm going to get that poisonous bitch out of my house and away from him, my wonderful, wonderful son, because she's manipulating and lying to him. But I don't say it out loud. Silently, I stand and go to the door, touching it gently where his face might be on the other side.

'Love you, Mum,' he says. 'I'll be gone for a couple of hours.'

He walks away. I listen intently. The front door opens and closes, his car starts up outside, and I hear it crunch the gravel, pause to let the gates swing open and drive away. I wait for fifteen minutes to make sure he doesn't return and exit the bathroom.

I go immediately to his bedroom, bang on the door, cross my arms. There's no more polite Jen now. Lily is leaving. Tonight. If I have to drag her into the lane by her hair, then I'm ready for it.

When there's no answer, I open the door. Seth's bedroom is empty.

Blaring heavy metal music makes me jump. My house is usually so peaceful and calming, but now screechy shouty male vocals penetrate it like toxic fumes.

I storm down the stairs to where the noise is emanating from – the main lounge.

The music comes from the telly, where a music video plays. A wave of heat from the faux fire hits me in the face followed by a cold breeze from an open window. All the lights are on. All the candles are lit. Lily is sprawled on the sofa, in my usual spot, her closed laptop resting on her belly. She's wearing my dressing gown – she must've snuck into my bedroom to take it off the hook on the back of the door. She's got her filthy boots on and her feet up on the sofa. Dirt smears the cream material.

And on the coffee table is a bottle of my mead, mostly empty, and the tub of my honey-roasted nuts, also mostly gone.

She sees me and throws some nuts in her mouth. And my anger rises. That's the last of the goods I made with my bees' honey. Now all dead, it has more meaning. It should not be being scoffed by the bee killer.

She makes no attempt to move. She smirks at me as if she owns the place and I'm the intruder.

'This ends now,' I shout. 'Get the fuck out of my house!'

Lily presses the remote control and the volume increases until it's deafening. She cups her hand to her ear and gives me a withering look as if to say, *you're going to need to speak louder, I can't hear you.*

I stride over to the telly and wrench the plug out of the socket. The telly dies and the music stops. I turn to face her.

'Get the fuck out of my house and get the fuck away from my son. Get your things and don't ever come back.'

She snorts derisively. Slowly, she opens the lid of her laptop. 'You have a lot of secrets, Victoria Prince.'

The name clangs in my ears like someone hitting a gigantic gong. The vibrations reach right to my toes, as devastating as a powerful earthquake. I haven't heard that name spoken out loud since 2006. I shook it off; it no longer belongs to me. It belongs to another lifetime. How did she find that out? She can't know *everything*, can she? Sweat trickles between my shoulder blades.

She continues, 'You ran away from Norwich – and not from Milton Keynes as you like to tell everyone – with your baby, changed your name and ended up in a shelter in Southampton. All your family are still alive in Norfolk. You're not an orphan.' She turns her laptop to face me. 'Family is *so* important, don't you think?'

My knees turn to jelly, and I almost tumble over. The screen is filled with pure evil: a photo of my abusive ex, Damian.

That face haunted me for years. I buried it deep, haven't allowed myself to see it in my mind's eye for nearly two decades. It stares at me. I want to look away, but I can't.

She taps the screen. 'And this here is Damian Butcher. Seth's biological father.'

I swallow heavily. I've always maintained to Todd that Damian had thrown us out, that he hadn't wanted Seth. But that's not quite true. Does she know the whole story? I have to pray she doesn't.

She continues, 'I think Mr Butcher would like to know where his son ended up. He posted a lot on social media about your disappearance with his son. There were missing persons campaigns and all sorts. But you hid well.'

I shake my head. 'No. You can't tell Damian about Seth's whereabouts—'

She cuts me off. 'Or maybe I should tell Seth about Damian and where he lives so they can reconnect?'

I take a step backwards from her. 'No, you can't... please...'

She sits upright on the sofa and takes a swig of mead right from the bottle. She spits it out with a spray all over the carpet. 'This tastes like crap.'

She throws the bottle on the floor. Precious golden liquid seeps out, and I know it'll leave a stain, just like all my lies have left a stain on my soul. But I had to lie. It was my only option, the only way I could save Seth.

Lily wipes her mouth on my dressing gown sleeve. 'What did you say to me earlier?'

I don't reply. All my bravado has scarpered.

She continues, 'Didn't you tell me to get the fuck out of your house? To get the fuck away from your son? Ha! As if. I'm not going anywhere. I'm perfectly comfortable right here, thank you.' She sprawls back on the sofa. 'Tomorrow, you'll tell Seth that Todd isn't his father.'

'No, it'll break his heart.' We should've told Seth long ago. There was just never a right moment.

That's not strictly true. Todd was waiting for me to take the lead. Would've supported me no matter what and no matter when. But I never pushed because it saved me from having to tell Seth about his real father, or, perish the thought, Seth ever wanting to seek that man out. I simply couldn't ever let that happen.

'If you don't tell him tomorrow, then I will.' She stuffs her hand in the tub of nuts and shoves as many as possible in her mouth, spilling some on the sofa. She chews and talks with her mouth full. 'And I'll help him to find his real daddy's contact details. And encourage him to reconnect.'

'If I do this, will you stop? Will all this be over? You'll break off the engagement and leave my family alone?'

She munches the nuts noisily and swallows slowly. 'You'll just have to find out, won't you?'

'Why are you doing this?'

Lily erupts into a cackle and taps the side of her nose like it's one big, hilarious secret.

I hurry from the room; her evil laughter follows me all the way back to the en suite. I lock myself in again. I stand very still, stunned for a few moments. And then I pace.

She can't know what I did to get away from Damian, can she?

CHAPTER TWENTY-SIX

The following day, we drive home in silence. Usually, I'd be working on a Wednesday but my work is still closed pending the outcome of the investigation. Penny filled me in this morning. My boss, Syreeta, has been released but is still a person of interest. Simon has been remanded in custody and not granted bail.

Lily went to uni this morning and is out all day in lectures – keeping up her farce. She's obviously avoiding me, playing up how scared of me she is following the 'slap'. It's all for Todd and Seth's benefit.

Yesterday, Todd's PA found a therapist in the city who had availability for a short notice appointment this afternoon. Todd booked it and told me. He said he'd drive me there, wait for me and bring me home.

I went along with it. I can't have him turn against me any more than he already has. But I didn't tell the therapist anything about Lily or about me. She knew I was holding back and could tell I wasn't being completely truthful. But I wasn't about to blab about my past. She'd go straight to the police, horrified by her patient.

'We'll have dinner, and then I can drive you to choir practice, if you like?' Todd says as we wait at a red light. He's being overly clingy, worried about me, wanting me to 'get better', to go back to the Jen I was before that bitch arrived in my home. He keeps glancing sideways at me, checking I haven't completely caved in on myself and further away from him.

Usually we'd be chatting away in the car, telling each other about our days, something funny, what we fancy doing at the weekend. But the only thing on my mind is Lily. And I've tried discussing that with him and met a brick wall. So he's being met with silence. I have to handle this on my own.

'I'm not going to choir practice tonight,' I reply.

'Really? You didn't go last week either. The only time you miss it is if we're on holiday.'

When I don't elaborate, he continues, 'I'm so worried about you, Jen. I wish you'd tell me what's going on.'

I grit my teeth and stare out the window. I want to yell, *I have told you what's going on – Lily is out to get me! But you've told me it's all in my head.*

He glances at me again as we pull into our driveway. 'I'm going to make lasagne and homemade garlic bread for dinner. Your favourite. Sound good?'

I don't reply.

We eat mostly in silence. Todd continually attempts to engage me in conversation. I shun his every attempt.

About an hour after we've finished dinner and cleaned up, the front door opens, and Seth and Lily come in.

'Seth, Lily, I'd like to have a family meeting, please,' I call out.

Todd frowns at me. Then he comes over all relieved. He must think my silence has something to do with the therapy session. Perhaps he thinks I'm about to apologise for my violent behaviour and make amends. I head over to my spot at the dining table, and he joins me, putting his hand over mine and giving it a supportive squeeze.

Seth comes in followed by Lily doing her Oscar-worthy shy-girl performance. They take their seats opposite us. My son looks at Todd and at me. Lily keeps her eyes down and leans into Seth as if she can't support herself without him.

I clear my throat. 'Thank you, everyone, for being here. I have something very important that I want to say.'

'Your mum went to see a therapist today,' Todd adds.

'There's no easy way to say this,' I say, looking at Seth and at Todd and completely excluding Lily. 'I love you both very much, and it might not feel like it now, but what I'm about to say is for the good of this family.' I have to believe that once it's done then Lily will have her fill of whatever sick game she's playing and leave us alone.

I continue, 'I should've done this a long time ago. I regret that. But you have to know that I'm the one to blame here. And not Todd.'

Seth's eyes narrow, unsure as to what is coming. Todd's firm hand pressing down on top of mine wavers, the pressure lightening.

'Seth, your biological father isn't Todd. You were a few months old when Todd first met you. He adopted you when you were a baby.'

Lily gasps. Todd swiftly removes his hand, absolutely shocked. Seth stares at me.

I wait a moment for that news to sink in, to see if Seth might say anything. But he doesn't, he just stares. I'm terrified of what this news might do to him – his entire identity shattered in an instant. But I know him. He's a sensitive soul but is also resilient and open-minded and doesn't hold grudges. He'll get through this; I have to believe he will.

He swallows, and his face crumples. He blinks rapidly, looking from me to Todd.

'Who is my biological father?' he asks eventually, as I knew he would. He's too curious.

'Not a man you want to know, Seth. He kicked us out when you were a tiny baby. He didn't want anything to do with us. This will be painful to hear, but he didn't want to know you.'

I don't mention he was violent. That we escaped from him. I don't want any questions about what happened. It's simpler for Todd and Seth to believe Damian booted us out.

Seth nods, silent tears roll down his face.

'But his loss was our gain, because we met Todd. And Todd absolutely did want to know you and love you and bring you up and be your dad. Todd loves you more than that man ever could. Todd is your father in every way apart from blood.'

Todd instantly reaches out across the table with both hands to Seth. Seth takes them, and they share eye contact for a few beats. It's a tender moment that fills my heart with so much joy. They love each other so much.

But Seth's eyes turn to me. They narrow, and his face screws up. Seth's beautiful features register shock, confusion, despair, and come to a stop on anger. 'Why didn't you tell me sooner? Why did you keep this from me?'

'We never really felt the moment was right—' Todd begins, but I cut him off.

'It's all my fault,' I say insistently.

Todd eyes me strangely. It was a joint effort; we both know this. But I don't want Seth's relationship with Todd crumbling because of this.

'What was his name?' Seth asks.

'I have never told Todd that, and I will never tell you. It's better that way. If you sought him out, he would reject you all over again.'

'You don't know that,' Seth says.

'I'm trying to protect you, Seth. That man wanted nothing to do with you then, and won't want anything to do with you now. I'm sorry, I know that's hard to hear. But your father is here, and he loves you and wants you.' I indicate Todd. Seth blinks at me. I continue, 'I really don't want you' – I swallow the bile that rises – 'or Lily to move out. You live here. We want you here. This is your home for a long while yet, okay?'

I don't want Lily to persuade Seth to leave – I want him, and that means her – under my roof. I can attempt to keep an eye on her, to try to keep Seth safe because he's not completely alone with her.

Seth stands abruptly, wiping tears from his face, and hurries out. Lily follows after him. The front door opens and closes and the sound of Seth's car leaving the driveway floats through to the kitchen.

'What the hell, Jen?' Todd says, when the sound of tyres crunching on the gravel has stopped. 'Why didn't you tell me you were about to do this? We could've done it together. We *should've* done it together. Planned it out better, waited for the right moment. Instead, you completely blindsided me. Is this why you've been acting so strange recently? It was eating you up, and you had to say something? You should've talked to me.'

His voice hitches and his eyes go watery, but he pulls himself together before any tears can spring.

I want to comfort him, but I know he wouldn't want that. I know him too well. In a minute he'll walk away for some space. I debated all day about telling Todd so we could say something together, but he wouldn't have understood the urgency, would've wanted to talk it through for a few days and delay it. But Lily said I had to do it today or she would. At least this way I could control what was said. And it keeps Lily's attention squarely on me. I did what she asked.

Todd stands. 'What's happened to our partnership? What's happening to our relationship, Jen? It feels as if it's crumbling… we've always been so solid, but I just can't believe you did this without consulting me first. I'm going out for a drive. I can't be anywhere near you right now.'

A few moments later he's out the door, in his car and gone.

And I'm all alone in the house. It's not comforting. I feel completely isolated from everyone I love. And the guilt that I still haven't told my beloved husband and wonderful child the full truth is eating me up.

The photo Lily showed me has become embedded behind my eyes: Damian. Seth's biological father, and my violent ex.

He's a dangerous man. And he must be employing Lily to screw with me.

I got complacent, thought he'd give up looking, thought he'd let it go. But I was stupid. Of course he wouldn't just let it go. He's not that kind of man. He's the sort to seek revenge on those who've wronged him until the day he dies. And he's finally caught up with me after all these years.

I misjudged him. I thought if he ever found me then he'd end my life quickly. He has zero patience, zero subtlety and zero imagination for anything else.

But I've underestimated just how much he loathes me. He's found Lily somehow – on some kind of con-artist-for-hire site on the dark web? Through a friend of a dodgy friend down the pub? – and briefed her to get Seth to trust her and to play games with me. I can just imagine him saying, 'Draw it out, torture her, make her hate her life. The worse you can make it, the better. And then once she's in pieces, introduce me to Seth because that'll destroy her all over again.'

'I'll beat some manliness into that pussy,' he'll tell me. 'Erase that pathetic pond bullshit.' Damian won't stop until Seth is brainwashed, until Seth's all about pints, pubs, being one of the lads, fighting, misogyny. Damian never wanted a son; he loves himself too much. He wants a mini me, a henchman, a kid he can control. He'll want Seth to fear him, not to love him.

Well, enough's enough. He's had his fun now. It's me that

he's after. He can leave Seth and Todd out of it. If I contact him, then he's won. He can call off his attack dog; there'll be no more need for her to be in my house. Whatever he wants to do to me, he can do it direct. I'll beg him to leave Seth be. There'll be something he wants; there always is with men like that. Some *thing* that'll make him feel as if he's won, as if he's got all the power.

I go out to my car and take my secret laptop and mobile phone out of the boot, head back up to my en suite and lock the door. Using the phone's hotspot and not the house's Wi-Fi so Lily won't know, I type 'Damian Butcher Norfolk' into the search bar.

My finger hovers over the enter key. In eighteen years, I've never looked him up. That part of my life was dead. But I have to protect my family from any more heartache.

I press enter, and the search results pop up. I scour them for anything relevant.

There are hits on Damian's window-cleaning business, apparently very successful in the area. Bile rises up my throat when I see photos of him.

And then I see it. An obituary in a local newspaper from four years ago:

> Damian Butcher, the disgraced Norfolk businessman who was jailed for beating his third wife so severely that she lost the baby she was carrying, has died in prison. Butcher became involved in a brawl with six other inmates and died from his injuries. The others sustained minor injuries. The 54-year-old had run Norfolk's largest window-cleaning business before he was jailed for domestic violence and was forced to sell it. It is believed he had one child with a partner before his first wife, but no other children. Rebecca Lush divorced Butcher after the incident and has since remarried and had two children.

I have to read it three times before it sinks in.

The monster is dead.

That news startles me so much I almost drop the laptop and have to place it gently on the floor to allow my entire body to tremble from head to toe. That poor woman, that poor baby still in its mother's womb. He was pure evil.

Damian isn't pulling the strings. Lily is working on her own. And I have no idea why.

Well, whatever her reason, that bitch is not going to get away with this.

I wait patiently until Seth and Lily return. They go straight upstairs to Seth's bedroom. A moment later, Seth comes out. I can tell his footsteps, his speed, from years of hearing him. He uses the family bathroom and heads back into his bedroom.

And then it's Lily's turn. Her footfall is lighter on the hallway carpet.

I rush from the en suite and run, as quietly as I can, to the bathroom down the hallway, just in time to catch her closing the bathroom door. I stick my foot in the way.

We glare at each other.

She whispers, not wanting Seth to hear us, 'You didn't tell them Damian's name. You failed your task. I'm going to tell Seth who his biological father is and where to find him.'

'Damian's dead.'

She smirks. She knows.

I continue, 'You are evil. I'm going to find a way to get rid of you, don't you worry.'

'Ha, well, go on then. You're going cuckoo, remember? No one will believe a word you say.'

She moves her hand, and it's then I notice it's in her pocket. She draws it out slowly.

Does she have a weapon? Is she about to stab me?

She'd concoct some story about me coming to knife her, and my attack going wrong when she fought back. She'd play it all innocent and claim that I accidentally got stabbed when she was defending herself. I can see all the lies she'd spin so distinctly.

Her hand comes out but there's no weapon. She waves it in front of my face and wriggles her fingers.

A huge sparkling engagement ring catches all my attention.

'We went to the shops today on our lunch break. Seth spent all his saved-up pocket money on it, bless him.' She pouts in an over-the-top way.

I'm mesmerised by the ring. She slowly and deliberately draws a finger across her throat and points it at me. A clear and explicit threat on my life.

Malice laces her tone, so vicious it sends shivers down my spine. 'Watch your back. You never know when I'll jump out at you.'

Speechless, I edge back.

She lunges forward. 'Boo,' she says. Then laughs.

It makes me jump, and I stumble. She slams the bathroom door in my face.

My heart pounds. An icy chill licks at my skin: she doesn't just want to toy with me – she wants me dead.

CHAPTER TWENTY-SEVEN

18 YEARS AGO

DAILY TIMES
Friday 15 December 2006

WOMAN FOUND GUILTY OF JERRY WARD MURDER

Natalie Owens sentenced to life in prison

Today a woman was sentenced at Southampton Crown Court to life in prison for the murder of 69-year-old Jerry Ward.

Natalie Owens, 21, was sentenced to life with a minimum term of eighteen years in prison.

Jerry Ward was brutally murdered at his Freemantle house at around 9 p.m. on Saturday 1 July, 2006. His body was found the following day by his daughter.

Detective Chief Inspector Rohan Bhatia said: 'Our thoughts remain with Jerry's family, who have lost a beloved father and grandfather in the most violent and cruel circumstances. This sentencing won't bring Jerry back, but I hope it brings them some comfort knowing justice has been done.

'It's clear from events that Owens is a highly aggressive and unpredictable individual. A random meeting at a pub led to Ward losing his life.

'I am pleased this woman is now safely behind bars and hope she will use her time in prison to think on the pain and heartbreak she has brought to a loving family.'

The jury submitted a unanimous verdict of guilty and Judge Nicolas Riley sentenced Owens today.

Ms Sanderson, Ward's eldest daughter and the person who discovered his body, said outside the court: 'Justice has been served. Our family can now fully focus on the grieving process and trying to heal the trauma.'

Senior reporter's opinion:

The sentencing of Natalie Owens has sent shockwaves through the nation. The jury took just two hours to come back with the guilty verdict, a pronouncement that led to a ripple of gasps throughout the courtroom.

Forensic evidence – that of a single strand of hair found near the body – strongly implied a second person was present.

But the jury decided that this wasn't enough to find Owens innocent. Her fingerprint close to the body, the CCTV and eyewitness accounts of Owens with Ward earlier in the evening and Owens' erratic behaviour on the stand was sufficient evidence to prove her guilt.

It's a question that will niggle for years to come – who was the second person, and will they ever be found? And – the most disturbing thought of all – will they kill again?

CHAPTER TWENTY-EIGHT

Frightened, I run straight to the kitchen, grab a large kitchen knife, and run back to the en suite and lock myself in.

She plans to kill me. What about Seth and Todd?

The police are not an option. And even if I did go to them, would they believe me? Everything points to me losing my mind. My husband and son will support that conclusion too, so swept up in Lily's web of lies.

There has to be something. Some clue I've missed.

I open my secret laptop. Googling Lily Hailstone didn't produce anything damning.

I take a deep breath and close my eyes. In my mind, I run through all the interactions I've had with Lily, forcing myself to do it slowly, to pick at every little thing.

And a shred of light illuminates something in my brain. Latching on, I realise it's to do with the dark web hoax that Lily instigated.

She'd said whoever had organised the hitman wanted me dead because of something that had happened eighteen years ago. I immediately jumped to Damian or Todd, or Seth's birth.

But what else happened eighteen years ago? Lily was born, she's eighteen – at least that's what she claims. But what else?

I google 'what happened in 2006', scan through the hits and know that huge world events are definitely not what I'm looking for. I narrow it down by adding 'UK' onto the end, and then further by adding 'Southampton'.

A name stands out: Natalie Owens. It was a huge scandal at the time, which I vaguely remember. I read through a few articles to remind myself – a young woman murdered an older man in Southampton in the summer of 2006.

The murder was on the same day as my first date with Todd. What an odd coincidence. I'm about to move on and continue my search when I see a photo of Natalie Owens.

The breath is snatched from my lungs.

She looks just like Lily.

The same natural, light-blonde hair, big blue eyes, face and nose shape. Lily has quite a distinctive, wonky nose. And so does Natalie.

I devour all the *Daily Times* articles about the case, dig deeper and find an obscure book written about Natalie Owens. The grey-haired male author's other six titles are also books about young, pretty female murderers. He claims to spend hours interviewing the perpetrators while they're still in prison. And I get the sense it is some kind of creepy hobby. The book about Natalie is still available for sale as an ebook. It has four reviews, so not widely read.

I immediately buy it and download an ebook app onto my laptop so I can read it.

The author spent six hours interviewing Natalie in her first year of prison at HMP Bronzefield in Ashford for the book. Apparently, she gave her full support to its publication, insisting she wanted her 'truth' to be told.

An 'ambitious glamour model', the author spends a long time detailing Natalie's looks, her 'perfect hourglass' body and her 'fake, very perky' breasts. She was a 'regular' in lads' mags and 'yearned for a glitzy life full of luxury' and was 'on the up' and 'destined for great things'.

Which is why it was such a shock to everyone that she brutally murdered a sixty-nine-year-old man.

After a few chapters of deliberating, making clear that Natalie insisted she left Ward when he was still alive, the author delicately suggests that Natalie has a serious mental health condition. He concludes, even though Natalie vehemently denies it, that the unhinged Natalie snapped, randomly picked Jerry Ward and murdered him. And that the poor old man was simply in 'the wrong place at the wrong time'.

A little-known fact: Natalie was in the early stages of pregnancy when Ward died. She didn't know. She gave birth in prison soon after she was convicted, and the baby was immediately taken off her.

Is Lily the baby?

A memory tickles then jumps squarely into my head – Lily told us she'd been born in Ashford, Surrey. The location of Natalie's prison.

I delve deeper into the book.

There are a few photos that Natalie supplied to the author. The quality isn't great, and they are in black and white. I flick through them and stop. I screenshot a photo so I can zoom in on it.

It's Todd.

The photo caption reads, 'Natalie with friends in 2006 shortly before Jerry Ward died'. It shows Natalie, Todd and a couple of others in a group photo. Todd is standing next to her. He has his arm around Natalie's shoulders, but he has his other arm around another woman's shoulders on the other side. It's not obvious it's him because he's turning his face and it's a little blurred. But I know it's my husband – he's wearing what was his favourite leather biker jacket at the time. He hardly took it off, he loved it that much. And he wore it to our first date. It looks as if they're in a nightclub.

A heavy rock lands in my gut.

It could just be he was posing with fans on a night out. He has his photo taken with randoms all the time, even now. But why would Natalie select this photo to put in the book? Was she trying to make out she was famous because she was hanging out with football players? Or did Todd and Natalie know each other, as 'friends' or something else?

The sound of a car crunching on gravel outside chimes a warning in my mind. It's Todd back from his drive. I turn off my laptop and phone and hide them in the linen cupboard, at the back and under some towels.

I pick up the knife and listen.

There's a knock on the bathroom door that makes me jump – how did he get up here so quickly? So silently? Or is that Lily out there pretending to be Todd arriving home?

The gentle knock comes again, followed by Todd's soft voice. 'Jen? Are you okay in there?'

Relief sweeps through me. It's my husband. Not *her*.

I swing open the door, lunge out at him, pleased he's home.

Todd jumps back, startled.

His eyes shoot down to the large kitchen knife in my hand. His hands fly up, his face pales and terror flashes across his eyes.

'No, Jen. Please don't hurt me,' he begs.

CHAPTER TWENTY-NINE

'No, this isn't for you. It's for Lily,' I reply.

'For Lily? Fucking hell!'

'No. No! I mean it's to use as self-defence if she comes after me. I'm not going to do anything to her!'

'Okay, sure. Let's put the knife down, shall we?' Todd lowers his hands and gestures to a tall chest of drawers by the door.

I place it on the top of the chest of drawers. With zero preamble, I blurt, 'How did you know Natalie Owens? That woman who murdered the grandfather, Jerry Ward?'

Todd winces and has a reaction similar to the one I had when Lily said my real name again. It's as if something buried deep inside of him suddenly cracks open and spills its guts. It's clearly not a name he's heard for a long time.

He steadies himself by placing his hand on the chest of drawers. He looks at the knife. It's almost touching his middle finger. An ominous ripple seems to pass right through him. His muscles tense.

Oh fuck, is he about to use it on *me*? Have I just uncovered something extremely dark from Todd's past that he'll do anything to keep quiet?

All the air is sucked out of the room. Neither of us breathes.

But his eyes meet mine again, and he steps away. 'Let's get into bed.'

He undresses, stripping down to his boxers, which is what he usually wears to sleep in. It's normal for us to chat in bed. It feels like exactly the right thing to do. I get changed into my pyjamas. We get into bed and sit upright with our backs against the padded headboard and turn inwards so we face each other.

Once we're both comfortable, Todd begins.

'I met Natalie in a nightclub in Southampton. I didn't want to be there. I hate nightclubs. But I was single and that's where all the single footballers went, so I was pressured into going. All the lads were gawking at her, and she could've got with any of them, but she threw herself at me, like all the women I met at that time.'

Todd isn't being big-headed, he's stating a fact. Women *still* throw themselves at him, even though he's happily married and has been for many years.

He continues, 'It was clear her only goal was to marry a wealthy footballer. I really wasn't interested, but I'd never met any other kind of woman, so we dated for a few weeks – very casually. She was sleeping with other men, keeping her options open. She didn't keep it secret. The relationship was so brief the media hadn't even picked up on it, and no one knew.

'She had a way of wheedling me and getting under my skin. I knew she was manipulating me, but I didn't know any different – I thought perhaps this is what a relationship was like... I had nothing to compare it to. But then I met you.'

He leans over and kisses my cheek. 'I was blown away by you. Finally a woman I actually connected with, could be myself with, could have a conversation with. The day before our first date, I called it off with Natalie. I didn't think she'd be that bothered. In my mind, it wasn't going anywhere – we didn't really get on and had nothing in common. It had mostly been sex.'

He shakes his head remembering. 'But she went crazy. Said she thought we were getting married, said I'd broken her heart, said I was a piece of shit for leading her on. I felt bad, of course I did, but she wasn't the one for me. You were.'

He rubs his face and sighs. 'We had our incredible first date, and I knew we would get married and be together forever. I just *knew*. After saying goodbye to you that evening, I checked my phone. I had hundreds of missed calls and messages from Natalie. It was insane. She told me she had a surprise for me and to come to an address that I'd never heard of before. It wasn't her Ocean Village apartment.

'She called me again, and I answered and told her no. Reiterated that we were over. Told her I'd met someone else. But she said she'd kill herself if I didn't come. She was a total headcase. So I went. I couldn't bear the thought that she might go through with it and it would be all my fault. I'd have it on my conscience until I died. I thought maybe she'd bought a new house, or rented it, or something, and wanted to show it to me, wanted to show me the life we could have together. Well, how wrong I was.

'She opened the front door covered in blood. I was so shocked that I let her hug me, so the blood soaked me, too. I thought she'd slit her wrists. I thought it was her blood. But then she led me inside.

'And I saw a dead body on the floor.

'"I did it for you," she told me, "to prove my love for you."

'"Who the hell is that?" I said.

'"Jerry Ward. I tracked him down. It wasn't hard."

'And then I took a proper look at the old man. And I knew him.

'In a moment of absolute drunken madness, I told Natalie

about my childhood. I deeply regretted it the next day. But she never mentioned it again, so I prayed she'd been too drunk to remember. But she'd remembered, all right.

'My mum was an alcoholic and drug addict, as you know, and she dated Ward for a few years when I was a kid. He'd come round, they'd drink, she'd pass out on the sofa, and he'd come into my room. He abused me from age six until nine. Three years of horror. I never told Mum. I never told anyone. I was so ashamed.'

I reach out to hug Todd, and he clutches me tightly. We stay this way for a long while.

'I'm so sorry that happened to you,' I say gently.

He pulls away and takes a deep breath. 'I've dealt with it in my own way. But in that moment, I had no idea what to do. Natalie was off the rails, she kept babbling that she'd done it for me, that she'd killed the paedophile bastard who had ruined my childhood, that it was proof of her love.

'I should've gone straight to the police, I know that now, and told them the truth. But back then I was terrified. My football career was taking off. I had Ward's blood all over me. I was the one who had the motive – Ward abused me, not Natalie. It would look like I'd murdered him and she'd helped, I knew it would.'

He rubs his face again, looks up to the ceiling and back to me.

'So I helped her clean the place up. We went out into the forest in the dead of night and burnt our bloody clothes. How was I supposed to know that we'd missed one fucking fingerprint? That the police had her fingerprint on file from a shoplifting incident years before that she'd never told me about?'

I ask, 'And the single strand of hair that was found – that was yours, wasn't it?'

Todd nods. 'The police arrested her. Rohan – my best mate

– led the investigation. I kept waiting to get arrested, for Natalie to say something, for Rohan to say something.'

'But the police never came.'

'No. I've never been in trouble with the police, so they don't have my information on file to match that hair. And no one remembered her from the nightclub; no one linked her to me.

'After she was jailed, Natalie sent me letters telling me how much she loved me, how we'd be together again when she was out, that she'd understand if I didn't come and see her in prison, that she knew I loved her deeply and always would. She never mentioned what had happened; she knew the letters would be read by prison staff. She sent them to the football club. I'd moved in here by that point, and she didn't have my new address. I told Jeanie, the lady who sorted post at the club, to bin all that came from her because she was an obsessed fan. Jeanie told me when she retired recently that the letters went on for years – there were thousands of them. Then one day they just stopped coming.

'I've waited for Natalie to say something, to implicate me. But she never has. She sees it as her proving her love for me by taking the blame – even though she was the one who committed the murder. I debated for a very long time about coming forward and telling the police I was the second person at the house that night, that the hair belongs to me. But I never have. I guess I'm a coward.'

He holds his head in his hands. 'It eats me up,' he says and sobs. 'I thought I'd done enough to keep her out of prison. But... she's a psychopath, and prison is the best place for her. And I'm... glad... she's in there because she's not been able to hurt anyone else. But, fuck, I feel so guilty about it.'

I hold him tightly while he cries on my shoulder. 'Oh, Todd, you were tricked into going to Ward's house. It's not always easy doing the right thing.'

He sniffs a few times and looks up at me.

I continue, 'It said her jail term was eighteen years minimum. Do you think she's out now?'

'No idea.'

'It also said she was pregnant when she murdered Ward. Did you know?'

'What? No.'

The shock on his face tells me he's telling the truth.

'I reckon she must've been two or three months gone when you were seeing her, because she gave birth after the trial.'

He shakes his head. 'I had no clue.'

I draw in strength. I know he won't like what I'm about to say, but I have to say it. 'I think Lily is her child. They look alike. Maybe Natalie has something to do with why Lily is after me? Maybe Natalie has set her child on me.'

Todd sighs impatiently. 'Oh, Jen, why have you got it in for that lovely girl? It needs to stop, now. It's pure coincidence that they look alike. Lily is a wonderful girlfriend to Seth and is a really sweet person.'

I change tack; he still has Lily-wool pulled over his eyes. 'I need to tell you something.'

'I'm listening,' he replies and looks at me intently.

I brace myself with a deep inhale through my nose and drag everything up from the depths.

'I'm not from Milton Keynes. I'm from Norwich. I'm not an orphan. My parents didn't die in a car crash. They're very much alive. I come from a huge family on my Greek side. Including a brother. I had an awful childhood, not a boring one. The reason I had that funny turn after the baby shower was because the place reminded me of the pub they left me in after a big family event when I was eight. They told me to play outside and completely forgot about me – all of them. Parents, brother, grandparents, aunties, cousins. One of the staff found me, terrified, hiding under the table we'd been sitting at. They managed to get in touch with my drunk dad to tell him I was there. And it took them four hours to come and get me. The staff sat me on my own at a table by the door. They were too busy to look after me. Hours sitting there alone felt like days.'

I shudder at the memory.

I continue, 'Damian used to beat me, and my awful family took his side. He scared all my friends away, so I had no one.

'I met him at seventeen. He was much older. He love-bombed me. I know this now, but at the time I got completely sucked in. I moved out of my family home at sixteen. I could only find a low-paying job and was living in a tiny one-bed flat with three other women. It was a hovel, really, but it was the only thing I could afford.

'Damian asked me to move in with him. I did. I thought it was love. But it wasn't. I was so screwed up from a loveless childhood that I lapped up any shred of attention he gave me. Slowly, slowly he took over my life. He controlled my finances, my technology use, when I went out, who I saw. Eventually he convinced me to stop working. He made me wear sexually suggestive clothes, trowel on make-up and curl my hair. I'd doll myself up to 'receive' him when he got back from work. And every night he'd come in the front door and force himself on me before even saying hello.

'This went on for nine years.

'Twice I tried to leave. Twice he found out. I was punished severely. But that didn't stop me from saving cash here and there in a rumpled plastic bag at the back of a kitchen drawer that he rarely went in. Stashing it away, just in case the opportunity to escape ever presented itself again, just in case I could ever summon up enough courage to attempt it a third time.

'And then I got pregnant.

'One night, Damian was enraged by Seth's crying. He beat me, then he went for Seth. And I snapped. Just as he was looming over Seth's cot, his big fist about to connect with Seth's tiny face, I snatched a large glass ashtray off the coffee table and smashed it over Damian's head.

'He stumbled backwards, blood pouring down his face. He was furious and came at me again, but his balance was off. I ran into the kitchen; he teetered after me. He was about to kill me, I knew it. And then he'd kill my baby, I knew that too. So I picked up a knife.

'I stabbed him multiple times. It was the only way to stop him. I should've called an ambulance, the police. But I didn't. While he was bleeding out, I showered, got changed into clean clothes, grabbed the measly sum of cash, picked up Seth and left.'

I look at Todd. His mouth hangs open in a perfect O.

'Damian survived,' I say. 'But I was wanted by the police in Norfolk for attempted murder. If I hadn't have run, if I'd called the ambulance and police immediately, if I'd stabbed him once and not multiple times, then I might've been able to convince them it was self-defence and got away with it. But I couldn't take the chance. I couldn't risk Seth being taken off me.

'I changed my name, got a fake passport from a woman at the Southampton shelter who knew some people. Hid. Met and married you. Have always stayed away from any kind of limelight or social media. Damian died a few years ago. But the police might still be after me.'

'Shit, Jen,' Todd says, wide-eyed. 'That's a lot to take in.'

I feel undone, as if someone has unzipped my skin and let everything rotten in me right out, exposed to the world, to scrutiny, to inspection. But I'm thankful I've told him. A great weight has lifted.

'I told myself that I'd never be in a relationship again. I'd focus on being a mum and making sure Seth had the best life possible. But we just clicked, didn't we? I could be myself, and you loved me, properly *loved* me. I'd never experienced that before. It was like our two broken souls were drawn to one another to heal together.'

He takes a moment to gather his thoughts, and I expect he's going to ask me what my old name was. But he doesn't. He takes my hand and kisses my knuckles.

'Everything is out in the open,' he says. 'No more lies.'

I stroke a fingertip gently down his cheek. 'I love you, Todd.'

'I love you, Jen.'

We kiss tenderly and snuggle down into the bed.

'We should tell Seth everything,' I say.

But Todd goes rigid. 'The only people who know about Jerry Ward are me, you and Natalie. And I want to keep it that way. We're not telling Seth about that. Or anyone, for that matter. I don't want the world to know I was abused as a child. I've dealt with the shame; it's in the past. I don't want to bring it all up again and have to deal with the trauma a second time. It would destroy me. Do you understand?'

'Yes, I understand,' I tell him, and I do. 'But one day I'd like to tell Seth about my past.'

'Okay. But probably not right now. You just dropped the bomb that I adopted him.'

'No, not right now,' I agree. Because my number one priority right now is to prise that poisonous snake off my son.

CHAPTER THIRTY

My alarm goes off at 6.30 a.m. I wake with a start, squirming with a distinct feeling that someone was standing over me. I turn on the light, but there's no one there.

Todd is already gone. He was up early to exercise and head to the club for a breakfast meeting. He'll be out for most of the day. It's a Thursday. Usually, I'd be heading into work. But it's still closed. Usually, Seth would be going into uni for all-day lectures and Lily would be going to her morning lectures. I know their schedules. I listen carefully for any movement in the house. But hear nothing. I quickly shower and change.

The knife is still on top of the chest of drawers where I left it. I pick it up. I feel safer with it in my hand, in case Lily attempts anything.

I hear the toilet in the bathroom down the hallway flushing. Seth and that bitch are awake. I head straight to Seth's room and knock on the door, tucking the long knife up my jumper sleeve.

There's some mumbling, and Seth opens the door. Behind him is Lily, sitting on the edge of the bed.

'Yes?' he asks sharply, still upset with me after last night's revelation.

'I just wanted to check how you are this morning,' I say.

He sighs. 'I'm not ready to talk to you just yet.'

'I understand.' I attempt to make my tone light. I glance over his shoulder at Lily. She stands and walks a few steps so she's right behind him. 'Are you and Lily going into lectures this morning?'

'I'm going in, but Lily's lecture got cancelled,' he replies.

Behind his back, so he can't see, Lily silently mimes shooting Seth in the head and blowing the smoke from the top of the 'gun' she's made with her fingers. She grins at me.

My breath is punched from my chest. My body does one big tremble.

Seth sees the shocked pallor of my face. 'You all right, Mum?'

I steady myself. 'Can I speak to you in private?'

He rolls his eyes but steps forward out of his room and closes the door.

What should I do? I need to get him away from that devil, but how? There's no way he'd come willingly if I told him that she'd threatened his life. He thinks he's in love with her. He thinks she's in love with him. They're engaged, for fuck's sake. He'd say I'd imagined it.

The only other option is to force him. Pull this knife out of my jumper sleeve and hold it to his chest so he'd come with me. But the idea makes me judder. I'd essentially be kidnapping my own son using the threat of violence. Would it be worth it to get him away from her? Would he understand eventually that I was doing it to save his life? But where would we go? And for how long? I'd be holding him against his will. He'd think I was mad and still had it in for his girlfriend for no reason. Everyone would think I'd gone insane. And he's stronger than me – would he attempt to overpower me to escape? Would we struggle, would I hurt him?

How can I threaten my own son with a knife? I can't do it.

Maybe I should barge in and threaten Lily with it – hold it to her neck and get her to admit to everything, leave the house, promise to stay away from us forever. And then what? Lily would act innocent, scared. Seth would no doubt go to the police about me, worried for his girlfriend. And I'd look bonkers.

Maybe that's what Lily wants. To make me do extreme things to get me put away.

I take a deep breath. 'Do you fancy skipping uni today to spend a bit of time with your dear old mother? We could go anywhere and do anything that you like.'

He looks at me like I've just spoken to him in Latin. In normal circumstances, there's no way I'd ever ask him to skip his lecture because I know he loves his course. He'll likely be one of the few students at the end of the year who will have a one hundred per cent attendance record. It's a desperate attempt to keep him with me and away from *her* for the day.

I continue, 'A bit of mother-son bonding time? What do you reckon?'

He shakes his head firmly. 'No, Mum.'

'Just know I love you very, very much, my darling boy. And no matter what, I have your back. Look after yourself today, okay? Make sure you're around people, not just... Lily, okay? Call me if you need me, for anything, however small, and I'll be there as fast as I can.'

He frowns at me.

I hold out my arm for a hug, keeping the arm with the knife up my sleeve hanging by my side and slightly behind me. It's a weird angle to go in at, but I'm sure he's found this entire exchange weird, and he doesn't seem to notice. He hugs me reluctantly, turns and heads back into his room.

I see Lily waiting for him. He goes past her, and she reaches out to hold his hand. It's a tender gesture, but she smirks at me while she's doing it.

'Didn't you say your mother was called Natalie, Lily?' I ask.

Seth turns.

'No,' Lily says, her sickly-sweet voice tinged with confusion.

'Why?' Seth asks.

I shrug. 'Oh, no reason.' But there is a reason – now Lily knows I'm on to her, that I'm not giving up without a fight. 'See you later on.'

I leave quickly, grab my coat and car keys, exit the house and jump in my car.

As soon as the car door shuts, I yell. Roar at the top of my lungs and slam my palms onto the steering wheel. It goes against everything in my mother's bones to leave my son with that murderous stranger in my home.

But it's only a matter of time before I expose her. I have a plan.

Following discreetly in my car, I watch Seth drive on his own to his campus, park up and enter the university building. Then I drive straight to Bevois Mansions. I park down the road and stare at the apartment block. The waft of weed worms its way into my car. The vibe of this run-down housing estate puts me on edge. People stare brazenly at me as they pass the car and groups of teens with hoods up and bandanas covering their faces slouch by pushing bikes.

The building has eight floors and probably at least sixteen apartments.

And in one of them is Natalie Owens.

Lily's mother must be behind all this. She's the missing link that connects everything.

She's been released from jail and is back in Southampton. She's sent her daughter to infiltrate our family. She wants revenge because Todd left her in jail for eighteen years without coming forward or visiting her or replying to any of her letters. Or perhaps she's jealous of me and wants Todd back. Yes. And that's why I'm the target and not Todd.

I make sure my car doors are locked and pull out my phone. I google Natalie. But there's nothing about her release. The media seem to have lost interest in her, in her story, after she was jailed. Apart from that book, there's not been anything reported on her for ten years.

I put my phone away and stare at the building again. I'll knock on every door, break it down or smash a window. I'm not about to give up now. Not when my son is in the clutches of that fraudster. I'll make Natalie call her child off my child. We can deal with this mother to mother.

I still have the knife with me. I get out of the car, lock it, unzip my coat and hold the knife behind one side. I stride confidently up to the entrance doors of Bevois Mansions, Block 3.

The large dog jumps out at me and snarls. The man follows, stepping out of the shadows and blocking my path.

Shit.

The way in had looked clear from the car.

He folds his arms and glares at me. The dog barks, pulling at the chains that keep it tethered to the railings by the doors.

'Hi again,' I say with a big smile, hoping to disarm him with politeness. 'I'm just going up to see Natalie. Natalie Owens.'

He looks me up and down. 'No one here by that name.'

'Ah yes, you might know her by a different name. She's blonde, blue eyes, late thirties. Very pretty.' I take a step forward. I just need to edge past him.

But he blocks me, leans forward so his face is inches from mine. My hands go clammy, and a nest of spiders writhes in my belly. I fight the instant urge to run.

'Stay off my patch, bitch. Stay away from everyone in it. They're all under my protection. Fuck with them, you fuck with me. Understand?' He leans back and jerks his chin in the direction of my car. 'Get the fuck out of here.'

But I'm not giving up.

I pull the knife on him.

'No,' I say defiantly.

Surprise flickers across his features. But his expression hardens. 'You pull a knife on me then you'd better be ready to use it.'

I stand my ground, raise the knife a fraction so he knows I'm serious. 'I'm going inside. Get out of my way.'

He steps aside.

I move towards the doors. The dog lunges and snaps at my ankles. I dodge out of the way. The man takes full advantage of my lapse in focus. He seizes my wrist, bends my arm behind my back and pushes up. I scream in agony. He twists my wrist. The knife drops and clatters on the ground. He plants a large black boot on top of it.

He shoves me away and picks it up.

I stagger back, fall over my own feet and land in a heap on the pavement.

He points the knife at me. The dog barks and bares its teeth.

I scramble backwards, get to my feet and run for my car. His dark cackle follows me.

I fumble with my keys, finally let myself in and speed away.

What do I do now?

My heart races, my wrist throbs where he twisted it and there's an excruciating pain in my lower back and left hip where I fell.

I drive chaotically for fifteen minutes, breathing shallowly, terror pulsing through my veins. I come to a stop at a red traffic light at a busy crossroads and take a few deep breaths.

A flashing light catches my attention in the rear-view mirror. A large pick-up truck is hurtling at speed towards the back of my car, headlights flashing, horn blaring.

A whoosh of adrenaline floods my senses: it's not going to stop in time.

I catch a glimpse of the driver – Lily's intimidating neighbour.

The pick-up shunts into the back of my car, bumping it into traffic.

Fuck!

Vehicles beep, swerve, emergency stop. I brace myself for a horrible collision, but by some kind of miracle nothing hits my car.

The traffic lights change. It's my right of way. I put the car into gear and drive. A hideous metallic scraping and thumping noise comes from the back – no doubt the bumper hanging off – and there's a heaviness dragging at the car, but I put my foot down nonetheless.

The pick-up truck follows, slamming into the back of my car whenever I'm forced to slow down.

In the rear-view mirror, I see the man's face is one of pure joy. Each time he bumps me he laughs maniacally.

I weave in and out of traffic on The Avenue, a long and straight road heading out of the city and towards the motorway.

He tails me. I can't shake him off.

In a split-second decision, I head in the direction of nearby city Portsmouth. Southampton and Portsmouth have always had a bitter rivalry when it comes to football, with violent clashes between fans over the years.

But also with gangs.

I join the motorway, cut across two lanes into the fast lane and increase my speed. The pick-up accelerates to keep up, swinging into the middle lane and jerking into my lane in an attempt to make me steer into the central barrier.

Everything in my body clenches. Terror pulsates. Even though it's damaged, the car responds to my foot pressed hard on the accelerator pedal. I've never driven a car this fast, and I'm teetering on the edge of control.

The pick-up veers in front of me and slams on the brakes. I brake, swerve into the middle lane, lose control and the car spins.

Fuck, fuck, fuck.

Brakes squeal. Cars scatter out of my way.

The pick-up slows to watch.

My car hits a pothole. I'm about to tip and spin over and over until there's nothing left of my car. Until it's crushed into a little box, with me in the middle, broken and in pieces.

I cling to the steering wheel, turn into the spin, slow the speed, gain control.

And come to a stop facing in the right direction.

My lungs scream with the lack of air.

The pick-up truck is a few cars behind me, crawling in the fast lane, obviously waiting to see what happens.

But I didn't crash. I'm not dead yet.

Lily's neighbour speeds up to reach me, undertaking and weaving in and out of lanes. Cars are strewn across the motorway, stopped in haphazard positions. But no one appears to have collided.

I put the car into gear. And tear off towards Portsmouth.

The pick-up follows.

But as I reach the very outskirts of Southampton, edging ever closer to the boundary of its rival city, the pick-up lurches across three lanes to take the exit.

I called it right: Lily's neighbour won't set foot in this city. He's part of a gang that's not welcome here.

I slow right down and drive sensibly, turning off the motorway and into a lay-by on the main route into Portsmouth.

It takes a few seconds for me to prise my stiff, bone-white fingers from around the steering wheel. I kill the engine and breathe. In and out. In through the nose, out through the mouth.

Chased out of Southampton. Will he be waiting for me to return? How long will he wait?

Just breathe.

I'm not sure how much time passes as I calm my body

down, grateful that I didn't just die in a gruesome road traffic collision.

My phone pings and brings me back to the present.

Seth has messaged in the family WhatsApp group.

It's Halloween and time for our annual spooky shindig! Don't think it's not happening because of a little revelation about my biological father yesterday.

He ends the message with an emoji winky face. My heart swells with love for my beautiful son. He'll get over it, process it and see the bigger picture – he has a father who loves him dearly. We always make a big deal for Halloween, play silly pranks on each other, wear our favourite costumes and put up decorations.

Normally, I would've decorated the house by now. But that hasn't been a priority this year, for obvious reasons.

My phone pings again. Seth has messaged me direct.

Mum, get back by 7 p.m., no earlier. Lily and I will sort everything. Love you xxx

I reply with a thumbs up emoji. Then add:

I love you too, very much xxx

My head drops into my hands. I sob desperately. Howl. Snot streams.

What the hell am I going to do?

Maybe I can draw Natalie out by threatening Lily somehow? But how would that interaction even play out? I kidnap Lily and get her to contact her mother to organise a meeting? I'm not some kind of criminal mastermind to plot all this. And would it even work? Natalie is violent, would she turn on me?

No.

There's only one way I can see: to save my family, I need to tell the police everything.

We'll get Todd's best friend and chief constable of the Hampshire and Isle of Wight Constabulary over later and tell him about our past in front of Seth and Lily. Rohan will have no option but to investigate Lily and her connection to Natalie Owens. Todd and Seth will know the truth about her, learn all her lies, see her for what she really is – a manipulative game-player and fake. And Lily won't be able to threaten me with revealing my secrets when they are already all out there in the world. And Natalie will have nothing on Todd either.

And then this little game of theirs will come to an abrupt halt.

But, almost two decades later, would Todd go to jail? Would I?

It would be a big scandal – a local legend and his wife thrown in jail eighteen years after they both committed terrible crimes – the famous footballer helping to cover up a murder and his wife almost killing her ex and leaving him for dead.

It would tarnish Todd's name, that's for sure. I'm not famous; I don't earn a living off my good reputation. But the victim was his abuser, and the murderer was caught and put in jail where she belonged, so would people understand what he did?

Would they understand what I did? Saved my life and that of my son by fighting back? And changing my name and hiding so I could give Seth a good life away from an abusive man and an awful family?

I get out of the car and go for a very shaky walk up and down the lay-by, needing to stretch my tense legs, needing to get some air. There's a footpath sign hidden behind some bushes, and I take it. There's no one around. I wander down the overgrown footpath, stare into space, linger aimlessly, wander some more.

The dilemma goes round and round in my head – save myself and my husband from jail by keeping our secrets, or save my son by confessing all?

What is best for Seth? Lily with her claws in him and threatening his life, or him free from her and safe but with both his parents behind bars?

My legs move automatically while my thoughts whirl. My brain attempts to search out different routes, different ideas on how to stop the evil mother-daughter duo once and for all.

But it always circles back to confessing all to the police.

I choose Seth, of course, and I know Todd will too. I've saved Seth once before, and I will again. I'm fully prepared to sacrifice myself and my life to save my family.

Todd will understand. He loves Seth more than anything. He doesn't know the full extent of Lily's evil, but he will as soon as Rohan investigates. Jail for us but freedom and safety for Seth – that's what is important. And once Rohan looks deeper into Lily then Simon will be released, my charity reinstated and the shelters reopened for all the women in desperate situations, like I was eighteen years ago.

On a wider part of the deserted path, I pause and dial Todd. He answers almost immediately.

'Hey, where are you?' he asks. 'Your reception is patchy.'

'I'm somewhere near Portsmouth,' I reply.

'How come?'

I debate whether to tell Todd about Lily's neighbour, the terrifying car chase, the almost accident. But I don't. I simply don't have the energy.

'Doesn't matter…' I mumble vaguely. 'I've been thinking, and we need to tell the police about our pasts. Admit everything.'

'No, Jen,' Todd explodes.

His vehemence takes me by surprise.

He softens his tone. 'No, Jen. I do not want to do that. Why would you even say that?'

'It's to save Seth from Lily.'

The fury returns. 'You're talking absolute nonsense. The only person Seth needs saving from right now is you.'

'But—'

'End of discussion!'

The line goes dead. I sigh. I'll just have to make him understand.

A dog barking attracts my attention. I can see the path in front of me for about ten metres before it goes behind bushes.

A man dressed in black with a large dog turns onto the path, heading straight towards me.

My chest constricts. It's Lily's neighbour and his huge dog.

She must've put some kind of tracking app on my phone. He's tracked me, parked up nearby and was creeping up on me from the other direction, from wherever this path leads.

I turn on my heel and run.

I glance over my shoulder. He's running too.

He bends and lets the dog off the lead. It charges after me.

CHAPTER THIRTY-ONE

I pull the keys out of my bag while barrelling my way through the overgrown bushes. I open the car, jump in and slam the door just as the dog leaps up. It scrapes its claws on the door, barking and leaving drool on the window.

The man, with my knife in his hand, thunders towards me.

I shoot out of the lay-by without looking and speed deeper into the heart of Portsmouth. I drive, drive, drive, my heartbeat racing as fast as my speedometer.

What would've happened if he'd caught me? Would he have knifed me and left me for dead down that path to be discovered by a dog walker days, weeks, months later? That route is clearly not well used.

While driving, I turn off my phone. Hopefully that'll stop the tracking app. I keep glancing in my mirrors, but there's no sign of the pick-up. I follow signs into the city centre and park up in the middle of a busy shopping area. I get out of my car, slip in and out of shops, hide in crowds, keep looking around me, check if I'm being followed.

As I'm leaving Marks & Spencer a prickle passes across my

shoulders and all the hairs on the back of my neck stand on end. Someone's behind me who shouldn't be.

Fuck.

I take two steps out of the shop and spin around.

'Watch out,' the woman grumbles, head down, as she almost stumbles right into me.

Miranda.

Her face clocks mine. She freezes. 'What the hell?' she hisses.

'Why are you following me?' I demand loudly so that everyone around – including the security guard standing just inside the shop doors – can hear.

She reels back. 'I'm not following you, you crazy cow.'

'Bullshit. What are you doing here?'

'Shopping,' she spits back. 'What are *you* doing here?'

'You're in on this, aren't you?'

'In on what, exactly?' Her expression darkens. 'You've lost the plot!' She waves at the security guard. 'Hey, excuse me! This woman is harassing me. I need help.'

The security guard comes forward, speaking on his walkie-talkie.

'I'm not harassing you. You're following me!'

'Ladies,' the security guard says, an edge of warning in his tone as if he really, *really* doesn't want to deal with this kicking off. There's a crowd gathering, all whispering and pointing at us and blocking the entrance to the shop.

'Get out of my way.' Miranda attempts to barge past me.

But I block her. 'Why are you following me? Tell me!'

'I'm not. You just happened to be in front of me. I want to go to the pharmacy and then head home.'

'How do you know Lily?' I insist.

Her face screws up in confusion. 'Who?'

'Why are you doing this to me?' I shout.

'Leave me alone!' She shuffles around the guard and pushes through the crowd.

I'm not sure why I do it. Why I don't just let her go. But I lunge after her, grab her coat and yank her back.

She trips, falls hard on her bum, lets out a little 'Ow!' The crowd collectively gasps. Guilt at hurting her cuts through my tunnel vision, and I bend towards her to help her up, but she mistakes my gesture and screams in my face, 'Get away from me! You're insane!'

The security guard pulls me back. Miranda shakes her coat out of my grip and scrambles out of my reach. A man in the crowd helps her to her feet. She hurries off, wiping a tear from her face.

'Ma'am, why don't you come with me for a minute,' the guard says.

And I do. We sit in his little office out the back of Marks & Spencer and he gives me a cup of tasteless tea. He talks to me, but I don't really hear. Something about how he won't get the police involved but I can't be causing a scene like that again. How I seem like a normal, sensible, reasonable woman and that I'm just having a bad day. It happens to the best of us. Things wind him up too. Perhaps I should consider anger management classes...

I let him talk. I slowly sip the tea. I figure if I'm in here then I'm not out there with the man and his dog going to jump out at me at any moment. My head swirls with thoughts of Miranda. She must've hated me from the start because she sensed Simon had feelings for me. But I acted impulsively just now. She isn't part of this. I'm sure of it.

The security guard tells me I can leave. I dilly-dally for as long as possible until he – politely but firmly – orders me to get out of his office. I thank him and tell him he's a very nice man.

Hours have passed. I turn my phone back on. It pings with a string of direct messages from Seth.

Wanted to share some exciting news this evening, but don't know how you'll react, so I'm telling you in advance so that you can process and calm down and be excited when you get home.

You're going to be a grandma! Lily is pregnant! Huge surprise, but we're over the moon.

I forgive you for not telling me sooner that Dad adopted me, so I'm hoping you can be cool about this.

Love you, Mum. Let's have a wicked Halloween party to celebrate.

Pregnant!

My heartbeat, only just back to normal, soars sky-high again. I need to stop this game *right now*.

I message Todd:

We need to admit everything to the police. And then Lily will have nothing on us. I know you don't understand right now, but you need to trust me on this. We should call Rohan and get him to come over tonight. We will tell him everything in front of Seth and Lily. It's the only way. It's to save our family. It's to save Seth. We need to do this together.

The two ticks turn blue, and '*Todd is typing*' shows on the screen. I'm surprised when I notice the time is 5 p.m. – the entire day has raced by in a blur. No return message comes through. He's changed his mind to think about it rather than a knee-jerk response.

I send him another message:

I'm heading home now. I'll be back around six. Are you home already? If you're still at the club, then head home now, and we'll be back around the same time. I know Seth said not to get back until seven, but we need to talk.

I wait to see if he'll read the message, but he doesn't. His last seen time is a minute before I sent it. I wait two more minutes to see if he comes back online. When he doesn't, I set off home.

For the entire journey, I'm hyper-vigilant for the pick-up truck. But I don't see it.

A carved pumpkin with a flickering candle inside greets me on the porch. I open the front door and step inside the house. There are no lights on, but there are lit candles lining the hallway. All the usual Halloween decorations are up in the usual places. Seth must've done it. Music blares from the kitchen – *The Addams Family* theme tune. The party is in full swing.

But I'm about to burst the party mood. I'm ready to call Rohan. I'm ready for Todd and me to tell all about our pasts to ensure Seth's future.

I pause on the threshold of the kitchen. It's lit with candles too, and in the dim light, it takes me a moment to see Todd sitting on a dining chair in the space between the dining table and the kitchen island. An odd place to put the chair. He's wearing his favourite Count Dracula Halloween costume, the one he gets out every year.

My eyes adjust. He's tied up, his arms behind him. There's a gag stuffed in his mouth.

Next to him on a chair slumps Seth in his beloved frog costume. He doesn't appear to be tied up. He appears to be unconscious.

For the briefest moment, I think they're pranking me.

But Todd's eyes tell me otherwise. They bulge out of his skull, eyelids drawn right back. He's frightened.

He flicks his gaze urgently from me to a space next to the doorway where I'm standing and back again.

I understand his message: *there's someone dangerous there.* I take a small step in and look.

CHAPTER THIRTY-TWO

It's her.

I'm too late.

Lily sneers at me as she strides over to where Seth is slumped on a dining chair. She brandishes a knife and holds the sharp tip to Seth's neck.

'Welcome to our hellish Halloween party. Come on in,' she says.

I take a few steps into the kitchen, not taking my eyes off her.

She's wearing a devil costume: red dress, long red gloves, horns on her head and a pointed spade-shaped tail. A small red trident sits next to a syringe, which still has some liquid in it, on the dining table.

She nods towards the syringe then indicates Seth. 'This one will be out for a while yet.' She nods towards Todd. 'That dick-head was so eager to get tied up when I told him it was a prank for Halloween. Seth was still in the shower, and I said it would give him a right fright when he came down.' She puts on a mockingly childish voice. 'How could Todd resist his son's sweet and innocent girlfriend?'

Todd snorts and jerks in his chair, attempting to shout through his gag and break free of his bindings. But it's no use. Whatever Lily has used to tie his wrists behind his back and onto the chair isn't budging.

Lily continues, 'And when Seth came down, I met him at the bottom of the stairs and told him I had a surprise for him. I asked him to close his eyes, led him to that chair and got him to sit. And stabbed that syringe in his neck. He was out like a light. And will have no idea what happened.'

My entire body goes heavy with a devastating regret. I shouldn't have left Seth with this bitch, should've trailed him all day, should've forced him to come with me. What was I thinking? I let this snake strike. But I can't dwell on that now. I need to focus on the current situation. I need to save my family.

'What do you want?' I say shakily. 'Please don't hurt Seth or Todd. If you need to hurt someone, hurt me. Leave them out of it, please.'

'Shut up,' Lily snaps.

But I'm not done begging. 'I'll do anything, please.'

'I said, shut the fuck up!'

I chew my lip. She's enjoying having the upper hand. She looks taller almost. Pumped up.

She continues, 'I know all about the murder of Jerry Ward that he' – she points at Todd – 'committed.'

My jaw hangs open. *Todd murdered the old man?*

Lily glares at Todd, her face screwing up in utter disgust. 'He told Natalie she had to prove her love for him by helping him to murder his junkie mother's paedophile boyfriend. The man who'd abused him for years as a boy. Natalie was blind with love and did it. She flirted with Ward at a pub, and Ward invited her back to his house. When she was there, she secretly opened the door to Todd. And he was the one who killed Ward, not Natalie. But it landed her in jail for nearly twenty years. She never dobbed Todd in because she loved him so much.'

Todd attempts to talk through his gag again, but it comes out in unintelligible grunts. He shakes his head desperately.

'None of that is true,' I say. 'Todd is not a murderer. Natalie did it in an attempt to win Todd back after they'd split up. She lured Todd to Ward's property after she'd killed Ward and got Ward's blood all over Todd. Todd tried to help her, and together they cleaned the place up. Except they missed a fingerprint.'

Lily snorts. 'What a load of bullshit. Todd deliberately left that fingerprint so Natalie would get caught. He knew exactly what he was doing.'

'That's not the truth,' I insist.

'What do you know?' she yells. 'You weren't there, were you?'

'And neither were you,' I reply, and a surge of power bolsters me. She has nothing to say for a moment, so I press on. 'You're Natalie's daughter, aren't you?'

'Woo, you worked it out. Well done,' Lily says sarcastically.

'Who is your father?' I ask.

Lily glowers at me. 'I have no idea. Natalie never told me. I doubt she knew either. But Natalie was so obsessed with him' – she points at Todd – 'that she named me Frankie.'

Todd shifts in the chair. Frank is his middle name.

Lily continues, 'I was Frankie for all of three hours, before social services took me off her. And then I was renamed Freya and had that name for eighteen years. And now I'm Lily.'

'Natalie is out of prison and living in the flat at Bevois Mansions. That's what all of this is about, isn't it?'

But Lily laughs. She makes an incorrect buzzer noise as if I'm on some game show. 'Wrong!' She shakes her head. 'Natalie is dead.'

That revelation thrashes my body like an unexpected wave, and I struggle to keep my balance. 'Did you kill your mother?'

Lily looks affronted, as if she can't believe I'd ask that.

'No,' she snaps. 'When I was seventeen, I did some digging,

hacked some confidential files and found my biological mother. It was a shock that she was a notorious murderer, that's for sure. But I went to visit her in prison. She was months from being released but dying from cancer. She'd dreamed of me finding her since I'd been ripped from her arms as a newborn. We talked and talked. They let me stay with her for longer than the usual visiting times because she was near the end.'

Lily's face crumples with sadness. 'She's the only person who has ever loved me for me. I'd only just found her and only saw her three times. Then she died, still behind bars.'

Her face just as quickly hardens. 'I made her a deathbed promise. I promised to make you suffer and kill you. Natalie told me Todd would've been with her if it hadn't been for you. They were about to get married. And then you swanned in and stole him off her.'

I frown – no loving, sane mother would ask their child to kill someone for them. 'She manipulated you, Lily. She didn't love you. She's used you to carry out her revenge—'

'Shut up,' Lily yells at me before I can go on. She glares at Todd. His cheeks are bright red from all the exertion of trying to break free and shout through his gag. 'My mother loved you so much, Todd. But I don't love you. I hate you. You made my mother take the blame for a murder she didn't commit and let her rot in jail without so much as a letter. So, you die too.'

Todd jerks in his chair so violently he almost tips over into Seth. He stares at his son and at me. He shakes his head. I know what he's communicating.

'Seth hasn't done anything,' I insist. 'Let him go. Please.'

'Ha, nope. Ickle Sethy here is mine now. To manipulate, torture, make suffer. He's so in love with me, it's sickening. He'd do anything for me. Take the rap for a murder? Yeah, he'd do it. Just like Natalie took the blame for Todd.'

'Todd did not murder Jerry Ward,' I say adamantly. 'Natalie murdered Jerry Ward.'

'You can't handle the fact that you've been married to a murderer all this time, can you?'

I shake my head. Todd's eyes plead with me, *it's not true, you have to believe me*. I turn back to Lily. I need to keep her talking, delay whatever she has planned and try to work out what to do. Perhaps Todd will break free. Or Seth will wake up. Or someone will come round, maybe some trick-or-treaters will see the light coming from the windows and buzz the gate, or perhaps Rohan will come for an impromptu visit and let himself in... I'm clutching at straws. And I know it.

'You plan to kill us and frame Seth for our murders?' I say.

'What? No! Much worse than that.' She points at her outfit. 'I am the devil, after all.' She cackles. 'Here's what's going to happen. You kill Todd tonight and go to jail. Seth and I will get married and, as the dutiful mummy's boy that he is, he'll visit his murderer mother for all the years that you are incarcerated. I'll make his life a misery, of course, but we'll live here in this fancy house. I'll fake a few more pregnancies and miscarriages and dash his hopes of becoming a father, just to break his heart over and over.'

'You'd do that? Why?'

'To make *you* suffer! I promised my mum. You'll scream until you're blue in the face about how I'm lying and faking and blah blah, but he won't believe you. Because everyone will think you're deranged.'

'You don't need to do this. Your mother is dead. You can break that promise, you don't need to live your life bound to a woman who never loved you.'

But Lily ignores my pleas, relishing all the ways she's devised to torture me for her mother. 'Better for Seth to live another twenty years than die at eighteen, wouldn't you say?'

'Yes, of course...' I mumble. The thought of Seth no longer being in this world at any age shreds my soul into pieces.

Lily smirks. 'But the day before you get released from

prison, Seth will suffer a terrible, fatal accident. And you'll be all alone. And one day, I'll catch up with you. You won't know when. But I'll always be watching you, I'll always be crushing any joy or happiness in your life, and, when you're least expecting it, I'll strike. And I'll make it a long drawn out, painful demise.'

'Don't do this. You're young and have your whole life ahead of you.'

'I promised my mother I'd make you suffer, and that's exactly what I'm going to do.'

'And if I don't agree to murder my husband?'

Lily shrugs, as if it's obvious. 'Then both Todd and Seth die, right now.'

'Please, Lily, let's stop this. Walk away. We won't tell anyone. Just walk out of this house and don't look back.'

'Certainly not. When I make a plan, I execute that plan. I don't walk away! I finish what I start. I tick things off. Get stuff done. Your choice is: Todd dies, Seth lives. Or, Todd dies, Seth dies. Either way, Todd is taking his last breaths.'

I desperately hold out my hands to implore Lily. 'Your mother wanted revenge; I can understand that. But you are not your mother. You're taking on her anger when you don't need to.'

'Wrong! I'm fucking angry. All this' – she gestures around the large room – 'should've been *mine*. Natalie should've married Todd, and *I* should've been the golden child adopted by Todd, growing up in this wealth, in this house, with a rich and famous dad, with everything I could ever want. But instead, it was you and your fucking brat.' She grabs Seth's hair and yanks back his head.

'No! Don't hurt him!'

Seth's eyes roll up in his head. He's completely out of it – so helpless, vulnerable, lifeless.

'My mother went to jail, and I got shipped off into the care system. First sent as a baby to a family who kept me until age eight, when they decided they'd had enough of me and "returned" me like an unwanted gift. Then I spent the next eight years in and out of foster families and hostels. No one wanted to adopt the nerdy, computer-obsessed, weird kid. I was sent to meeting after meeting with prospective parents and was always rejected. I had to fend for myself from sixteen. I've never had a cosy family. But I should've done. You and your child stole that from me. And you,' she points at Todd, 'manipulated my mother into helping with a murder and deliberately left that fingerprint so the police would trace her and put her away because you had no further need of her.'

Todd shakes his head.

I sense Lily is reaching the end of her tether. 'You must see that Natalie has manipulated you into believing that story—'

Lily shouts to silence me. 'Enough talking! Let's do this. Pick up that knife, Jen.'

But I don't move. 'How do you expect to get away with this?'

Lily's smug face is sickening. 'Your fingerprints are all over that syringe. Very easy to lift them and plant them when you know how and have the right stuff purchased from the dark corners of the internet. And I know how to beat myself up. You see that glass? I'll smash that over my head and fall so I knock my head on the edge of that table. And you know I'll do it. So then it'll just be you still conscious, with Todd dead, Seth drugged and me out cold. What version of events do you think the police will believe? Especially when Seth eventually wakes up and tells them that recently you've been losing your mind. And then they'll find all the evidence on your laptop of you purchasing the sedatives.'

Terror slithers into every last crevice of my body. I watched Lily punch herself in the face with zero hesitation, and I know, without a doubt, that she'll harm herself and throw herself against that table. She's unhinged. She'll go through with everything she's saying. It's not a threat. She's telling me how it's going to be. She's planned all this out meticulously and not left anything to chance.

'Pick up the fucking knife. Now,' Lily yells at me.

CHAPTER THIRTY-THREE

'No,' I reply.

Lily presses the knife tip into Seth's neck. His skin dents but doesn't break.

'Stop,' I yell. 'You won't hurt him, you can't!'

'You wanna bet?' Lily replies. She picks up Seth's hand and, without a flinch, slices the knife down the palm. Blood gushes from the wound. Seth doesn't stir.

I lurch forward, arms outstretched, desperate to go to him, to soothe, to stop the blood, the pain. *My boy! My poor boy!*

'No closer,' she yells, halting me in my tracks. She presses the knife tip, now smeared in his blood, back to his neck.

I stop, hold up my hands.

'Stab Todd with that knife. Or Seth dies right now. What's preferable to you, Victoria Prince?'

The use of my old name sharpens my focus. The last time I owned that name, I had to do something drastic, something violent, to save Seth. He's my only child, my flesh and blood. He is not dying tonight. I pick up the knife and head over to Todd.

My husband is staring at me with tears in his eyes, shaking

his head and grunting through his gag. My heart shatters at what he knows I'm about to do. He knows I have no choice. His entire body tenses. Snot flows from his nose. He's weeping, resolved, maintaining steady eye contact. He wants to look me in the eye as I do it, as I knew he would. He knows I'm doing this for our son. He'd do the same. He knows I love him and will always love him.

I heave, blink back tears, steady myself.

And wink.

Lily doesn't see.

I pray he remembers.

He raises his arm ever so slightly, to expose his armpit. This was a Halloween prank we did years ago to fool Seth. With a fake knife, of course. I stabbed Todd in his armpit. He squeezed tomato ketchup everywhere. His black Count Dracula cape hid the knife angle, and it looked as if I'd buried the blade deep into his flesh.

This has to work.

'I'm so sorry,' I whisper to him, for Lily's benefit.

I stab him.

But before my knife can wedge in his armpit, I'm shoved forward so forcefully that I land face down and all the breath is knocked from my lungs. I lose my grip on the knife.

Lily gasps behind me. 'You're meant to be dead,' she stammers.

I frantically suck down some oxygen and muster the energy to flip myself over.

'Penny?' I say.

Just as Lily blurts, 'Mum?'

But the woman ignores us both and kisses Todd on the tip of his nose. 'I saved your life,' she says to him. 'You're mine forever now.'

If Todd didn't have the gag on, he looks as if he'd be vomiting everywhere.

She turns and sits on Todd's knees, wriggling her bottom back into his crotch.

Penny looks completely different. Gone is all the black. She has long, naturally blonde hair and blue eyes. Penny sees my confusion.

'Wig and contact lenses.' She points to her nose. 'Nose job, fillers. I got a new name and a new face when I left prison. Daddy helped me. All the rest of the family disowned me and didn't want anything to do with my daughter, but I was always a daddy's girl. He bent over backwards to help me when I got out.'

I'm frozen on the floor. I can't stop gawping at her. My colleague, who I trusted and whose company I enjoyed, is Natalie Owens. Nausea swirls in my gut, and I swallow back bile.

Lily makes a mewling, painful noise, and Penny's attention flicks towards her. 'Of course *you* recognised me. My weirdo daughter.'

'You were dying of cancer. You *died* of cancer.' The shock turns Lily's face ashen, and she sucks in shallow, rapid breaths.

'I was in remission when you showed up at the prison hospital. You were so desperate for love. You reeked of it. Ugh. So, I told you what you wanted to hear. And then when the prison staff told me you'd asked to book another visiting slot with me, I told them to say I wasn't available anymore knowing you'd assume the worst.'

'But what about the longer visiting hours...?'

'A blow job for the right person in charge gets you all kinds of perks.'

'You let me believe you were dead?' Lily's voice comes out very small. She blinks back tears.

Penny – Natalie – laughs. 'Yes. I couldn't believe I had an insipid little computer nerd as a daughter. I made you make me a promise, but I never thought you'd go through with it. I wanted shot of you. Natalie Owens became Penny Nichols, and I got a job with that man-stealing whore over there' – she points at me – 'and set about learning everything about her. For the past year, I've been moulding myself into her to win back my man. Then you showed up and started causing chaos. Fine, I thought. No skin off my nose. I've been watching closely.'

Natalie's face darkens. 'But I told you not to hurt Todd. He's mine. He's always been mine and always will be. And here you are getting his whore to stab him. No. You're getting shut down, Frankie.'

Lily judders at the name. 'You've been watching me?'

'No, not just *you*.' Natalie sweeps her hand around the room. 'I've been watching everything. I have my own keys to this place. I copied that whore's keys when she wasn't looking while we were at work. And the stupid idiot uses the same PIN code for her phone as for the gate, typing it in right in front of me. I let myself in and out of this place all the time, to listen in, to watch over my Toddy here while he's sleeping.'

All those moments I felt like I was being watched. I was. By Natalie. I do a full-body shudder.

She points to me again. 'A number of times I came close to suffocating that one with a pillow so I could cuddle up next to my man.' Her nostrils flare in disgust. 'But I resisted. I knew I had to play the long game, to seduce him and get him to fall in love with me and out of love with her. I wouldn't get him any other way. So, while the whore has been at choir practice for the past few months, Todd and I have been meeting up for a drink in the Jockey Arms pub. The first meeting was a "chance encounter".' She chuckles. 'And then it was deliberate. And he was slowly falling for me, because I acted so much like her.'

Todd shakes his head frenziedly.

He'd sometimes go to the Jockey Arms when I was at choir practice to meet his ex-coach pal for an orange juice and a catch-up. I didn't think anything of it. *But he was meeting her?*

Natalie twists and puts her arm around his shoulders. 'Oh, Toddy, my love, you can't deny it. Another few weeks and you would've been mine.'

A fat tear rolls down his cheek. I catch his gaze. And for once I can't tell what he's thinking.

Natalie licks the tear away and smacks her lips together. 'Mmm, you taste just as delicious as I remember. You had no idea I was once Natalie, did you? But I made myself irresistible to you.' She points at me. 'Thanks to you I learnt all about eighties cartoons and ThunderCats. I mean, sooo boring, but we had a long conversation about that, didn't we, my love.' She nuzzles her face into his neck. He recoils.

I gulp back the vomit that charges up my throat. I remember telling her the story about how we met. She told me how she'd met her girlfriend. We were opening up to one another, making conversation on a slow afternoon. How fooled I'd been by 'Penny'. I'm utterly stunned.

'And what about me?' Lily demands, her shock turning into anger.

'What about you? You promised to take care of the whore. You were doing that. I was quite enjoying watching this little show – the way you lured Todd and tied him up – *ha!* Brilliant. I was almost proud of you. But then you took it too far – planning for it to go on for *years*. I don't want to wait *years*. And then about to kill Todd! Well, it's the end for you. You are no longer required. You can piss off now. I'll take it from here.'

Natalie flicks her hand at Lily, dismissing her. She bends down and sweeps up the knife that I dropped. She stands and points it at me. In a voice like a news reporter, she says, 'Woman kills son and then herself while forcing husband to watch in bizarre murder-suicide.'

I'm rigid with fear. My eyes sweep the room for any kind of weapon, for anything to use to fight off this maniac. Natalie moves towards me.

'You lied to me,' Lily hisses. 'You never loved me. You never wanted me.'

Natalie tuts in annoyance at the interruption. She pauses her advance to glare at Lily. 'Are you still here? You're a freak. I don't love you. I don't want you. I told you to piss off. So, piss off. Go and crawl back into whatever tedious little hole you came out of.'

Lily's heartbreak is evident: her shoulders slump, her eyes go to her feet. She puts the knife she's holding on the table and steps dejectedly towards the door.

Natalie turns her attention back to me.

I kick out at her and attempt to stand, but my body betrays me in its sluggishness.

'Goodbye, whore,' Natalie says. 'I've been dreaming of this moment for eighteen years.'

I push off the floor and grab for the knife on the table. My fingers graze the hilt, and it spins out of my reach. Natalie thrusts her blade at my ribs, and I dodge back, the tip snagging the material of my top. She stabs again, quicker, more determined to find her mark. I scramble back, tipping over dining chairs. She comes after me, swiping. I push and shove and scream and attempt to grab hold of her wrists. She thrusts the knife in my side.

I brace myself for pain, but it doesn't come.

Lily is on Natalie's back, yanking her mother's hair in one hand. With the other, she stabs her in the neck with the syringe. Natalie swings and jerks, dropping the knife to grab Lily and attempt to pull her off. But Lily clings on. She pushes the plunger down all the way to the bottom.

'That amount will kill you in a few seconds, bitch.' Lily lets go and stands back.

Natalie slaps at the syringe, dislodging it and chucking it across the floor. She pitches towards her daughter and throws a punch that dies mid-swing. A flash of surprise dances across her face. She lurches backwards into Todd, knocking his chair.

His eyes go wide for a second before the chair tips sideways. There's a sickening *thump* as his head hits the side of the kitchen island and is flung back at an awkward angle.

I scream.

The chair, with Todd's limp body still strapped to it comes to a stop in a position where I can only see his feet and legs. He's not moving. Not making a sound.

Oh, fuck, no. It's as if one half of my soul is ripped from my body. Todd's shining bright light can't be extinguished from this world, it just can't.

'Todd!' I clamber up but Natalie ploughs into me, knocking me back down again.

She collapses in a heap in front of me.

Lily spits on her.

Natalie's eyes roll back in her head. She twitches twice and is still.

Lily roars. It's a guttural sound, like an animal celebrating the slaughter of an enemy.

She scans the room, the fury in her eyes burning. 'Now, all of you die,' she bellows.

She swipes the knife off the table and launches herself, blade-first, at Seth.

I spring up and shoulder-barge her away from my son. I headbutt her, and she stumbles backwards.

She steadies herself and comes at me with the knife.

But rage bubbles up and explodes. Damian's face flashes across my mind. His face when he was about to murder my son. An energy surges through me – I took down a six-foot-four man, I can take down this skinny teen.

Red clouds my vision.

We tussle, and I grab the handle of the knife. We thrash, grunt, spit, hiss. Two feral cats fighting for their lives.

I twist her wrist, and the knife drops.

And that is it. I punch her in the face, take out her feet and throw all my weight onto her. We drop to the floor. She yanks my hair, bites my arm, claws at my skin.

But I don't feel any pain.

All I know is I have to end this.

I punch and elbow and knee and pummel. This bitch is not getting up again.

She weakens, slows, grinds to a halt. She flops like a limp rag doll in my arms. But I don't trust her.

I pull my arm up for one final hit. To take her out for good. To save my family.

I strike, but my arm is wrenched back before it connects, and I'm dragged off Lily.

CHAPTER THIRTY-FOUR

'Mum! What are you doing?' Seth bellows, hauling me along the floor a few paces away from Lily.

My arms swing madly for that bitch, and my feet kick out. Seth uses all his body weight to restrain me.

'Mum,' he yells again.

This time his voice cuts through the rage trance I'm in. My arms drop, and I take in his face. My attention snaps back to him, my precious boy. He's safe. I reach up to touch his cheek.

But he drops me, turns and goes back to *her*, falling to his knees and cradling her beaten and bloody face in his arms. He reaches out and touches her belly, where he believes his unborn child is growing.

Lily groans, half-conscious, her eyes fluttering open and shut.

'Seth! You're awake, thank goodness,' I say.

'Yeah, I'm awake. You drugged me. And I wake up to see you beating the life out of my fiancée. And did you do this too?' He holds up his bleeding palm. His arm trembles, and I realise he's still a little woozy from whatever drug Lily gave him, slurring his words ever so slightly. He jiggles his torso to revive his body, forces his eyes open wider. 'You're insane. Stay the fuck away from us.'

I scramble up, my entire body sore from the fight, and take a step forward. 'No, Seth, that's not what happened. It might look that way, but that's not the truth.'

'Don't come any closer. I'm warning you. Take one step nearer and we'll be fighting – do you understand? Do you want to fight with me like you did her? Do you want to punch me until I'm no longer conscious? Is that what you want?'

I pause, holding up my hands. 'No, of course not, Seth. I don't want to fight you. I saved you. From her. I love you.'

'You're psycho! You tied up Dad, stabbed me with a syringe of fuck-knows-what and went for her. You've hated her from the beginning. Were you going to murder her? Kill your own grandchild?'

'Lily isn't pregnant. She's evil!'

He shakes his head. 'You're the one who is evil.' It's then he notices the dead body. His fuzzy brain takes a moment to process what he's seeing. 'Who is that?' His voice is a few pitches higher than normal.

'Penny,' Lily mumbles before I can reply.

'Penny who you work with? Oh, Mum, what have you done?'

'It's not Penny. It's Natalie. Lily's mum. Well, technically it *is* Penny...' I stumble over my words trying to tell Seth everything all at once.

He holds up a hand. 'Please, stop talking.'

'Lily killed her!'

He shakes his head. 'Lily wouldn't hurt a fly.'

'She killed my bees!'

'Mum, please, you're delirious.'

'Seth – your father! He'll tell you the truth. He'll tell you who this woman really is and what Lily did. Lily manipulated you. She's made you believe a pack of lies. But I think... I think he might be...' I can't bring myself to say it.

Seth takes in Todd as if he hadn't, until that point, remembered he was there.

I hurry over to Todd.

'Stop,' Seth says. 'You go and stand over there, away from all of us.' He points to the far corner of the kitchen near the doorway.

I back away from Todd into the corner where Seth is pointing.

'Stay there,' Seth orders.

I nod.

Seth gently lays Lily's head down, steps over Natalie and rushes to his father, not taking his eyes off me.

'Dad?' he says as he checks his father. 'Dad?' he repeats, desperately. He checks his pulse, puts a hand over his mouth and nose, shakes him. 'Oh my god...' His voice cracks. Tears well in his eyes.

My world implodes.

Seth sobs once, wipes his face, turns to me. 'What have you done?'

'I... didn't... do... this,' I manage through choking emotion.

Lily groans and props herself up on her elbows. It's all she can manage. She forces her heavy eyes open to look at me.

'Your mother is crazy,' she says.

Seth stares at me. Sadness creeps across his face.

'She's sick in the head,' Lily continues. 'She tied Todd up, drugged you, got her colleague here and injected her with some lethal drug because of a mad idea that Todd is cheating on her with this woman on Wednesday nights when she's at choir. Then she went for Todd, told him he'd watched his mistress die and now it was his turn. Then she turned on me. It was awful. She planned to kill me and our baby too.' She gently rubs her belly. 'She said she wanted it to be just you and her again. We need to call the police. We need to restrain her somehow. She's having a massive mental health meltdown.'

I watch closely as surprise, confusion, then acceptance pass across Seth's face. Eventually he nods, agreeing with her.

'Thank... goodness... you... woke up when you did, Seth,' she mumbles with great effort, hamming up her injured state. She lifts her hand up and rests her knuckles against her forehead, as if having some kind of Victorian swoon.

Seth laps it up. He's still completely spellbound by her.

My legs give way, and I land in a heap on the floor.

He thinks I'm crazy. It's my word against hers. If I attempted to tell Seth about Jerry Ward and Natalie Owens now, he wouldn't believe me. He'd think I was rambling, delusional, making up a paranoid version of events.

No one will believe my side of the story. I'll be put in a secure unit for the rest of my life. Everything I say will be dismissed as the nonsensical blathering of a madwoman.

'Seth,' I beg. 'Please, you have to believe me. I love you so much. I only want the best for you. I was so happy that you had a girlfriend. But she's not who you think she is. She's lying to you. Don't believe the lies, please, Seth.'

'Shut up,' Lily hisses. 'We're sick of hearing all this bullshit, Jen. You murdered Todd and Penny right in front of me. Seth, we need to restrain her, call the police and an ambulance. Listen to me, baby. Use what she tied Todd up with.'

'I don't think we need to tie her up,' Seth says, still looking sadly at me.

'Seth, I know you love her but she's murdered two people. She's unpredictable and dangerous. We need to restrain her. You didn't see it – I did. She's insane. Please, do it for me.'

Seth nods, moves behind Todd to untie his hands. He looks down. Pauses.

Lily groans. 'Seth,' she says weakly. It's not even put on this time; she's barely conscious. My beating and her acting has taken it out of her.

Seth's face is unreadable. I channel all my love into the look I give him.

I understand, it says. *I understand that you believe her, that you'll condemn me without even realising. She's set you up so perfectly, and you're so trusting. I understand.*

Tears spring to my eyes. My future life spans out in front of me. I'm going to get taken away, charged with murder and put somewhere where I won't be a threat to others ever again. Perhaps with good behaviour I'll be permitted visitors. Perhaps my darling boy will visit me. Perhaps I'll still get to see him grow up from behind a glass screen in a secure visiting room. Better that than him dying tonight.

I take a very long, deep breath and resign myself to my fate. My son is alive. Ensnared by a liar, but alive. He'll marry Lily. They'll live here. Lily will get the life she always wanted in a fancy house. Seth will find joy. I have to believe that he'll be happy... perhaps not in his marriage, but in his work, in his hobbies...

Seth takes a step back.

He doesn't untie Todd's hands.

He doesn't go to Lily.

He comes over to me. And picks me up off the floor.

'Mum,' he says over Lily's whimpering. 'I believe you. Let's call the police.'

EPILOGUE

ONE YEAR LATER

It was the knot.

We're a family of sailors, spending time on Todd's powerboat, doing many a sailing lesson on the Solent and even spending three weeks in Croatia on a sailing boat one summer when Seth was still at school. We know knots. And as soon as Seth saw the chaotic way the rope around Todd's wrists had been tied, he knew I hadn't done it.

We're sitting next to each other on sunloungers around a large pool at a hotel in Fuerteventura. We needed a holiday after everything that happened.

Lily's Bevois Mansions flat was searched. It had been full of tech equipment and fast-food wrappers. It took the police a while to sift through all her data, but they soon discovered evidence to prove everything I told them. Turned out she was a bitcoin millionaire from running a ransomware-on-demand service. She'd hired out-of-work actors from London to pose as Kiah Wong, Hadley Perry and the two film crew, rented a dilapidated and rat-infested 'student' house and hired more actors to play her housemates to fool Seth. She'd paid deepfake specialists to create photos and videos of Todd and 'Gemma'. The police seized as many of her assets as they could find. It was confirmed she wasn't pregnant.

Her neighbour was arrested. Lily had made some of his criminal charges 'disappear', and he was repaying the favour by intimidating me on her orders. He chased me in my car, and was also the person hanging around outside my house on the night I stayed at a hotel and sitting at the café opposite my work dressed in a black outfit.

They looked into Lily's past, and she was telling the truth about Natalie, about her childhood known as Freya with an adoptive family and about the conveyor belt of foster homes and hostels. There was no aunt in Inverness. All three of her meetings with Natalie had been recorded. They were analysed and, although there was no sound, lip-reading experts confirmed Lily – or Frankie, as Natalie kept calling her – had made a deathbed promise to her mother to make me suffer and kill me for stealing Todd, for taking what should've been their lives in a lovely home. Natalie had completely manipulated Lily.

Penny Nichols was confirmed as Natalie Owens. Police found evidence that she'd been in our house many times, including a handprint on my bedside cabinet, strands of her hair in the cupboard under the stairs and even fingerprints on the steering wheel of my car and in Seth's bedroom.

I've not been able to sleep properly since, always jerking awake with the sense someone is standing over me. Or having vivid nightmares of Natalie hiding in my wardrobe or under my stairs about to jump out at me.

Todd survived. It was touch and go for days, but he pulled through.

He woke up and told the police everything about what happened in 2006: Natalie murdered Jerry Ward and lured him to Ward's house, and he helped her clean up. They reopened the investigation. Looked into everything again from a different perspective. Did not give him any kind of special treatment as a celebrity. But the estimated time of death was when Todd was with me on our first date. The police tracked down and interviewed people who had been working at the restaurant that night. Found old CCTV from a traffic camera that showed Todd's car driving towards Ward's house much later in the evening. Ward had died before Todd had arrived at his house, and there wasn't any evidence to suggest otherwise.

But, despite all the lies that Natalie fed Lily, Lily insisted that her mother's story was the correct version – Todd was the murderer, and Natalie had been framed for it.

Based on all the evidence, the police decided Todd was telling the truth.

Todd was given a short sentence for perverting the course of justice. Lily was charged with murder and attempted murder. And I was given community service for acquiring and using a false passport and fake documents. It turned out Norfolk Constabulary had stopped looking for me and closed the case when Damian had died in prison.

Todd admitted to me that he'd met with Natalie a few times.

'She told me her name was Nicole,' he'd said to me while lying in a hospital bed, his head still in bandages. 'I had no idea she was your colleague Penny. I bumped into her at the Jockey Arms and had a bad feeling. Something about her reminded me of Natalie. And I had to know if Nicole was Natalie. I knew that if Natalie was back in Southampton, it meant bad news for us. I had to keep her away from you and Seth. I should've put two and two together quicker. I should've told you. I'm sorry, Jen.'

It turned out that Todd wasn't the only one who'd thought there was something familiar about Penny. Natalie had followed me into the forest on the day that I'd been caught by Seth and Lily. And Miranda had been following her. Miranda Sanderson. Jerry Ward's daughter. She'd found his body.

Miranda had met 'Penny' on reception when she'd come in to meet Simon after work. And the hunch had been so strong that she'd come back to see her a second time when I'd been working. She'd followed Natalie back to my home in the middle of the night, seen her putting in the gate code and letting herself into the house. Miranda had returned, believing that was where Natalie was living, but I'd caught her. Bumping into Miranda in Portsmouth had been a coincidence, though – she had just been shopping on that day.

Miranda told police, 'You don't forget the face of your father's murderer. Nose job or not.' She hadn't been informed that Natalie was being released and, as she'd said, 'I couldn't believe she'd have the nerve to come back to Southampton after what she did. I had to confirm and then make a complaint.'

I'd had no idea that Natalie had been following me. I try not to think about it too much. I'd never leave the house otherwise.

Todd came clean to the media about his history and that he was a victim of child sexual abuse. He was ashamed and terrified for years to talk about it. But he reclaimed his story and has lots of charity work and sponsored fitness challenges planned to help others like him. He also gave a TV interview, set up by the PR gurus at his football club and signed off by the lawyers, all about what happened with Natalie.

He is more loved than ever by his fans. And by his wife and son.

Due to the media coverage and, unfortunately, my face splashed everywhere as Todd's wife, my parents and brother came crawling out of the woodwork scrounging for money. Not asking to be in Seth's life, or to make amends with me, just leeches, same as they always were.

Todd got the club's lawyers to deal with them. Slapped restraining orders on them and tied them up in legal knots that meant they could never contact us again without risking a jail term. They scurried straight back into their holes.

My husband makes his way back to us and plonks three drinks on the small table.

'Three strawberry daiquiris,' he says and puts one on the table nearest to Seth before settling himself on the lounger.

'Lovely,' I reply and take a noisy slurp. It's not even lunchtime and this is our second of the day. I snap a photo and text it to Simon.

Once the police had gone through Lily's computers, Simon was immediately released and the charity and shelters reopened. She'd done it all. Planted everything. She'd sent him that email he thought had come from me and then wiped it.

Rohan said to me that if she'd chosen to use her computer skills for good, she probably would've been working for the NCA by now tracking cybercriminals. But she'd never been encouraged or shown the right way.

Simon and I are good friends. I made it clear I don't want anything more than that. Todd is, and always will be, my everything. Simon is dating his neighbour, Everly, who was interviewed when he was arrested. It's going well. I'm pleased for him. I think she could be the perfect woman for him.

Next to me, Seth reads a book about peat, peatlands and the environmental problem with harvesting peat. He's enthralled, turning the pages like I would a gripping thriller. It took him a while to get over Lily, to process how she'd used him. He'd only woken up when he did because she'd made the slightest error in the amount of the drug she'd injected him with.

But, Seth being Seth, he's taken it in his stride, opting to immediately go to counselling sessions to help him work through it in a healthy way. He's grateful the truth about everything has come out. Todd and I told him absolutely everything about our past lives. No shame or embarrassment, no more lies. I told him if he wanted to meet his relatives in Norwich and Greece then I could try to arrange it. But he wasn't interested.

'You and Dad are my family, Mum. You guys are all I need,' he'd replied.

My heart had swelled with pure love. And we're closer than ever.

A woman about Seth's age walks past us. Her eyes go down to look at the book Seth is reading. He's oblivious to her presence.

'You're kidding me,' she says in an American accent. Seth squints up at her. She pulls a book from her bag. 'I'm reading the same book.'

She holds it up to Seth.

He grins.

She sits immediately on the empty sunlounger next to Seth. He sits up and swings his legs over. They chat animatedly about peat.

I smile.

Could this be Seth's new girlfriend? He deserves a good one next.

A LETTER FROM NORA

Dear Reader,

Thank you so much for reading *His First Girlfriend* – I hope you loved it as much as I enjoyed writing it for you!

If you'd like to keep up to date with all my latest releases, please sign up at the link below. Your email address will never be shared and you can unsubscribe at any time.

www.bookouture.com/nora-valters

His First Girlfriend took me quite a while to write. That's because it started off as one half of a completely different book. But then I realised that it was a story that deserved its own full-length novel, so I pulled the original apart and rewrote it into the tale you've just enjoyed. (The other half will be another novel coming soon!)

This is my sixth psychological thriller so please check out the other five for more edge-of-your-seat tension and did-not-see-THAT-coming plot twists.

I'd be very grateful if you could leave a review on Amazon. I'd love to hear what you think, and your review will help new readers to discover my books. I massively appreciate your help in spreading the word.

Fancy a chat? Have a burning question about a character? Please get in touch! You can contact me through social media.

My next novel is in progress and will be in your hands very soon. I promise it will be just as thrilling as this one!

All the best,

Nora

www.noravalters.com

facebook.com/noravalters

instagram.com/nora_valters

tiktok.com/@nora_valters

x.com/nora_valters

ACKNOWLEDGEMENTS

Huge love to my family and friends for always supporting me and my books! Special mention to Becky HH for all your inspiration and wise words. Big thanks to all the team at Bookouture and to my wonderful editor, Cerys. And thank you to all my readers – I couldn't do this without you.

Nora xx

September 2025

PUBLISHING TEAM

Turning a manuscript into a book requires the efforts of many people. The publishing team at Bookouture would like to acknowledge everyone who contributed to this publication.

Audio
Alba Proko
Melissa Tran

Commercial
Lauren Morrissette
Hannah Richmond
Imogen Allport

Cover design
Lewis Csizmazia

Data and analysis
Mark Alder
Mohamed Bussuri

Editorial
Cerys Hadwin-Owen
Charlotte Hegley

Copyeditor
Laura Gerrard

Proofreader
Jenny Page

Marketing
Alex Crow
Melanie Price
Occy Carr
Cíara Rosney
Martyna Młynarska

Operations and distribution
Marina Valles
Joe Morris

Production
Hannah Snetsinger
Mandy Kullar
Nadia Michael
Charlotte Hegley

Publicity
Kim Nash
Noelle Holten
Jess Readett
Sarah Hardy

Rights and contracts
Peta Nightingale
Richard King
Saidah Graham

Made in United States
North Haven, CT
10 February 2026

88507887R00162